# losing step

## stacy mcwilliams

# ACKNOWLEDGMENTS

Oh my god, I can't believe I'm here again, writing another set of acknowledgements. My first thanks goes out to my girls. Thank you for believing in me and encouraging me to write this story. Thank you for reading it before anyone else and thank you for your amazing feedback. I love you guys.

Next I wanna thank my hubs and my boys. Thank you for sharing me with these fictional characters. Thank you for letting me write, edit, promote and for everything you all do for me. I love you guys more than I can ever express. You are my world boys and you'll always be my babies and hubs, I couldn't do this without you. You are so fucking amazing and I'm so blessed to be your wife. I love you so much.

Next I wanna thank my amazing editor. Karen you are honestly the best person I've ever worked with on edits. You make my books better, make me better and I honestly can't thank you enough for all your hard work.

To my amazing Beta's, arc readers and my writing girls. I wouldn't be who I am without you. My words would be nothing without your feedback, encouragement and support and I love you all so much for it.

Next Sienna and Freda, thank you both for your proofreads. You guys are amazing and you caught the mistakes that we missed on edits. I honestly can't thank you enough for everything. You girls are my freaking rocks. Love ya both.

Lizzie, thank you for making my book so beautiful and Kirsty, thank you so much for the stunning cover. I hope the story does it justice. Loves ya both.

To the readers, thank you for reading my words, for supporting me and for sticking around when I was off having my babies and getting my degree. There are some really exciting things coming up, so make sure you sign up for my newsletter here and stay abreast of all things Stacy related.

Well, that's all folks.

To those I've undoubtedly missed, thank you and I love you.

Stacy

# Chapter 1

# SLEEPING INTERRUPTED

## Chase

FOUR A.M.

That can't be right.

It's four in the fucking morning and I've only been in bed for an hour.

My cell rings and rings, and I sigh as I ponder answering. The incessant ringing irritates me enough that I grab it from the nightstand and glower at it.

Unknown caller.

I think about not answering it, but very few people have my number, so I sigh, giving in, and say hello, but it's too late. The call has dropped.

For a moment, there's silence, and then the ringing starts again.

"Hello," I all but growl, trying to stow my ire until I know who's waking me up at stupid o'clock in the morning.

"Uh, Chase?" a cautious voice mutters breathlessly down the line, and my dick stirs in my shorts.

"Mmmm."

My answer is non-committal because my last number got leaked, and I was getting calls at all hours of the day and night from groupies.

"Chase, it's Cassie."

Her voice echoes in my head, and I sit up straight in bed, my irritation forgotten as I realize it's my stepsister. Well, that's a fucking joke because I barely know her, and she doesn't really know me.

"Cassie? What the fuck? How did you get my number? Why are you calling? If this is for concert tickets or some shit..."

"Chase, shut up and listen to me."

Her chastising tone and the fact she told me to shut up makes my heart race. I want to bite back, but her next words rob me of my will to snap.

"It's your dad. He collapsed at the office. It's not looking good. Can you come home?"

My blood pounds in my ears as I remember the last time I was home. My dad and I got into it again. He was furious with me for blowing off college, but my band, Deviant, was and still is, my passion.

*"You're throwing your life away on chasing a dream that might never happen."*

*"It's my life, Dad."*

*He met my eyes with fury on his face, slamming his fist onto the table and making me jump. "Yes. It is. But I'm cutting you off. You leave college and you'll get no more financial help from me."*

*I'd only gone home to tell him that my band had been signed, but he didn't care. All he cared about was that I wasn't following the path laid out for my future, by him.*

*"Fine. I'm out."*

*I turned around and began walking towards the door when he stopped me with his words.*

*"You walk out that door, son, and you and I are through. I mean it."*

*My eyes stung with unshed tears, and my throat burned as I tried to speak.*

"Okay."

Although my dad's wife, my stepmom, Janie still reaches out to me from time to time, my dad doesn't, and we haven't spoken in five years.

"Chase, you still there?"

Cassie's voice breaks into my thoughts, and I swallow the pain I'm feeling at not reaching out to my dad sooner. I anonymously donated to his charity, but I haven't spoken to him since that day, although he did message me about a year ago. I never replied because… what would I say? *I'm sorry I'm such a fuck up in your eyes. I'm sorry I wasted my life according to you.* There was no getting around me disappointing him.

"I'm still here. What do you want me to do?"

My history with my dad and my hurt at not trying to fix us makes me lash out, even though it isn't her fault.

"Can you come home? My mom's a wreck and I don't know what to do."

"Uh… he won't want me there."

I try to get out of it, but Cassie is tenacious. I remember that about her. Even as a ten-year-old, she was always determined to get what she wanted.

"He's your dad!"

Her tone borders on disbelief, and I know I have to go. I'll never forgive myself if I don't, so I swallow my pride and suck in a breath.

"I'm in Tokyo right now. I'll fly out on the first flight and see you tomorrow."

"Thanks, Chase. Let me know when you're getting in and I'll pick you up."

"That won't be necessary. I'll get a car from the label."

She sighs, and the sound goes straight to my dick. *Down, boy. She's almost related to you.*

"My mom wants me to pick you up, so you can just text me and I'll be there."

"Fine. I'll see you tomorrow."

I run my fingers through my hair, waking myself up a bit more, and sit up in the bed as she hesitates before she says bye. She ends the call and I rub my exhausted eyes.

We've been on tour for six months, and I can't even remember what my flat looks like, or what a home-cooked meal tastes like.

The tour has six weeks left, but I guess we need to reschedule some dates. I call my manager, our PR person, Mason Michaels at the label, and my band mates.

Everyone but Mason answers, sounding pissed, but they're with me on tour.

"My dad collapsed, and I need to go home. Can we move a few dates around?"

"Chase, come on. We have six weeks left," Derry mutters, and then Kane speaks in an angry whisper.

"Can you not just see your old man when it's over?"

"He might not be there. Do you think I'd be fucking calling and asking to postpone our tour if I didn't have to?"

"It's fine. We'll sort everything out here. Go back to bed, boys. See you in the morning."

The guys all grumble and hang up, which eventually leaves me and Tony, our manager, as the only two on the call.

"Chase, there's a flight home at eleven. Do you wanna be on that one, or a later one at two?" Tony asks, and I sigh in relief.

"Put me on the eleven o'clock one. Where am I flying to?"

"You're flying to JFK, and the flight's almost thirteen hours."

"What time will I land?"

"Ten tonight."

"US time or Tokyo time?"

"US time. Will you need a car?"

"No. My… uh… my stepsister is picking me up."

It sticks in my throat calling her that. I don't even know this girl, so calling her my stepsister seems messed up, but what else am I supposed to call her?

"No problem. I didn't know you had a stepsibling."

"I met her when I was like sixteen and she was a kid, but then I took off for college and I didn't go home much after that, so I haven't had anything to do with her."

Something about my tone must stop him asking anymore questions because he refrains, and his next words make my body relax. Speaking about home makes me tense, but speaking about my dad's new family hurts me in a way I can't describe.

"Okay, well if you need anything, let me know."

"I will. Thanks, Tony."

"It's fine. Text when you know what's happening."

He ends the call and I lean back up, wishing I could go back to sleep, but I know that I'm not likely to fall asleep, so I get up and shower, then pack my bag.

My eyes sting as I whittle away the hours answering fan questions on social media and writing song lyrics. Eventually, my cell goes off, and I go downstairs with my hold-all, guitar, and laptop, grabbing a coffee and drinking it on the way.

Tony is there, handing me my passport and my tickets.

"Thanks, man. I appreciate it."

He nods stiffly at me as he walks me to the door. Once I'm in the car on my way to the airport, exhaustion hits me again, but I manage to stay awake. I have a few hours at the airport to kill, and when I see an unknown number has text, I open it up and see a message from Cassie.

> ### Hey,
> *It's Cassie. Your dad's in critical cardiac care or something, in Presbyterian. He's still critical, but stable. Did you get a flight okay?*

The message was a few minutes ago, and I swallow a mouthful of coffee before I answer.

> *Hey.*
> *I'm at the airport now. My flight lands at ten tonight. I'll call you*
> *when I land.*
> *C x*

She doesn't reply to my text, and I spend the next hour trying to remember what she looks like. Eventually, I cave in and let my curiosity take over. She was like ten or eleven when we met, and I didn't want anything to do with her or her mom, so I avoided her. She must be about seventeen or eighteen now, so I search Instagram for her, but her account is set to private. I scan the picture on the cover and realize she looks nothing like I remember.

Next, I try Facebook, and my heart sinks like a stone when I see her public pictures. There are a few of her and her friends, but one is of her with her mom and my dad. My eyes scan the photo and I'm drawn to her. The picture is recent, or so the date underneath tells me. She's wearing dark jeans, a light grey camisole top, and her hair hangs in loose curls. She's actually fucking hot, with long brown hair, hazel eyes, and a smoking body.

Her eyes glitter in the picture, and my dick swells in my pants, but I groan, moving my eyes to my dad. I stare at him and try to put the image of her out of my head to try to forget her, but my eyes keep skipping back to her. She's my stepsister. I can't have her, but telling myself that only makes it worse because I always want what I can't have.

Eventually, I force myself to look at my dad, and my fucked-up desires deflate like a burst balloon as pain and regret swim through me. It can't be that old, but my dad looks older, greyer, and worn. The longer I look, the more I'm sinking, until I feel completely numb, and not even her pretty face can break me out of the shell I've erected around myself. I stare at the image on my cell and wish I could feel something, anything else because now, staring at that picture, all I feel is a strange numbness.

The announcement sound reverberates overhead, and I startle

when I see my flight's been called. I jog to the gate and flash the attendant a brief smile as she scans my ticket and passport. Her gasp of recognition follows me onto the plane as I'm led to a seat in the main area.

A frustrated sigh leaves my lips as I place my guitar and carry-on overhead. When I take my seat, I see a girl watching me curiously from across the aisle.

I pull my ball cap down over my face and sink back into my seat. The plane fills up, and soon most seats are taken, but no one sits beside me, and I'm grateful for that.

As the flight takes off, I lean back and close my eyes, drifting off into a deep sleep. The flight passes quickly, and before I know it, we're preparing for landing.

My heart races as the flight lands, and I'm on my feet seconds after the seatbelt sign is off. I grab my bags and guitar and wait for the aisles to empty as I follow my fellow passengers through the airport.

As we walk, I put my cell back on and see three messages from Cassie.

**Hey,**
**I'll pick you up at the arrivals lounge.**

**I'm wearing a grey sweater and dark jeans.**

**I'm by the seats on the way out. Text when you are near.**

I quickly respond that I'm off the plane and making my way through the airport. As I pass through customs and follow the signs for the exit, a few girls spot me, and I tug my hood down, wishing I had security with me.

My heart hammers in my chest, and I squeeze my hand around the case of my guitar. As I move out of the arrivals lounge, my heart sputters for a whole other reason because I can see her. I can see

Cassie, and the sight of her makes my footsteps falter. She's even hotter in person than in her photo, and I know I'm in big trouble because I fucking want her. I want to take her home and show her a good time. I don't care that she's supposed to be my stepsister. I don't care what anyone will think, and as I stand staring at her, completely frozen, I acknowledge that there's a small, fucked up part of me that would take pleasure in knowing that we aren't supposed to be together.

She's worrying her necklace and craning her neck as she looks for me. For a few minutes, I observe her from a distance. She's so beautiful it hurts to look at her. Her heart-shaped face, long brown hair, and hazel eyes that sparkle, make me stop for a moment and I swallow the lust that swells inside me.

*She's related to you, doofus. Down, boy.*

Her eyes meet mine, and she rushes towards me, throwing her arms around me. As soon as she touches me, all thoughts go out of my head and I never want the moment to end.

# Chapter 2

# AFFECTION & AFFLICTION

## Cassie

MY EYES SCAN the crowd for Chase, and I wonder what my reaction will be. No one at school knows I'm Chase's stepsister. My surname isn't Crawford, it's Danson, so unless I tell someone that we're stepsiblings, no one would know.

My friends all have a massive crush on him, but I usually make non-committal noises when they talk about him.

He is gorgeous, with bright green eyes, a jaw that looks like it's been chiseled from marble, and a body that's hotter than hell. His eyes are hidden behind sunglasses, but just the memory of his eyes from his music videos sends a thrill through me.

I impatiently move from foot to foot, and then I see him. He takes my breath away, but before I can think too much about it, I rush towards him and wrap him in a hug.

His body stiffens in surprise, and he disentangles himself with ease. Taking his glasses off, he smiles gently down at me, and my breath catches in my throat.

"Where's your car?"

His voice is low and sends a thrill through me.

*Get a grip, Cassandra.*

My internal chiding makes me dopey, and he stares down at me with an irritated expression. "Your car?"

I give myself a mental shake as Harvey's death plays out before my eyes again. "This way."

I lead the way to the parking lot and begin the drive back home to the house in Woodbury. My mom and I decided not to tell him about his dad until he was home, but when he asks why we're heading home instead of the hospital, I don't know what to say.

"I uh… we… I…" I stammer as we stop at a stop sign.

"Cassie?"

I risk a glance at him to see him biting his lip as he stares at me. For a moment, we just stare at each other while I'm waiting to be able to move.

His eyes drop to his lap, and when he looks back at me, his eyes are filled with tears. "He's gone, isn't he?"

I can't say anything because I feel Harvey's death hit me again. He's the only father I've ever known, and it kills me that he and Chase were on such bad terms before he died.

"I'm so sorry." My voice is barely a whisper, but before I can say anything else, the cars behind us begin beeping, and I'm forced to drive. He doesn't say another word for the entire journey, and my heart breaks as he wipes away the few tears that fall. He doesn't break down or acknowledge what I said. When we pull into the driveway, he's out of the car before I even turn the engine off.

My mom is a mess, and nowhere to be found, so I end up ordering pizza because I'm starving, it's been the longest few days. It took me almost three days to get a contact number for Chase; I hate that he found out his dad had died in my car.

I sit staring morosely at the TV with *Friends* on, but even the antics on the screen can't distract me from the pain I'm feeling.

Harvey was a good man. He wasn't my dad. My dad had left my mom when I was five, and he cut all contact with me when he left.

The doorbell rings, and I stand up, going to get my pizza as Chase comes downstairs. It's a little after one a.m. and he's changed into loose shorts and a t-shirt that's seen better days.

Once I pay for my pizza and garlic sticks, I take them into the sitting room and spread them out on the table, pouring myself another Coke then sitting down to eat.

"Can I join you?" Chase asks nervously from the door, and I give him a smile as I nod. I watch him as he walks into the room with a confidence I could never manage and slips down onto the floor beside me.

He picks up a slice and takes a bite of my favorite pizza. Meat feast, mushrooms, sweetcorn, with extra garlic. My mom thinks I'm nuts, but it's my comfort food.

He groans, and the sound vibrates through my chest, making my body ache in a way that Taron, my boyfriend, has never managed.

I quickly pick up a slice and take a bite of the heavenly goodness. Taron doesn't eat junk food. He's a health nut, so I usually end up with smoothies or salad when we're out together. I shake off my thoughts, focus on eating my delectable snack, and press play, watching Monica dress up with a turkey on her head. This episode always makes me laugh, and I can't help the small giggle when Joey sees her.

Chase doesn't speak, but he sits there, right beside me, and his arm runs down the side of mine, sending bolts of electricity through me when he moves.

We finish the pizza and the breadsticks, and neither of us move from the floor. My soda bottle is on the floor near him, and while I want to get a drink, I don't want to move, but Chase saves me the trouble when he tops up my glass and pours himself another drink.

I wonder what he's drinking and wish I was brave enough to ask for a taste. I've had a few drinks over the last few months, but I've never really drunk enough to let my guard down.

My heart thrums loudly in my ears as we both sit and watch *Friends*. He sips what I think is a whisky from the smell, and he drinks it neat, just like Harvey did as I sip my coke.

For the next few hours, we sit in silence, and he pours himself a few more drinks from the decanter he has beside him.

Eventually, I pluck up the courage to ask for a taste, but before I can, my mom appears at the door. She's sobbing, and by the time I put her back to bed, I realize It's after five a.m.

When I go back downstairs, Chase is nowhere to be seen, so I settle back down and press play on the cable box.

I sit there trying to quell my anxiety about going to sleep, and I don't even flinch when I feel Chase's warm body slip down beside me. My eyes dart to his when I feel his burning gaze on me, and he gives me the briefest smile. It doesn't reach his eyes, but it affects me, nonetheless.

As I shift my gaze back to the TV, he shifts slightly closer to me. He's so close that his arm is touching my leg, and the heat from it is blisteringly hot.

My breath stutters as I chance a quick look over at him. He's so beautiful, and his sex appeal is through the roof. It's no wonder he's one of the most eligible bachelors in the world. Everybody wants a piece of him.

His body shifts again, and he's even closer. There are no sounds other than the TV, our breath, and my thundering heart. I wonder if he can hear it, but he's focused on the TV and isn't looking at me at all.

In fact, I'm beginning to think he's forgotten I'm even there when his finger runs across my bare ankle. The contact makes me gasp, and he turns to face me with blazing eyes, lowering his head towards me, when a loud bang makes us spring apart.

He jumps up and bolts towards the door, leaving me sitting there with a rapidly strumming heart and a feeling of chagrin. I have a boyfriend. I'm supposed to be in love with Taron, but in the year and a half I've been with him, I've never felt as turned on as I do right now. My head is swimming, and I lean back, closing my eyes as I imagine what would have happened without that loud bang.

I imagine how his lips would brush mine, and his hand would tangle in my hair, angling my face up so his tongue could invade my mouth. I envision him pulling me around onto his lap, and his mouth would move down my neck, and how he'd pull the top over my head before capturing my nipples and biting down on them.

I want to continue with my daydream, but there are loud voices coming towards me, so I climb up on the sofa and curl up, pulling the comforter down over my body as Chase appears back in the living room with his Uncle Phil.

I watch through my arm as Phil gives me a once over, but then he starts speaking to Chase in a hurried whisper. I know he thinks I'm asleep, but I hear every single word.

"I need to go over the accounts again, but I'm pretty sure your dad gambled away most of his money. He owes big on this house, and on Cassandra's schooling. He's even spent her college fund, and his business is on the verge of going under."

My vision swims as I imagine not being able to go back to school and not being able to see my friends again. My heart breaks for Chase, who's come home and is now responsible for the mess Harvey left behind.

"I'll sort it." Chase speaks in a whisper that makes my insides coil. "Does Janie know?"

"I don't think so. Nobody really does, but Chase, the amount owed on this property is hundreds of thousands. And Cassie's school isn't exactly cheap."

"I'll take care of it. Does he at least have life insurance?"

"Yeah. It's worth half a million and you're the sole beneficiary."

Chase sighs, and I'd give anything to peek at his face, but if I move, then Phil will know I've overheard everything.

I feel Chase looking at me and his warm gaze stays on me for a few moments before it's gone again.

"I'll cover the school costs and the mortgage. You can't tell them though. You can't tell anyone. I'll sort it out today. And I don't want the insurance. Give it to Janie and Cassie. Make sure a college fund gets set up for her."

Phil mumbles something inaudible to me and they both leave, closing the door softly behind them. I lie with my eyes closed and think about how generous Chase is, but as my body drifts off to sleep, I wish Phil had waited a few more minutes before inter-rupting us.

I feel warm hands around me and I moan in my sleep, turning my face into my pillow and feeling a rock-hard chest that smells like heaven instead of my pillow. My eyes open, and I see I'm being carried up to my bed by Chase.

He's padding along the corridor to my bedroom, and if I don't stop him, he'll see my posters of him and the other members of Deviant covering my wall.

"Chase, what're you doing?"

My voice is a husky whisper, I clear my throat and lift my eyes to see him staring down at me. I can't read his expression and his mouth is a thin line, but his eyes are darker than before.

"Putting you to bed. That sofa is hella uncomfortable and you'll get a sore neck."

"I can manage."

I try to move, but he holds on firmly to me.

"Let me do this, please?"

His voice sends a shudder through me, so I quit moving and prepare myself for the embarrassment of him seeing my room.

He opens the door and walks in after turning on the light. His eyes automatically go to my guilty pleasure wall, he smirks when he sees a few topless pictures of himself covering the pretty pink decor.

My face flames, and his smirk grows wider when he sees the concert stubs and album covers pinned to my notice board.

"Have you been to my concerts?"

His voice is a quiet rumble, and there's a hidden emotion in it that makes my heart race.

I can't speak, so I nod slowly, and he leans down, brushing a whisper-soft kiss against my cheek.

"Why didn't you tell me? Or ask me for tickets?"

"Uh, your dad said not to. Plus, when I called you to tell you about your dad, you weren't exactly happy to hear from me."

I watch as the shutters close and he drops me down on the bed. I bounce a few times as he turns and begins to make his way towards the door.

"Chase, that's… uh… that's not the only reason. I… uh… I didn't want… people don't know that you're my… that we're…"

"What? Spit it out, Cassandra." His voice is low, and the command has my body tingling, but his stance puts me on edge, and I spit out the word that I wish I could suck back in immediately.

"Related," I finish in a lame whisper, wishing I could explain to him why I've hidden our connection. Why I don't tell people he's my stepbrother, but I knew it was out of the question.

He freezes by the door and then spins back around, coming towards me in a way that has me both turned on and terrified.

"We are not related. Your mom married my dad. That's it. We are nothing to each other. Nothing at all."

He hovers over me, and I swear I feel his indecision as he glowers at me on the bed, but after a second, it's gone, and he spins around and storms out of my room, slamming my door behind him.

I collapse onto my pillows and draw a deep breath in as my heart slams against my rib cage, reminding me that Chase is oh so off limits and so very dangerous to me.

Having a celebrity crush is one thing but having a crush on your stepbrother who's a worldwide superstar is quite another. With that thought, I try to force the image of his lips brushing mine from my mind. I fall asleep feeling the whisper of the kiss we almost shared and dream about finishing it. Even though it's wrong, and dirty, it turns me on and makes me feel something I never thought I'd ever feel—a connection with someone else.

# Chapter 3

# FURY & FUCK-UPS

## Chase

I HAD to leave her room before I did something beyond stupid. Her lips were right there, and seeing posters of me on her wall made my dick so hard I could hardly see straight because she clearly likes me too. Part of me wondered if she'd got herself off to the image of me, and although I know it's completely fucked up, the thought of her playing with herself while staring at me made my cock so hard that I had to clench my fists to stop myself reaching out to her. Then she said we were related, and my hard-on wilted immediately. My heart hammers in my ears as I storm back over the bed and say in a low whisper, "We are not related. Your mom married my dad. That's it. We are nothing to each other. Nothing at all."

Her eyes dart about my face, and I have a moment where I want to reach down and fuck her mouth. Let her say we're related then. But I can't. I'm only here because my dad died, and not only did he die; he left a huge clusterfuck of a mess for me to sort out.

I turn away from her and almost sprint out of the door,

collapsing against it as my desire to show her I'm not her fucking stepbrother battles with my desire to run away.

I storm into my room and turn the shower on as low as I can stand it. Cassie's supple lips, full tits, and peach of an ass play across my vision as I try to get a handle on myself.

She's no one to me, yet she's affected me in a way very few have, and I'm intrigued by her. She's innocent, sweet, and a temptation I don't need. Not now. Not when I have to bury my dad.

He raised me alone after my mum died giving birth to my baby sister, who didn't make it either. Ruby was born at twenty-seven weeks and managed three days, but then she died too, and my dad was a broken man. He changed completely after that, but I still remember my fun-loving, carefree dad, who taught me to ride my bike and how to play my guitar.

I close my eyes because I think I'm about to become emotional, but the pain I'm waiting for doesn't come. I'm leaning on the shower, thinking I should feel something, feel anything, but instead, I feel nothing.

The only emotions I can detect are lust over Cassie, which is not helpful right now, and exhaustion.

I scrub at my skin and then wash my hair, wishing I knew how to feel something else.

Why don't I feel anything? What's wrong with me?

Once I'm out of my shower, I put my Spotify playlist on and fall asleep to Imagine Dragons. I sleep for a few hours, but after such a long sleep on the plane yesterday, I don't need much, so I get up and decide to hit the gym.

As I make my way downstairs, I can see Cassie, Phil, and Janie sitting at the island in the kitchen.

"Janie, I'm so sorry," I tell her as their eyes swing towards me. Cassie won't look at me as Janie rushes over and hugs me tightly.

"He really loved you, Chase. I'm only sorry you never got to patch things up."

I open my mouth to say something when Phil comes over and

leads a tearful Janie back to the table. My eyes automatically go to Cassie, and I watch her run her hand over her neck. Her hand stays there, and I freeze at the edge of the table as her fingers rub at her skin. My mouth dries up, and I have to count backwards from one hundred to stop my semi from becoming a full hard-on. It shouldn't be erotic, but it is, and I know right then that I'm going to hell.

My dad's dead, and all I'm thinking about is how much I wanna run my fingers all over her delectable little body. How much I wanna sink into her and fuck her 'til she's screaming my name.

I'm not like this. I don't get hung up on girls. Fuck, I don't need to, but there's something about her that calls to me and makes my heart sprint like a jackhammer when she meets my eyes.

Something is broken in me and I don't know how to fix it. I try to shake it off and think of my dad and what he'd be thinking of me to take my boner away, but then her head turns to me and I'm trapped like a deer in headlights. She holds my gaze for a moment before she looks down at my shorts, flames bright red, and turns back to the table.

My exercise shorts, while practical, do not hide anything, so I rush to my seat at the table without taking my eyes from Cassie's soft fingers. I wonder what they'd feel like wrapped around my cock, and my boner is clear for all to see. I slump down on the seat and feel her legs under the table. She jerks them away from me, but while I want to slip under the table to taste her, I need to stop acting like a complete psycho, so I finally swing my eyes away from her and glance around the room, staring anywhere but at her.

Phil meets my eye and gives me a tight smile, sliding some papers towards me. Before I read them, I need a coffee, and the pot is right in front of Cassie.

"May I?" I ask no one in particular, and Janie smiles at me as I meet her eye.

"Of course. Cassie, stop hogging the caffeine and pass your... uh, pass Chase the coffee, please?'

I glance up and meet Cassie's eyes as she slides the coffee pot towards me. Our fingers brush, and my arm tingles at the contact, but she pulls away quickly as Phil starts to speak.

"I'm taking Janie to the funeral home to make some arrangements. Can you check everything over and make sure everything's in order?"

He stands and helps Janie from her seat as I open my mouth to ask if they need anything from me, but he'd have said, and to be honest, I don't want to plan my dad's funeral. I just want to get it over and get away from the temptation of my stepsister.

I give him a sharp nod as I watch them leave, and then I turn my attention back to Cassie, who is staring determinedly ahead and not looking at me. I spend an inordinate amount of time watching her, and her nipples pebble in her top, so I know she's as affected by me as I am by her.

I push up from the table after stowing my constant hard-on in my waistband and walk over to the cabinet to grab a mug. I walk slowly back, standing right behind Cassie and brushing against her back as I reach across her for the creamer pot. My lips brush against the soft skin of her neck. She sighs when my hand moves her hair out of my way and my lips lick, suck, and nibble on the skin as I slowly drag the coffee pot towards her.

"Chase," she mutters in a breathless whisper as I drop my hand down her arm and over her tit, teasing her nipple until she's squirming beneath me. I pull my lips away and give her nipple another pinch as my mouth moves towards hers.

She inhales sharply and my arm brushes her breast as I bring my hand up and tease her nipples. My lips are a breath away from hers, and she's breathing heavily when I hear footsteps approaching.

I spin away and pour my coffee at the counter, taking a sip as Phil jogs back into the kitchen for his cell. He scoops it up and bolts back out to the car. I stand salivating at the sight of Cassie as she stands up and brushes herself down. She glides towards the door and brushes her fingers across my abs as she passes, making me suck in a deep, shuddering breath, but then she's gone and I'm alone again.

Part of me wonders if my fascination with her is because I've been single and not sleeping around for the duration of the tour.

The guys and I made a bet that I wouldn't last until the tour was over, but I'm sorely tempted right now.

I want to follow her, but I know I need to read the paperwork Phil left, so I go sit and read what he left. Basically, I'll be paying the mortgage off and providing Cassie's school tuition until the end of term.

I call the number on the school paperwork and ask to speak to the finance office. It's when I'm speaking to them that I find out my dad hasn't paid the past two terms tuition and that Cassie is at risk of exclusion.

I quickly settle the balance until the end of the year, even though it costs one hundred and twenty grand, then I call the bank, clearing off the mortgage. I had my PA call and offer to do this years ago when our band topped the billboard charts, but my dad told me he didn't want a penny from me, so I donated it to his charity.

He never knew I was the anonymous donor, and now he never will, but I don't care. I had enough to spare.

I have a house in Malibu, an apartment in Manhattan, and a beach house in Hawaii. I don't need anything else. I don't want cars, although I have a few. I don't want models or girls who want me for who I am. I just want a simple life and to record my music.

After I've paid for the funeral and set up an account to keep Janie and Cassie going, I'm done helping out.

I sign the insurance policy over to them, stipulating that a college fund is to be set up for Cassie, but when I'm done, I'm filled with a restless sort of energy.

I decide to go for a run and take my ear pods out of my pocket, plugging in some random music before I grab a water bottle from the fridge.

I jog to the door and open it to see Cassie kissing some preppy little douche in a red corvette. My heart thumps loudly in my chest as I think that she's mine, but I know she's not, not really. Part of me wants to go over and take her inside to punish her for kissing him, but more than that I want to rearrange his face. The jackass doesn't see me. Cassie does though, and she closes her eyes when her gaze meets mine. I force myself to ignore her and bolt down the street, taking my favorite trail and running until my legs shake, my lungs burn, and my heart feels as though it's coming out of my chest.

I drink my water and begin to jog back when my cell rings. I answer when I see that it's Tony.

"Hey, I'm just checking in. How's your dad?" His soft voice makes me want to hang up and bolt, but I swallow my instincts and answer in a detached voice.

"He didn't make it."

"Fuck, I'm sorry, man. Did you make it in time?"

"No. I was too late."

And that was the story of my life. I'm a screwed-up mess because I didn't get to say goodbye to my mom, my sister, or my dad, and my head is swimming with how much I wanted to fuck my stepsister. Yeah, I'm a delight.

"The boys and I are here if you need anything. Just let me know when the funeral is, and we can sort your return date then. I'll handle Michaels."

"Thanks, man. I appreciate it."

He genuinely sounds sorry, but I don't care. I give him a non-committal answer and end the call, walking back.

We hang up and my cell goes a few minutes later with a message from Tony. He offers his condolences again and tells me he's managed to postpone the dates for a week and a half, but after that, he needs me back.

I'd run further than I thought, and I'm jogging back into the driveway when preppy douchebag reappears behind me. He beeps the horn and skids around me, trying to block me from the door, but I'm tired, pissed, and frustrated as fuck, so I ignore his stupid attempts to get my attention as I cross the drive.

Within seconds, he's out, jogging across the drive and grabbing my arm. I shrug out of his grip and spin around to face this annoyance.

His eyes dart up to mine, and I'm a few inches taller than him. The recognition that flickers in his eyes proves to me that Cassie hasn't told anyone about our connection.

Color me impressed.

"Chase Crawford, what are you doing here?"

It's on the tip of my tongue to say I own this fucking house, but I swallow it back. I'm about to tell him that Harvey was my dad when Cassie opens the door and sprints over to us.

The tiny cocksucker turns to her and excitedly says, "Chase Crawford is here in your driveway. We gotta tell everyone."

He makes a move for his cell when Cassie captures his hands. She glances at me and I can see the apology all over her face before her eyes go back to his.

"You can't. If the media finds out Chase is here for his uncle's funeral then he won't get a moment's piece. Promise me, Taron. This has to be our secret."

I hear her lie and I don't say a word about it. My eyes are on the dickhead she's with. I want to fuck him up, but I can't. If I move though, he's a dead man. He licks his lips as he looks at her, and I want to punch him so hard he'd swallow that tongue, but I bite my lip and stay stock still.

"What's in it for me if I keep my mouth shut?" His voice is low as he runs a finger over her breast. I have to clench my fists to stop myself from decking the little snot rag.

"What do you want?" she asks in a seductive voice that makes me want to rip the douche limb from limb, but it's when he leans forward, kissing her in a way that makes me want to throw up or throttle him that I have to look away.

"You. I want your first time, and I want tickets to the Deviant concert in Madison Square Garden."

Cassie meets my eye for a brief second, begging me not to intervene, and then turns back to him with a soft smile.

"Done," she mutters, and he kisses her again.

My vision blurs, and there's a red tinge to it. "Not fucking done," I hiss, and Cassie pushes Taron towards the house.

"Go on. I need to have a chat with Chase. I'll be in in a minute."

Taron grins at me like the cat who got the cream before he turns and bolts into my fucking house, leaving me seething.

"Chase! Chase!" Cassie snaps her fingers in my face, and I glance down at her, fury seeping through every pore as I take in her pouty lips. My body reacts on its own, and I lean forward, brushing a strand of hair from her cheek before my fingers close on her shoulders. My penetrating gaze burns into her, and I have to stop myself from dropping my lips to taste her delectable little mouth. Her scent is intoxicating, and I breathe through my mouth as I try to keep my desire for her at bay.

After a moment, I bear down and speak into her ear, holding her shoulders tightly in a way that'll leave marks, but I don't care.

"You are not going to give that jackass anything to keep my being here a secret. And no way in hell am I giving a guy who'd illicit sex from a girl to keep a secret a fucking ticket to my concert, especially when *you* are that girl."

My body vibrates with fury and the desire to knock that fuckwad out.

Cassie touches my arm and her touch burns through me.

I don't look at her. I can't, but she reaches up and touches my cheek until I glance down at her.

"It's fine. It's just sex."

"It is not just fucking sex. He's not the kind of guy… No, Cassie. I'm not… you're not…. no fucking way."

"What if I promise not to have sex with him until after you're gone and then I dump his pathetic ass?"

My eyes burn into hers, and I wonder how she has me so twisted up. I usually don't give a fuck about anyone, and it baffles me that she had gotten under my skin so quickly.

"Chase?"

Her quiet voice makes my dick hard, but I can't show her that.

"He'll never go for it! He'll know…"

"No, he won't. I'll give him something, but I swear I won't have sex with him."

She breaks off as I lick my lips. Her mouth is right there, tempting me and teasing me, and all I want is to kiss her. I want to do it so fucking badly that I can barely think about anything else.

Her soft fingers move across my lips, and I part them, ready to lean down and take her mouth, consequences be damned, when my cell vibrates in my pocket.

"Cassie," I mutter as she drops her hand and steps back from me.

"Don't. I'll do what I need to do to protect you."

"It should be me protecting you!"

"No, it shouldn't. I'll keep myself safe. I always do, but you do have to give him the concert tickets. Don't give him them until you leave, and if his seats should accidentally be double booked, then that's too fucking bad."

She pleads with her eyes and I give her a sharp nod, wishing I could figure out a way to stop her from letting him anywhere fucking near her, but I'm powerless to stop it. I step back and let her go into the house. As her ass disappears out of sight, I make my way around the farthest garage, which is my gym room.

I go inside and spend the next few hours beating the shit out of a punchbag, pushing my body to my breaking point, and I'm walking back outside since the side door is locked when I see that little fuck leaving.

He's smirking and watching something on his cell that he tries to hide when I approach him.

I snatch his cell out of his hand and see that he'd not only gotten his fucking way, but the cretin had filmed it.

I delete the video before he even opens his mouth to protest, then I drag him around the corner and pin the fucker to the wall. My body vibrates with the fury I feel at seeing her hand moving up and down his cock, and I want to fucking kill him.

"Listen here, you dipshit," I say as I slam him hard against the wall. "You ever pull a stunt like that again and I'll make sure the only place you get a job is the prison kitchen. I know the teachers at your school and I'm pretty sure if I put your name on blast, no college will ever accept you."

He nods and smirks up at me, but I know I have to let him go. My fingers don't want to oblige, but I do it anyway, and my muscles tense as I watch him walk away without his cell.

I pocket his cell and go back into the house, intending to try and find Cassie, but Phil and a few of my dad's friends drag me into the sitting room.

# Chapter 4

# SWEET & SOUR

## Cassie

I WATCHED Taron leave and went to wash my hands. I'd given him a hand job to show I was going to go ahead with it.

It's just sex. It's not a big deal, although I'm still a virgin, but from Chase's reaction, you'd have thought I was selling myself to Taron.

My heart begins to hammer as I remember the look in his eyes as I brushed my fingers across his lips.

I wanted him to kiss me. I needed it, and then he didn't. My fingers ache, and I decide to go for a shower to wash Taron off my skin. I turn the water to warm and strip out of my clothes, stepping inside.

I start washing and imagine that Chase is with me as I scrub my breasts. I tease and squeeze my nipples like he did earlier and think about what would have happened if Phil hadn't come back. My eyes close as I remember how it felt to have him kissing my neck before I move my hands down and running them down my waist until I part my folds. Taking the shower head off, I turn the pressure up. I slowly move it down my body as I lift my knee and push my fingers inside, curling them up.

The jets hit my nipple, and I groan softly in pleasure before moving the spray down and hitting my clit with it as my fingers pump furiously inside me.

My nipples brush against the tiled wall and the cool tiles sends an electric thrill through me that tosses me over the edge as I picture Chase's hands instead of my own. My legs shudder under me as my climax shakes me and I throw my head back, moaning and biting my lip as shockwaves hit.

After a few minutes, I put the showerhead back in place and wash my hair, trying to ignore the fluttering in my abdomen as I think about facing Chase again.

I'd teased myself with him before, and it wasn't the first time I'd brought myself to orgasm picturing his face, but it was the first time since he was back in my life. Somehow it felt wrong. Dirtier and naughtier, but so much more thrilling too.

My body is like a coiled spring as I step out of the shower and pad back into my room in my towel.

I'm getting dressed and have just pulled on my bra and panties when my mom knocks at the door, calling me to dinner.

My hands tremble as I tug on my joggers and a tank top, but it's as I'm tying my hair up that I feel someone watching me.

My eyes dart around my room, and I see Chase by the door. His eyes are low, fixated on my ass, and his arms are curled around his chest as though he's trying to stop himself from reaching out to me.

He can't meet my eye, and when I walk towards him, he backs up a step.

"Cassie, uh… your mom wants you down for dinner."

His voice is hoarse, and when I reach him, all I can see is his massive erection. Before we make it out of my room, he shoves me back in and spins me with my back against the door, trapped by his enormous frame.

He leans down and pushes his lips against mine, shoving his tongue into my mouth and grinding his cock against my already tender clit.

"You feel that?" he hisses against my mouth as my tongue licks along his lips and he pushes into me even harder. "This is all because of you."

His lips kiss a path down my neck, and he grips my hands firmly as his hot mouth sucks on one of my now aching nipples through my tank. He bites down on it and I moan, dropping my head back until it bangs off the door, and then he moves across to the other side.

"You want me, Cassie?" he asks in a low voice, and I whine in response. "Answer me." He nips at my nipple. My clit rubs against his leg, desperate for some relief when he bites again, and I swallow the sound I want to make. "Do you fucking want me?"

He pushes my hands into one of his, dropping his other hand to my joggers. His rough hand pushes inside, and before I can say a word, he's pushing a finger into me, then another, and he starts fucking me in time with his sucks on my breast.

"I think you really fucking want me inside your tight little pussy."

My clit grinds on his hand and he comes back up, holding his lips a breath away from mine.

"Do you fucking want me?" he asks as his hand stills and I stare at him.

"Of course. I want you. Please, Chase."

My begging works, because as soon as the words are out of my mouth, he slams his lips to mine and kisses me with a passion I've never felt before. His thumb presses against my clit, and I turn into a loud mewling creature under his masterful strokes. My head moves back, and he licks and sucks on my neck, biting gently and caressing my skin with his tongue.

His hand still holds both of mine above my head as his mouth comes back to mine. He kisses me like a man dying of thirst, pushing harder and harder against me and breathing hard into my mouth, but we both ignore my mom's calls. I'm too caught up in the fact that his rough fingers are inside me. His lips drop again to my nipples and he bites down hard, making me convulse against him as my orgasm washes over me.

His fingers keep moving, taking every single bit of it from me, and then he steps back, kissing me gently before nipping my lip with his teeth.

He lifts his fingers to my lips and brushes the wetness along my skin before he lifts his fingers and sucks on them.

"Mmm, you taste delicious. I can't wait until my tongue gets a taste from the source."

My body shakes with desire, and he drags me into his arms, kissing me and pushing his rock-solid cock against me before stepping back slightly. I move to follow him, wrapping my hand around his cock, when we hear my mom yell even louder this time, and he drags himself away from me, bending over and clutching his chest.

My heart thunders in my ears and I can't move. I'm so turned on I can't think, and I certainly can't walk, but it's Chase's next words that steal my ability to speak.

"I came up here earlier to see if you were okay and I heard you moaning in the shower..." He straightens up and stares at me in both accusation and awe.

"I... uh..." I want to say something, but I have nothing, and when we hear footsteps, he turns away from me and crosses my room. I watch as he walks into the bathroom and closes the door, just as my mom knocks.

The sound makes me jump, and I spin, opening my door and following my mom to the kitchen. After a few minutes, Chase follows me, but I can't even look at him. My pussy is throbbing, and I want his mouth on me so badly that I can't think straight. My blood still thrums under my skin, my lips tingle, and my body feels like a spring about to snap.

I try to eat my food and listen as my mom tells us about the plans for the funeral. She talks on and on as Phil plies her with wine, then she begins sobbing. Chase and Phil quickly leave, and I sit with her as she cries on my shoulder for an hour, and then I put her to bed.

Once she's settled, I go downstairs and sit on the sofa, but Chase is nowhere to be found. I lie on the sofa with *Divergent* on, trying to distract myself, but it's no use.

Eventually, I close my eyes and try to think of something other than my stepbrother and how fucking hot our make-out session was, but my mind is reeling. Feeling his fingers push into me is something I don't think I'll ever forget. I try to think about school and how much work I'm missing to get that image out of my head, but my fingers brush my swollen lips, and I lean back on the sofa, reliving it. I try to think about my vacation that probably won't be happening because of Harvey and his gambling, but all I can think about is Chase.

None of it matters. I don't care about missing school that much, and I hadn't really wanted to go on vacation anyway.

I lie for four hours trying to think of anything but Chase, trying to force my mind to watch the movie, but it's a pointless exercise, and when he finally appears, my stomach drops out. He strolls drunkenly into the sitting room as if he doesn't have a care in the world, accompanied by a buxom blonde, who's kissing his neck between giggles.

I can barely look at him as I get up from the sofa and go into the kitchen, but before the door closes, I hear him answer the girl when she asks who I am.

"She's no one. My dad was married to her mom, but I don't know her and she's nobody to me."

Hurt makes my eyes sting, but I refuse to cry. I won't let him see me hurt, so I grab a couple of sodas, a bag of chips, and a bar of chocolate to take upstairs with me.

As I pass the living room, I see him kissing her, but his eyes are open, and the kiss looks different to our kisses earlier. There's no passion, no lust, and if anything, it looks a bit forced. One of the sodas drops from my shaking hands as his hand wraps around her neck. It skids across the floor and bursts open, spraying juice everywhere.

I wish the ground would swallow me up, but when a cataclysm doesn't happen, I'm forced to clean up my mess.

The table next to the stairs will be fine to drop my candy stash onto, but it clatters as I drop it down, and the girl titters. "She's a noisy thing, isn't she?"

My blood pounds in my ears and I storm back into the kitchen, grabbing cleaning supplies as I rush back out to the sodden mess on the floor.

I refuse to even look in their direction as I march over and drop to my knees, wiping at the mess with one of the cloths. My knees are soaked, and my hands shake as I dry up the soda.

Warm hands cover mine, and I glance up to see Chase trying to take over.

"Let me help," he says in a whisper, and I shake my head.

"I got it. It's my mess."

"It's okay…"

"No. I got it. Go back to your *date*."

My mouth curls around the word date, and I know I sneered it by the shocked look on his face, but he stands and turns, heading back into the sitting room.

A few minutes later, I'm done cleaning, but the sounds from the living room turn my stomach as I stand up. My feet carry me back into the kitchen and I drop my supplies into the cabinet before running upstairs. I don't see Chase or his fuck buddy when I check in on my mom or when I go to bed. I bolt by my snacks, leaving them downstairs as I climb into my bed with my ear pods in my hand.

I debate for a moment whether I should go get my food but decide against it. I glance around my room once before shoving the ear pods into my ears and listening to the loudest, most obnoxious band on my playlist. As I drift off to sleep, I wonder what it would be like to be wanted back by the one person you truly desire.

My body relaxes and I drift off, wishing my life was different, and that Chase wasn't Harvey's son or that I wasn't his stepsister.

I wake up after a few hours and get up to go to the gym when I can't force myself to go back to sleep. I drag on my yoga pants and a sports bra then go to get a bottle of water from the fridge in the kitchen.

My feet thump on the stairs, and I pass the living room, averting my eyes in case there's something to see. My eyes don't follow my commands and dart towards it frequently, but there's no one there.

I bolt towards the gym and try to ignore Chase as he whales on a punching bag before I start running on the treadmill, only to be interrupted a few minutes into my workout by him. He taps me on the arm, and I slow my treadmill down to a walk, ignoring the quiver in my pussy as I glance at him.

"What?" I ask, and he points to his ears, so I take a bud out, waiting on him to speak to me.

"Are you nearly done?"

His voice is cold, and my body instinctively goes into fight mode.

"No. I'm not."

He disappears shortly after that, and I ignore him, finishing off my workout before going for a swim and a sauna. I put the sauna on to warm before my swim, and I'm struggling to relax when, after ten minutes, the door opens and Chase steps in wearing only a towel. My eyes drink in the sight of him, and I watch a bead of sweat run down his chiseled chest and down his abs, hitting the towel just below his V.

# Chapter 5

# SINFUL DESIRE

## Chase

I HAD to leave the gym. I couldn't stay in there with her because I wanted to cave. I'm craving another taste of her, I'm only fucking human, so there's only so much of watching her ass move on the treadmill I can take. Her gorgeous eyes glistened when they looked at me, and I still feel like shit over bringing that fucking girl back last night.

I shouldn't have done it, but I couldn't get the taste of her pussy out of my head. Hearing her moan as she came made my knees weak, and seeing her head thrown back, eyes closed, and tits bouncing as she rode my hand almost undid me.

It's so wrong, dirty, and fuck, I want it so bad, but I can't have her. She's my fucking stepsister. I need to keep reminding myself of that fact. I'm not supposed to kiss her. I'm not supposed to know how it feels to have her pussy pushed against my cock, or how her pussy tastes as she gushes on my fingers, but I do, and I don't know what to do about that.

Her face when she saw me makes me push myself harder on my

run. My feet pound on the pavement, and each step pushes me harder as I think about what I've done to her so far.

Her surprised gasp as my lips pushed down on hers.

Her tongue dancing with mine.

Her tight little pussy moving against me as I shoved my cock against her.

Her gushing as she came against my hand.

As I run, I remember Phil's words in the bar last night, and I push myself even harder.

*"Your dad adored Cassie. He thought of her like his own daughter, and I know he'd want you to take care of her and her mom."*

I'm pretty sure my dad wouldn't want me to take care of Cassie the way I really want to, so I force myself to go even faster. My lungs burn and my heart hammers in my chest as my breath comes in short, sharp gasps as I try to outrun the desire I feel for Cassie. I know I've fucked up and I want… no, *need* to apologize, but she was colder with me this morning.

I start to run back to the house.

My muscles are aching, and my legs are Jell-O when I get back, so I decide to go for a sauna when I'm passing, and the light is on. I grab a towel and shrug my running shorts off, kicking my sneakers off too. I tug my top off and toss it in my pile as I yank my socks off. My body is thrumming with lust, with muscle aches, and my chest is tight when I get to the door of the sauna.

As I open the door and step inside, I take a deep breath, closing my eyes, and then I open them to see Cassie sitting there.

*Can't I get a minute? Just one fucking minute?*

Her eyes are on my chest, and while she stares at my body, I can feel my dick hardening.

Fuck my life.

"Cassie," I mutter in a hoarse whisper, and she meets my eyes with a challenging stare.

"What, Chase?"

Her voice is low and irritated, but it sends a jolt to my cock, and

I want to rip that towel off her sweet little body and sink my cock inside her as she moans my name.

"I, uh…"

I break off as what I want to say to her gets stuck in my throat. She shifts, and her towel slips slightly, showing an inch of skin around her gorgeous tits.

"Chase," she growls, and before I can stop myself, I'm on her, kissing those delectable lips and taking what I so desperately want. My need overwhelms my senses, and our lips clash furiously. She bites my lip and then licks it before sliding her tongue into my mouth for a moment.

Her hands slip up my chest, and I let out a feral groan of need as her nails scratch my nipples, but she turns her head and pushes me away.

"We… can't…" she pants, and I can feel my frustration growing.

"Why the fuck not?"

"You're my stepbrother… and you slept with…"

"Cassie, I don't even know you, and I didn't sleep with that girl. I couldn't because I saw you. You've fucked my head up. You've made me want you, and I don't know what to do about that." I lean up and look into her eyes. I see the pain she's trying to hide there. "Cass, you have to believe me. I didn't fucking touch her. We kissed. That was it."

I slam my lips against hers, promising myself I'll take one more taste, just one, and her tongue tangles with mine as I grip her hair, angling her neck so I can plunder her mouth a little more. My free hand goes to the towel, and I start to loosen it when her hands come up and push against me.

"No, Chase."

"Kissing her was enough," she tells me, and I growl at her.

"And what was you giving that jackass a hand job? Was that not enough?"

Her body tenses and she tries to move but I slam my lips back down on hers until she concedes and kisses me back. Once she's kissing me back, I stop the kiss and pull back to stare down at her, wanting, needing to taste her pussy. My hand skims down the towel and I push it apart at her waist, sliding my hand inside. As I push her folds apart, her mouth pops open and she writhes against me.

Her eyes glitter as she stares at me, and I drop my lips to hers, giving her a quick kiss before I release her, dropping to my knees and pushing her thighs apart. The feeling of the rough floor, the heat, and the smell of her pussy completely overwhelm me, and I ignore her protests as I lean forward to take a lick.

"Chase, no. Stop."

She tries to close her thighs, but I use my shoulders to wedge them apart as I start devouring her.

"Chase," she mutters. "Stop."

My mind is overwhelmed with the scent of her while my fingers pump into her slick wetness. My tongue presses firmly against her tight little bud. I suck it into my mouth harder and harder, and although her mouth is saying no, her body is saying yes.

I pump harder and lick furiously until she starts quivering and convulsing on the bench. My tongue laps at her juices, and I don't stop pumping my hands until I've taken every single bit of her orgasm from her. Just as I sit back, her face heats and she shoves me away from her.

"I said no, Chase."

"You did, but Cass, your body was screaming yes at me and I chose to listen to it."

I lean up and press a wet kiss to her mouth, licking along her lips, and although she pushes against me, her mouth opens, and she sucks my tongue into her mouth. I pull back and run my fingers, still coated in her juices, along her lips.

"Suck," I command as she opens her lips, and I push my fingers inside her mouth. My cock throbs as she sucks on my fingers, and I hold her neck in place.

"Can you see how good you taste, Cass? Can you taste how sweet your juices are?"

Her teeth nip on my fingers, and I press soft kisses to her neck, to her collarbone, but then she shoves me away from her.

"No, Chase. I mean it."

I push my hand against her still wet clit, shoving two fingers roughly inside as I speak to her.

"This, right here. It's mine. Whenever someone gives you oral, you'll be thinking of me. Whenever someone slides their dick into your wet and willing pussy, you'll know it belongs to me, and I will be taking you. I will make you come so hard that you'll crave my dick forever."

I lean back away from her, withdrawing my fingers and sucking them into my mouth as she watches me. My dick throbs as I watch her sit up, pulling her towel tightly around her before she stands and starts to walk away from me.

"Cass." My hand reaches out and runs across her bare thigh, making her shudder, but she brushes me off and continues to walk away from me.

I stare at her as she walks out, closing the door behind her, and although I'm tempted to follow her, I know I have to let her go.

My hand closes over my dick as she leaves and moves up and down the shaft. My orgasm comes quicker than normal, and for a few minutes, I sit in the sweltering heat of the sauna, then when I lick my lips, tasting her on me, it starts to get too much for me. I get up and pace around.

What the fuck am I doing?

I can get pussy anywhere, so why am I so intent on tasting hers? Why does it feel like I have to have her and that another taste will satisfy the beast roaring inside of me?

My feet carry me to the sitting room, and I see Janie sitting with Cassie and Phil and I want to speak to her. I need to talk to her, to explain that I'm not an animal, but her tight little body is driving me wild.

I catch her eye and nod to the hallway, but she shakes her head and I bristle I just want a chance to talk to her, to explain and then I need to stay away from her. I go to my room and go for a shower, gripping my rock-solid dick and jack off in the shower to thoughts of her pretty little mouth. Why I can't get her out of my head I don't know, but as I picture sinking my dick into her tight little hole, my dick pulses and I come all over the tiles.

I lean back against the tiles and let the water blast down on me for a while, until I hear movement outside my room. I bolt from the shower and wrap a towel around my waist, as I run for the hall. Cassie is just passing my room when I open my door. I grab her and spin her into my room, pressing her against the closed door.

For a moment she just stares up at me and then her eyes wander down my body, scalding me with lust as they go.

"We need to talk"

My words are a hoarse whisper as I step closer to her, licking my lips as her breaths quicken. She reaches out and wipes a droplet of water from my chest making me bite my lip at the contact.

"Cass," I begin before she closes the small gap between us and presses a soft kiss to my shoulder. Her hand wraps around my cock and she squeezes, twisting and kissing a trail across my pecs. I begin thrusting into her hand when she lifts her head and slides her tongue into my mouth.

"Chase," she mutters between kisses and I wrap my arms around her, angling her head so I can fuck her mouth with my tongue. "If you ever push me into something against my will again, I'll come in when you are sleeping and cut this off."

Her hand tightens on my dick and I come hard, my legs shaking as her words bounce around in my head. She lets go, wipes her hand on the towel and pushes me back from her. Her cheeks are flushed and she's smirking widely at me, but as she goes to leave, I come back to myself and I scoop her up, carrying her into my bathroom.

I walk us into the shower, dropping my towel and turn it on as she whines against my shoulder. Her loose sweats are easy to get off, and her tank is sticking to her soaked skin, but she doesn't protest as my mouth closes over her nipple and my hand slips between her wet folds.

I push one and then both fingers into her as I suck on her tits before I drop to my knees between her thighs. I lick softly and she mewls loudly, as I push harder against her, pushing my fingers rapidly in and out of her.

"Cass, tell me you don't want this, and I'll stop. Tell me to leave you alone and I will."

Her head's thrown back and her body moves to the beat of my fingers, but I stop before her orgasm hits. I feel it building, but I stop just as she's about to crash over. I glide up her body and slam my lips against hers.

"Don't lie to me. Don't tell me you don't want me as much as I want you, because I can tell. Your pussy is soaked whenever I touch it, your nipples are tight little buds and your pupils are massive."

"I don't want you. I don'…"

I lean closer and her breath hitches, but my lips brush against her neck, tasting, teasing and claiming.

"Liar," I murmur, sliding my fingers back into her. "Admit it and I'll let you come."

She shakes her head and I step back from her, wondering if I'm punishing her more or myself.

"No orgasm for you then. You need to decide whether you want me or not, but Cass, if you threaten me again, I'll be forced to punish you.'

Her eyes widen and she stares at me in shock for a moment before we hear her mom calling her.

"Better run along now."

She scuttles from my shower and I lean back, lifting my fingers into my mouth and sucking away the remnants of her juices. My dick is throbbing so hard I'm almost worried he's about to lose his damn mind, but I just hope I didn't push her too hard. Having her hand around my dick made me lose my mind a little.

I quickly turn the shower off and dress, running my fingers through my dark hair as I tug on some clothes and head downstairs. Cassie is in the living room and it looks like she's alone, but as I move towards her, she shakes her head and within seconds Phil and her mom step into the room.

I watch her shift uncomfortably and I want nothing more than to push my cock into her, but it has to be on her terms. Holding back her orgasm has me on edge and I try to listen as Phil leads the lawyer into the living room to discuss my dad's will.

Cassie eventually leaves with her mom and doesn't come back in. I'm part thankful, part resentful, but before I can think too much about what I'm feeling, Phil arrives and tells me it's time to get ready.

He's organized a Catholic funeral mass for my dad, and his body is to be viewed today before it goes to the church tonight. I numbly follow his instructions and go up to my room to get dressed. I swallow the pain that's nipping at the edges of my numbness and get dressed into a loose black sports coat, a black shirt, and slacks.

Once dressed, I comb my hair and stare at myself in the mirror, wishing I could go somewhere, anywhere else.

My numbness keeps up until I'm alone in Cassie's car on the way to the funeral home, and then my thoughts sink back to doing this journey with my dad to see my mom and Ruby. The thought of that memory overwhelms me for a moment, and I bounce my leg up and down. I'm not ready to say goodbye to my last parent. Once I do, I'm really all alone. I have no one else, and it's that thought that has panic crashing over me like a tidal wave, consuming me and dragging me under.

*I don't want to see my dad's body. I can't do this.*

"Stop," I beg, and Cassie turns to glance at me as I undo my top buttons and open the window, trying to suck some air into my burning lungs. "Please, stop the car!" She pulls over, putting her warning lights on.

As soon as the car stops, I'm out and pacing up and down the side of the road.

"Chase," Cassie says softly, but I ignore her and continue pacing. My eyes burn and I stride faster until she comes over and puts a hand on my arm. I brush her off, but she's unfazed, and she steps in front of me.

"Move," I hiss at her, trying to act intimidating, but my heart's not in it.

"No."

Her simple retort makes me angry, and anger is easier to deal with. "I said move."

My eyes burrow into hers, and I want to push her aside, but my hands curl into fists at my side. I can see the defiance, and my fury is reaching boiling point when she answers.

"And I said no."

"Please. Just move." I beg her, and she steps into my space, touching my chest.

Anger gives way to the agony of knowing I can't fix things with my dad. I can't ever hear him say he's proud of me and it's killing me.

# Chapter 6

# PAIN & DESPERATION

## Cassie

MY EYES TRACK Chase as he fidgets, and I know something's building in him. He's like a powder keg about to blow. His glassy eyes dart from side to side, and his breaths are rapid.

"Please?"

His soft word isn't filled with the same anger as before, and my fingers brush up his shoulders to touch his cheek. For a single moment, he leans into my palm before he shrugs off my touch and begins pacing again.

I don't know what's bothering him, but I know my mom and Phil are going to notice if we don't get there soon.

I stand silently and watch him walking back and forth until he turns to face me.

"I can't do this. Please don't make me go."

His voice cracks and I can hear the anguish behind his words. He drops his eyes to the ground and runs his fingers through his hair, trying to hide his vulnerability.

"Chase, you can do this. You're so strong..."

He cuts me off with a snort… "You don't even know me. How can you possibly know if I'm strong or not?"

His words tear into me, and I want to back away and leave him alone. I swallow a breath. I wish I knew the right thing to say, but saying nothing isn't an option, so I opt to tell him what I think about him.

"I think I know enough about you to have an opinion. You left an easy life where you had your dad's support to follow your passion, and I've watched as you struggled. You always get back up again and it's incredible."

My words seem to have some impact on him because he spins towards the car and opens the door, calling over his shoulder. "We doing this or what?"

He's back to being the cocky asshole, and it makes me relax a little. I get back in the car and pull out into traffic, getting to the funeral parlor ten minutes late.

Phil and my mom are quick to admonish us, and I quickly glance at Chase, catching him shifting nervously from foot to foot as they speak.

"It's uh…" Chase begins, but I cut him off.

"It's my fault. We were halfway here when I remembered that I forgot my cell, so I had to go back."

"Honestly, you could have managed a few hours without it."

My mom's shrill voice makes my spine stiffen, but I don't miss the grateful look Chase gives me as the funeral director comes over to talk to Phil and my mom.

Chase follows the man and Phil into the side room, and I see him take a card from his wallet and pass it over through the crack in the door.

My mom isn't watching. Her eyes are fixed on the door to the left of Martin, the funeral director's office.

Once Chase and Phil are back, Martin shows us into the room. My mom and Phil go first, Chase and I following. I'm too busy staring ahead at the only father I've ever known, lying there, stiff and unmoving, that I don't see Chase falter at first. He stops a few steps behind me and then backs up and bolts from the room.

Phil turns and watches him go then quietly motions for me to go after him. I give a nod to show I understood, and I turn, slipping silently away.

My eyes scan my surroundings, and I hear a crash in a room to my right. I follow the sounds and open the door to see Chase sitting in the middle of the floor, picking up pieces of glass with tears streaming down his face.

He doesn't seem to notice me until I gently reach down, plucking the broken shards of a glass vase from him and dropping back on the floor.

"Chase," I say softly as he lowers his head and starts sobbing into his hands. I lean down on the floor, careful to avoid any shards of glass, and wrap my arms gently around his shoulders.

His head turns, and he buries it in my neck, breaking down as we sit amongst the mess on the floor.

"Hey, it's okay. It's going to be okay." I brush his hair from his head and hold him tightly with my free hand.

"How… how is this going to be okay? I'll never get to say I'm sorry for being so damn stubborn, and he'll never get to see me play or…"

I cut him off because there's something he doesn't know. Something huge.

"He did see you play. He saw you every time you played in New York, and he saw you twice in Toronto." Chase stiffens in my arms, but I continue. "He was so proud of you. It was him who took me to see you in concert, and it was him who bought all your albums. He kept your ticket stubs in his desk and proudly told his friends about you."

"What are you talking about? He never came to a concert."

"Yes, he did. Look."

My hands shake as I pluck my cell out of my dress pocket and scan through my pictures, finding the one of Harvey and me outside Madison Square Garden last September, next to the sign that said 'Deviant Live Tonight'.

Chase stares at the picture of Harvey in his Deviant cap and hoodie, next to me in my low rise dark blue cut-offs and my lemon and peach crop top.

Chase scans the next photos and sees another selfie of Harvey and me in our seats, and a sneaky video I took of Harvey as the concert started and Chase appeared on stage singing. Harvey was so proud of him, and it was so obvious. He was beaming as he watched his son on stage.

Chase stares down at the video and watches it three more times before he leans over, brushes his lips against mine, and helps me to my feet.

Once we're standing, he pulls me into his arms and holds me for a long moment, but as he releases me, we hear footsteps approaching outside and spring apart.

"Thank you, Cassie." Chase's voice is barely discernible over Phil speaking, but I hear it, and I step back into the viewing room after Chase, skimming my fingers over his back as we move closer to his dad.

"Can I… can I, uh… have some time alone?" he asks in a choked whisper, and my mom drags Phil and me outside.

He stays in the room for ten minutes, and I noticed every single minute of them pass on the clock. My eyes are so focused on the time that I miss the arrival of Calindra and Phil's obnoxious kids, Strewan and Stephanie. They are seventeen and fifteen, and horrible, spoiled brats.

Stephanie stands with her arms folded across her chest, popping her gum and whining to her mom about how she's supposed to be going out with her friends, and Strewan is staring at me in a way that makes me so uncomfortable. He's awful. He had tried to feel me up once at a party Harvey had, then blamed me for getting caught. I loathe him. My eyes dart to the clock and then to the hallway as Chase walks down and heads straight outside without saying a word to anyone.

"Oh my God, Daddy. You didn't tell me Chase was here!" Stephanie preens herself, and Phil glowers at her as I stand up.

"I'm his ride, so I'd better go."

"Yeah, I bet you are." Strewan answers in an undertone, and I want to smack the smirk from his face. My mom meets my eyes, and I grit my teeth as I storm outside.

I make it outside in time to see Chase hit the trunk of a tree that's lining the driveway.

"Hey, you wanna get out of here?"

My voice carries in the mild April air, and he smiles a little as he turns to face me. The smile doesn't reach his eyes, but his relief is evident when he looks at me.

"Yes fucking please."

I climb into the car and shove my belt forcefully into the clip as I start the car. My hands shake on the wheel as a memory of the sauna surfaces. I still can't figure out why I liked… no… loved what he did to me. My head is so confused because I feel like I should talk to him about it, but I don't know where to start, so I don't say a word to him as I drive us out of the crematorium.

After a few moments of silence, I finally speak, and I see him turn to look at me from the corner of my eye.

"Home or somewhere else?"

My voice is low, strained, and I check the dash to see how long we have. We've got a little over six hours to spare. The receiving mass or whatever it's called isn't until six, so I've got time to take us away.

"Not home. Take me somewhere… anywhere else, please?"

My fingers shake on the wheel. "Okie dokie. Any preference on where?"

"No. Just not home."

I glance up at the sky and see the mid-afternoon sun through the clouds. It's warm, but not hot, and suddenly, inspiration strikes.

He doesn't ask where we're going. In fact, he doesn't speak at all for the full car journey, and when I park in the beach car park, I see he's fallen asleep.

My eyes scan his face. He's even more beautiful when he sleeps. His forehead is less lined, and his eyes show no signs of the stress that's been hanging over us for days.

As my gaze moves down, he smiles and mutters in a hoarse whisper, "It's rude to stare at people while they sleep." He cracks one eye open and his smirk grows impossibly wider as my face catches fire. He glances around and then turns back to face me with a boyish grin. "Lake Welch Beach. This takes me back. I haven't been here in years."

My body tingles as he leans over and presses a soft kiss to my cheek before springing away from me and opening his door. For a moment, I can only watch, dumbstruck, as this beautiful, complicated man walks along the beachfront. I hop out and follow him.

We walk along for a while, but wearing pantyhose, Mary Janes, and a knee-length black dress with a white collar aren't suitable beach wear, so I tug on his hand to stop him.

"What's up?"

His voice is tender and sends a shudder through me, but it's the look in his eyes that has me overwhelmed. He looks open, honest, and vulnerable again.

"Can we stop walking? My shoes are filled with sand and it's killing my toes."

"Yeah, sure thing." He shrugs off his jacket and tosses it to the ground, tugging me down to sit with him. I'm seated on the edge of his sports coat, but he reaches out and pulls me closer until I'm between his legs.

For a while, we just sit on the beach, each of us lost in our own thoughts. Me between his legs, and his arms loosely around my waist.

As the breeze whips my hair around, I know it's going to take a while to style it into any order, but I don't care because, as that thought crosses my mind, Chase runs his nose along the back of my neck and presses a soft kiss onto my shoulder.

"Thanks for bringing me here, Cassie. I don't... I don't think I'd have gotten through the day if it wasn't for you." My body turns slightly so his face is in my view, and he leans over, capturing my lips in a kiss that melts me. "God, you are so amazing."

His soft words and the reverence in his voice make me feel brave and bold, and I say the one thing I never in a million years thought I'd be saying to my stepbrother, the rockstar.

"Chase, I want you to be my first."

He gasps in surprise, and his eyes widen. "Wait, I thought you'd just never done it with that douche. You mean you've never..." he asks without finishing the thought, and I see the horror that washes over his face. "You... I... I thought..." He shakes his head as he stammers, and then his face darkens as he stares into my eyes. "Cassie, you should have said. I never would have taken things that far I'd known you were still a virgin..."

He's silent for a moment as he stares down at my body wrapped in his arms, and when he looks back at me, his pained expression steals my heart.

"You should hate me. You shouldn't want me to be your first. What I did to you was fucked up."

My fingers brush his cheek softly, and he leans into my touch as a tear rolls from his eye. "Chase," I whisper when he won't look at me. My finger lifts his chin and his eyes reluctantly meet mine.

"I liked what you did. In fact, I really enjoyed it."

I want to say more, but his mouth is on mine and his tongue is pushing into my mouth. Our kiss heats more and his hand starts to move around my waist, up towards my breast until a commotion down the beach stops our moment in its tracks. My eyes follow the sounds that captured my attention, and he stands up when I look towards it.

"We better get back."

I don't comment on the fact that he didn't answer me when I asked him to take my virginity, and he doesn't comment on the fact that we both passed my 'boyfriend' kissing another girl. To be honest I don't care enough about Taron to be pissed. He's an asshole and I was only with him because he asked me out. No one else did. I want to end things with him, so this has given the perfect excuse.

Once we're in the car driving back, he turns the radio on and leans back, closing his eyes without a word.

The whole drive is filled with an awkward, uncomfortable silence, and when we get back home, it gets even worse. He's out of the car before I've even turned the ignition off, and he jogs into the house without looking back, leaving me confused and hurt.

I follow him inside and sit in my room, styling my hair and playing around with my make-up as I try to decipher what his reaction in the car was all about. Was he irritated with me? Sickened because I liked it when he took what he wanted, or was I not good enough? I thought he liked me, liked my taste, and liked commanding my body, but what if I'm wrong?

I wipe my face off and redo it, trying to ignore the swirling thoughts in my head until guilt washes over me.

Harvey is dead and he was so good to me. I miss him, but I can't think about him. I can't face it. My eyes brim with tears and I clean off my face again, doing my make-up one last time when my mom calls me to dinner.

# Chapter 7

# UNEXPECTED DEMANDS

## Chase

MY HEART THUMPS loudly in my ears as my head runs her words through my mind on a loop.

She's a virgin. A fucking virgin. She should have told me that before I thrust my fingers and my tongue into her tight little pussy. I knew it was tight and that she was likely inexperienced, but I never for a moment expected her not to have let someone fuck her. Her lips were an addiction, a habit I have to break, but kissing her, tasting her, having my fingers buried inside her makes me forget that I'm seven years older than her. Makes me forget that she's barely legal and I want to suck her pussy again until she creams all over my face.

The thought of taking her virginity pushes into my mind, and although I know it's sick, twisted, and wrong, I want to do it. I want to be the one to take it, to pop that cherry. Oh, how I want to fucking do that, but I'm a fuck up. I pushed her to let me taste her when she said no, and I ignored her protests as my mouth sucked on her sweet little bud.

I can't believe it. Her eyes dart to me as she drives, but I'm too lost in my thoughts to speak to her, and as soon as she's in the driveway, I'm out of the car, closing the door sharply behind me. Before she's even opened her door, I jog into the house and disappear into my room.

My instincts told me it was a bad idea to be near her because my body craves her. I want to take her to bed and taste her sweet pussy again and again before sliding my cock into her and making her come as she rides me.

I knew it was a bad idea to come home, but fuck. My blood thrums in my veins and my cock presses painfully against my fly, begging for release.

In desperate need of distraction, I check my cell and see a message from Tony, asking me to call him. As it rings, I stand up and pace around my room, fighting with myself to stop from going to her.

An image of the sauna rears up in my mind, and I groan aloud at how hard it makes me. I've already taken liberties with her. I should stay away from her, but her taste is like a drug, sweet and addictive, and I'm craving another taste.

I try to shake it off, telling myself she's a kid. I should have known she was a virgin. Just because I fucked my first girlfriend at sixteen, doesn't mean she was like that too. Even though she told me she liked it, what I did was so messed up. I can't say I wouldn't do it again, and that's the thing that's the most depraved because I know I would absolutely do it again to her, so I need to stay away from her for now. She's only just eighteen, and I'm fucking twenty-five. It was only her birthday a few weeks ago.

Her mom, my dad, and Cassie were all out for dinner, and she was wearing a black sheer blouse thing, with tight black skinny jeans that showed off her curves.

My dick had gone rock hard at seeing her, but as my eyes scanned the picture, I'd noticed that it was her birthday and that she was eighteen.

"Chase? Earth to Chase."

I shake my head as Tony says my name. "Fuck. Sorry, man. I was miles away. What's up?"

"Michael's called. He wants you back here for Saturday's show. Can you make it?"

My head swims, and part of me wants to say no.

I just lost my dad. I need time. Another part of me is desperate to get back, even though I know I'll be leaving the sexy brunette who is consuming me.

"Chase, are you still there?"

I swallow as guilt over where my head's at overwhelms me. I never, ever let a girl distract me from my band. It's my passion, and my soul is tied into it.

"Yeah, I'm here. Get me on a flight Friday and I'll be there. The funeral is tomorrow, so I'll be able to make it."

I know it's the right thing to do, but why does it leave such a bitter taste in my mouth?

"What time? Six a.m. or midday?"

"Go for midday!"

My heart stings at the thought of leaving Cassie, but I know it's for the best. I'm her fucking stepbrother, like it or not, and I have no business wanting her the way I do.

"Done. And Chase?"

"Yeah, man?"

"I'm really sorry about your dad. The boys and I are here for you."

"Thanks Tony. See you Saturday."

He ends the call and I collapse back on my bed, wishing I was someone else. My eyes close as I remember the feel of her in my arms, the taste of her on my tongue, and my dick hardens at the scent of her that wafted up when I shifted.

I roll onto my stomach and push my face into my pillow, yelling *fuck* and punching lumps out of it.

I need a shower. I need to wash her scent off my skin. I need to act my age. I'm twenty-five, not eighteen. I'm too old for her, even if having her in my arms felt right, and good, and I loved it. Plus, I'll only be here for two more days. Long enough to fuck her, but not have her.

I push up from my bed and walk to my duffel bag that has my clothes in it, digging through for something to wear until I need to dress for the requiem mass.

My hands touch on a pair of sweats, and I toss a shirt onto my bed as there's a knock at my door. I want to open it. I want it to be her, and for a beat, I debate with myself whether to open the door or whether to leave it. It opens and Strewan peeks his head inside.

"Hey, Chase. Can I have a word?"

I nod, grateful for the distraction from the girl down the hall, and he bounces into my room like he's got springs attached to his feet. He sits on my desk chair and I go back to my bed, sitting down and facing him. He spins on my chair for a moment and I just stare at him, waiting until he speaks.

"My mom doesn't want me talking with you. She thinks you're a bad influence or something."

I remember his mom. She's a stuck-up bitch, and I never liked her ever since she smacked me for crying about my mom when I was a kid.

The memory sits like a lead weight in my stomach, but I don't speak or move. After a moment of silence, he begins speaking again. His words all come out in a rush and my head drifts off as he praises our music and sound, but then he says something that catches my attention for a minute.

"So, I mean, if I could, that would be awesome."

I'm about to ask if he could what, when there's another knock at my door.

My heart races in my chest as I walk over and open the door. Chestnut brown hair and big hazel eyes that are swollen and puffy stare up at me, stealing my breath and my resolve to leave her alone.

"Chase, can I talk to you about earlier?"

I open my door wider so she can see Strewan, and her face instantly hardens. Without another look, she turns and storms away from me, slamming the door to her room.

My head is swimming with her reaction to him, and I want to go after her to find out what the fuck that was, but I can't. My hand shakes as I close the door and turn back to my cousin, who's staring at me suspiciously.

I take one step into the room, and he glances between me and the door.

"Did you fuck her? I mean, I know she's a pistol, but she blew me off last year. I managed to cop a feel though, and her body is sweet."

I close my eyes and pinch the bridge of my nose to stop myself swinging for the little fucker as he continues, oblivious to me wanting to fucking kill him.

"She's smokin', but she's, like, super uptight, man."

My ears are ringing and I wanna punch him out, but I clench my fists and swallow my fury.

"What do you mean? Of course I didn't fuck her! She's my stepsister!"

"Yeah, but you're not actually related, and she's a really fine piece of ass. I wouldn't mind trying again if she'd let me."

My hands are clenched so tight that I have to loosen them before I step towards him with my blood boiling.

"You stay away from her! There will be no more shots at her, no more touches… I mean it!"

I'm ready to pin him to the floor and beat the shit out of him when his mom barges into my room and glowers at me.

"Strewan, I told you to stay away from him…" Her whole body vibrates, and I turn to stare at her as she marches that douche from my room.

*Just in time, asshole. Just in fucking time to stop me making a mess of your face.*

I stand watching them and decide to take that shower, but my shoulders ache with the tension, and I decide to hit the gym for an hour first. My fingers fumble with my buttons, but I'm changed and ready to hit something. My knuckles are already scraped and bruised, and I know I should tape them, but I'm too furious to bother.

My black suit is hanging by the door, and I scowl as I pass it. My legs carry me downstairs, and I see a lot of people I don't know milling around, but I keep my head down and jog out to the gym.

I push open the door and see Cassie sitting on the weight bench, but it's the fucker kissing her that makes me see red.

"Get the fuck out!" My voice is full of fury, and I see her jump. Her sleazy douche of a boyfriend leaps back from her, and I see the blush crawling up her cheeks.

We saw him kissing someone else a few hours ago. At least, I did. I didn't mention it because I didn't want to upset her, but I will now to stop her sleeping with him.

"Hey, Chase. You still have my cell phone. Can I get it back?" the cocky shit asks me, and I give him the weight of my full glare until he backs down.

"Yeah, do I now? Did I accidentally drop it in the pool? Maybe."

His eyes widen and the stupid little shit actually tries to go toe-to-toe with me.

"That's my property. You can't…"

I'm about to punch him when he steps back and turns towards Cass as she speaks.

"Don't worry. He'll replace it."

I meet her stare and open my mouth to speak when he speaks again and I turn my attention back to him.

"Yeah damn right…"

My body tenses and I'm ready to go for him when Cass shakes her head, so I grit my teeth and spit out.

"How about you get the fuck outta here before I tell Cassie what you were doing at the beach today?"

He steps up to me, and for a minute, I think he's grown a set, but then he slinks away and out the door as Cassie stands and tugs her dress down.

Her fury is palpable, and her body vibrates with tension, but she won't look at me, and it kills me.

"Cass, I..." I start to speak, about to ask her what the fuck she's thinking kissing him when we both saw him playing tonsil hockey with another girl a few hours ago. I took her lead, not mentioning it, but the time for me to keep my mouth shut has long since passed.

"Why were you in here with him? What are you thinking? Didn't you see him on the beach kissing that skank?"

I don't know if the girl is a skank, and I don't care. All I care about is the beautiful girl in front of me who's looking at me like she's about to rip my nutsack off.

"Don't you dare lecture me. You also kissed another girl last night before you forced yourself on me."

My head rears back and I stare at her for a beat as her hissed words make my heart sink. I step towards her, lifting her chin and brushing her hair from her face.

"Don't, Chase." She steps back, breaking my hold on her. Her footsteps echo, and I want to follow her, but she doesn't want me too. After a moment of indecision, I jog over to her, closing the door before she can leave.

My hand closes over her arm and I spin her round, trapping her between my body and the door. I click the lock closed and lean down, running my nose along her jaw before brushing the sensitive skin on her neck with my tongue.

"Chase, no," she mutters in a breathless whisper that goes straight to my dick.

My head lifts, and I stare straight into her eyes as my lips brush hers, softly at first, and then more demanding as she kisses me back.

"Fuck," I groan as her leg wraps around my waist. I push my

cock against her and pour everything I'm feeling into the kiss. All my desire, frustration, and lust, but she pushes against my chest, and I back up a little.

"Stop." She sighs, and I keep pushing against her, kissing her lips, her neck, and down her chest. I push her dress down, opening the buttons and groaning at the sight of her lace-covered tits, but it's seeing her nipples pebbling as I suck on her skin that drives me crazy. It's not until I suck one forcefully into my mouth, scraping it with my teeth, that her body relaxes. Her fingers wind in my hair, and she tugs, almost to the point of pain, but I like it. Her nails on her free hand scrape down my arm and scratch at my chest.

"Chase," she cries aloud as I switch to the other side, still toying with the first with my hand, squeezing and releasing as she shakes under me. I drag my mouth back to hers and shove my cock hard against her, lifting her slightly and hammering against her as our mouths collide desperately. She begins to shudder, and I keep pushing, harder and harder until she starts moaning my name. My finger finds her nipple, and I tug on it hard, watching as she throws her head back and whimpers. Her body shakes as she comes apart in my arms.

As soon as her orgasm subsides, she shoves me away from her hand, bends over, and puts her hand on her heart. Our fingers are still touching, but she shakes my touch off, wrapping her hands around her waist.

"Why are you doing this to me? What do you want?"

*You!* My heart instinctively answers, but my head knows I'm so bad for her.

"You have to stop taking what you want from me when I say no. It scares me that you just push me and don't listen when I tell you to stop."

"I know you enjoy it and that you want me. It's written all over your body and your face. You're so responsive to me that I know you don't really mean no."

"But what if I do? What then? You rape me until I give in?"

I pull back to stare at her, and my eyes meet hers as I press myself against her again.

"If you didn't really want me, I wouldn't be standing between your legs right now having just given you an orgasm. Be honest with yourself and admit you want me as much as I want you."

"Chase, it's not about whether I want you or not, it's about you respecting me enough to take no as an answer when I say it. I'm not a toy or a plaything. I deserve better from you."

She does deserve better. She's got me there. I can't say a word because my head's overwhelmed with the fact that I want my step-sister. I want to taste her sweet pussy and make her come on my face again. I want to be her first, her last, and her everything, but I can't, and it's ridiculously unfair of me to want her like this when I have nothing to give her.

There is no future for us, and there's no way I can take her virginity when I'm leaving in two days.

"Chase," she whispers as I move my lips towards her.

My eyes bore into hers, and I push even closer so my rock-solid cock is pushed against her stomach, and our rapid breaths are the only sound in the room. I stare at her, and then my thoughts burst out of me as she starts pushing at me to escape from my hold.

"I want you. Don't you get it? Fuck, I want you so bad it's killing me."

I run my fingers through my hair and then bring my hands down, stroking her cheek with soft touches.

"Cassie," I continue, running my nose from her ear to her neck and back up again as she writhes against me.

"I want to stick my tongue so far into your pussy again that you scream, make you come so hard that you can't see straight, then slide into you while you moan my name, but I'm leaving on Friday and I won't be back. So I can't have you. But I need you to promise me one thing."

My heart stutters as a tear falls, and I brush it away with the pad of my thumb. I wait until she nods slowly, and I brush a gentle kiss against her lips.

"Don't give your v card to anyone. Wait until it's special, until it's someone who consumes you and knows exactly how special you are. Because you, Cassie, are so fucking special. You make a room brighter just by being in it, and you deserve a fuck load more than I or that tool Taron can ever offer you."

Her arms slide up my side and she wraps me in a hug, holding me tightly before she kisses me, and it's the first time, I've ever wanted to fuck someone so badly but denied myself the pleasure. I gently break the kiss because I know my resolve is about to shatter, but I don't move back or step away from her. I can't. I'm not strong enough to do that.

I'm usually the instant gratification guy, but as I'm kissing her, I know that I should savor every second, every taste, because I'm going back to my tour and I won't ever be home again.

"Please," she breathes into my ear and nips at my lobe. "I want you, but you have to stop pushing me when I say no. It has to be you, Chase. It just has to be."

Her begging is making me lose my mind, and when she brings her lips back to mine, devouring me, I can't think, can't breathe, and can't resist.

My tongue slides into her mouth, and I take everything she's willing to give and more. My hands slide up her dress, pushing it up until I lift it over her head, breaking our kiss for a moment before my eyes scour her body.

Her naked body glistens in the low light of the gym, and her hands rake up my sides, lifting my top and pulling it over my head.

"Are you sure about this, Cass?" My voice is low and unsure because I don't know what I'll do if she says no. My fear is quelled when she brushes her lips over my chest, muttering, "yes," as she goes.

Our lips clash after a moment, and the kisses become more and more frantic. I push against her willing body. My cock pushes against her clit, and she groans my name softly in a way that makes me lose my damn mind.

As I push against her, she scrapes her nails down my back, and I bite her shoulder to stop from moaning aloud. My dick is carved from granite, and I'm a few seconds away from lavishing her pussy with my mouth when there's a loud knock at the door.

"Chase, are you in there?"

I want to say no, but the knocking gets louder and more persistent. Cassie pushes me away, and I open my mouth to say something to her when she shakes her head. The loss of contact brings back a sense of reality, and I realize I was about to take her virginity. My cock thrums at the very thought, but I know I shouldn't be doing this. Not when I'm going to leave her. My eyes drink her in, and I want to tell whoever it is to fuck off and come back later, but they're probably doing me a favor. If I'm this addicted now, I can't imagine how bad I'd be if I pushed my dick into her, claiming her as mine and fucking her wet heat for the first time. Her eyes darken as she watches my emotions play across my face, and then she sighs as she wraps her arms over her tits.

I watch numbly as she steps out from my arms, scoops up her dress, and bolts towards the other door.

I want to ask her to wait, to ignore the person who's knocking, but when I look back, she's gone.

I quickly pick up my T-shirt and tug it on, stowing my boner in the lip of my boxers as I plug my earbuds in and crank the volume. I want another minute, standing and listening to the music before I pull the door open.

Phil is standing there, and so are Strewan, Taron, and Janie.

"What's going on?" I ask, and Phil points to my ears.

"Didn't you hear us knocking?"

His eyes dart around suspiciously, and I watch curiously as Taron shifts from foot to foot while Phil scours the room with his eyes.

"Where's Cassie?" Taron asks bitterly, and I clench my teeth as I answer in a low, deadly voice.

"How the fuck would I know?"

"She never came back out. She told me to wait for her. She's still in there." He pushes into the gym, and I laugh as he jogs around, opening the cupboard and then the shower room.

"Okay then. I'm going for a run. See you later."

I turn the music up and try to run my frustration off. In a way, I'm glad they interrupted, because my lips are on fire, my cock feels as though it's about to burst, and my heart pounds in my chest.

Fuck, fuck, fuck. I almost caved. I almost took what I wanted and damned the consequences. I can't let myself be alone with her again. She'd hate me if I took her and then left, and I can't have that. I never want her to hate me.

Fuck. The next two days are going to kill me, but I have to stay far away from my stepsister, or I'll forget that she isn't mine to take, break, and discard. Although, I'm sure I've done a fair amount of damage already.

# Chapter 8

## HOLY HOT HELL

### Chase

I BOLT from the gym and grab a swimsuit from the bucket, tugging it on and diving into the pool. My body is gliding through the water as Phil leads Taron and Strewan through the connecting door to the gym. I forgot I told him to wait. I was so consumed with Chase that I forgot all about Taron waiting on me. My head swims with confused thoughts as I think back to my interactions with Chase. Part of me is turned on when he just takes what he wants, and the other part of me is confused by the fact that I like it. He's pushing my boundaries and swiping them out of his way, and I don't know how to feel about that.

I watch as Strewan's eyes scan my body, and I want to cover up as Taron glowers at me, but I really can't find it in me to care. I wave at them and continue my swim, trying to clear the image of Chase staring down at me from my head.

Phil ushers them from the room, and I lay on my back, floating in the pool for a while and trying my best to put what happened out of my mind. I swim, wishing they hadn't interrupted. Wishing it was just Chase and me, and above all, wishing that I could just take what I want, like Chase does. He doesn't listen when I say no, and that's a little scary to me. He just pushes me until I crack, and although I love him dominating me and playing my body like one of his guitars, I'm also a little worried that something in me is a little broken because I enjoy it. If anyone else pulled what he did, I'd have their ass thrown in jail, but with Chase… I don't know.

It's not normal to want your stepbrother like I do, and it isn't normal to feel so electrified by his touch that I can still feel his rough hands on me hours later. The thought of his hands on me, pushing me, touching me, pressing roughly into my skin turns me on, and my body heats at the thought of him pushing that enormous fucking snake in his pants into me.

It takes me ages to calm down, and I swim for over an hour, trying to expel some of my energy. Once my heart rate is somewhat back to normal, I get out and shower, wrapping myself in a large towel and glancing at the clock.

It's a little after four, and I'm starving, so I go to the kitchen, grabbing a protein bar from the pantry. The house is oddly quiet and peaceful, but my nerves are on edge as I eat my bar in three bites and then go back for another.

Once I've eaten that one, I walk into the pantry to grab another one and a soda when the door of the pantry slams closed behind me.

I hate that door. It always sticks, and sure enough, it's closed, stuck fast.

"Help," I yell and bang on the door. My terror at the darkness makes me crazy, and I scream and bang at the door until someone opens it. I fly out, and Chase wraps his sweaty arms around me, holding me tightly as my breathing begins to calm.

He mutters soothing words in my ears and brushes my hair back from my forehead before wrapping my towel around me. I didn't even realize it was loose, but when he steps back, I can see something is off in his eyes.

He gives me a brief nod and then leaves me alone as my mom and Phil come into the kitchen, lambasting the caterer for only catering for three hundred.

I ignore them and go up to my room, dressing in my second best frilly black thong and push-up bra. I dry my hair and set to work on repairing my face, but it's slow going, and when my mom calls me down for dinner, I'm only just ready.

My dress is simple, knee-length, and lace. I have pantyhose on and black ankle boots that have a low heel on them. My clutch has my cell, my car keys, and my spare lip gloss, along with a hair tie.

As I leave my room, I see Chase coming out of his, and I stop for a moment and stare.

The man is heaven sent, but in a suit, he looks insanely hot, and I lose my train of thought. He doesn't even look my way as he passes me, and I wonder if he's angry with me.

It kills me that he won't look at me, and the whole way through our dinner, he won't make eye contact with me. He stares at his cell or at his plate and doesn't eat the chicken cacciatore his aunt made for dinner.

We all finish up, and I stay behind to clear up because my mom and Phil have gone to get the cars.

Strewan left to go outside, and Stephanie disappeared to finish getting ready in case any of Chase's band mates happened to show up. Calindra ignores me as I take the plates to her, but then she 'accidentally' splashes me with dirty dishwater ten minutes before the cars are due.

I know she dislikes me, but I accept her fretful apology before I dash from the kitchen and run back to my room to change.

The only other black dress I have is a scallop edged black bodycon dress that I wore to Alexa's birthday party last year. Without any time or another option, I pull my dress over my head and tug the other one on.

It's fitted, and there's a zip up the back, but it gets stuck and I can hear the cars downstairs. I know my mom will be furious that I'm not there, but I can't get the fucking stupid zip up my dress.

"Cassie, the cars are here," Chase calls in a dead-sounding voice, and I growl as I try to tug at the zip. "You okay?" he asks through the closed door, and I yell a string of curse words that would make a sailor blush.

"Stupid cunting fucking idiotic arsehole zip."

He opens the door and catches sight of me trying to get the zip to move.

His face lightens, and a smile crosses his lips before he comes over and brushes my hair over my shoulder. His fingers find the zip, and I feel like I can't breathe as he slowly pulls it up. His eyes meet and hold mine in the mirror the entire time, and he presses a soft kiss to my bare shoulder as he steps back.

He doesn't say a word as he leaves, and I grab my black cardigan from the back of the door, taking off after him.

The cars are here, and everyone is inside, but as I close the door, I see one door is open and there's one spot for me, right beside Chase. We don't speak the entire journey, and his head is bowed.

I can't take my eyes from the hearse in front of us, and it hits me that Harvey is gone. He's really fucking gone, and he didn't even get to tell Chase how proud he was.

My eyes fill with tears, and I sniff, causing everyone to look round at me, but it's Chase's gaze I can feel burning into me.

"What's the matter with you?" Strewan asks, and everyone looks at him.

Stephanie laughs when I don't answer and mutters in a harsh tone, "She's obviously upset that Harvey is dead. I mean, who's going to pay for her car and her college now? Her mom's as broke as a two-cent coin, and she doesn't even know who her real dad is."

My blood begins to boil, and I can barely hear over the ringing in my ears, but what makes it worse is that Chase doesn't say a word. He doesn't defend me or stop her as she continues to berate me.

"She's got that preppy school to pay for, and I heard Daddy telling Mom that Harvey is so broke that he owes back tuition. She's gonna need to sell her car to pay it off, so that's why she's crying."

I open my mouth to answer back when Chase finally speaks, but not to defend me or to tell his bitch of a cousin to back off.

"Enough. It's about my dad tonight, so can you give it a fucking rest?"

Stephanie shuts up and Strewan goes back to his cell as I turn and stare out the window with tears streaming silently down my cheeks. I almost feel bad for a second that I couldn't get a hold of Chase when his dad asked me to. I almost feel bad because I didn't know Chase well enough to have his number, and it took me days to get it. Because of that, he missed his dad dying.

My throat burns, and I want to break down, but I scrub at my face, glad I'm wearing waterproof mascara. I refuse to turn to look at him, even though I can feel him looking at me.

As soon as the cars stop at the church, I run out, stopping beside my mom. I walk in with her and sit holding her as she cries. Chase and his uncle carry the coffin, and I can't help looking at Chase, who has tears streaming down his face as he lowers the coffin.

I keep my eyes forward, but I can't help glancing at him as the priest speaks about how we all came from ash, and it's ash we'll return to. He doesn't shift his gaze, and when the mass is over and everyone leaves, I make sure I get a ride back with my mom.

When we get back to the house, a few of Harvey's friends, Phil, and some of the neighbors all come back too. We're all sitting in the living room, talking, when Chase gets back. He comes in, grabs a drink, and sits sullenly over in the corner. He smiles when spoken to, accepts condolences, but doesn't talk to anyone and leaves after an hour.

I want to leave too, but my mom needs me, so I begin to top my soda can up with vodka or gin whenever I get my mom a drink, and soon, I have a slight buzz. I go to the bathroom, kick off my boots, and take my pantyhose off before going back to my mom.

I leave after a few minutes when Cathy from next door comes to sit with her, and I decide to go to bed. I'm halfway along the corridor when I hear a noise that piques my curiosity. I follow the sound and push open Harvey's office door to see Chase sitting on the floor, surrounded by newspaper clippings, ticket stubs, and CDs.

I'm about to back out when he says my name.

"Cassie, wait, please…"

I shake my head and go to back away, but he's quicker than me, and in my drunken state, I'm not as steady as normal on my feet.

"Please, I need to talk to you."

Ha, that's a joke. If he'd wanted to say something to me, he could have said it in the car when I was being attacked by his cousin.

"No. I have nothing to say to you."

His face falls, and his arm drops from my waist as I take a step back from him.

"I don't blame you. I fuck everything up. It's just what I do."

A tear falls from his eyes, and I know I should turn and walk away. Logically, I know it's the right thing to do, but emotionally, I can't.

I move closer to him and wrap my arm around his waist as he crashes his lips down on mine. He backs me into the door, and I hear the click of the lock as he twists it.

"Cassie, you are so fucking gorgeous."

His tongue slides into my mouth, and he licks and sucks my lips, pressing hard against me. My body is awash with sensations, and I want nothing more than him inside me, around me, and over me.

His fingers dance up my sides, and I shudder as he brushes them under my breasts.

My nipples tighten, and he brushes soft kisses along my lips and down my neck. His hands spin me around, and he lowers my zip inch by inch as his lips and tongue dance along my neck and spine.

One more twist and I'm back facing him, with my dress pooled on the floor at my feet. His eyes darken as they scan my body before he drops to his knees and presses whisper soft kisses along my abdomen.

After a few moments, he stops and looks up at me with a determined expression on his face. "I'm so sorry about earlier. I didn't know what to say that wouldn't make it worse, but seeing how much it hurt you, killed me. Please forgive me?"

I nod once and he grins up at me before going back to kissing my abdomen.

My fingers push into his hair, and I let my head roll back as he dips his tongue into my belly button. His lips blaze a trail down, and he kisses me through my panties, making my knees buckle as a whimper leaves my mouth.

"Open," he growls as I press my thighs together, and I instantly shift my legs wider for him.

His tongue licks at my clit, and my fingers tighten in his hair as he slips a finger into my thong, pushing it inside me as he continues to tongue me.

My body shakes harder than ever, and I bring my hand up to my mouth, biting down on the back of my hand as he pushes into me harder and faster. His mouth and the feel of his finger inside me has me moving against him as the tension builds. He sucks my clit into his mouth and pushes hard against me before I come harder and faster than I ever have before.

His eyes glisten as he stares up at me, and he drags my panties down my legs while I'm still shaking from the orgasm rolling through me.

"Cassie, come down here."

He tugs me down and kisses me and then flips us so he's above me. His bright eyes show nothing but pure lust, and I know he wants inside of me. I'm ready, and I want him, but I can still see some reluctance in his eyes.

I lift my body up and begin taking his shirt off, one button at a time. My fingers tug each one off, and he tosses his shirt over to the desk when the buttons are open. My fingers fumble on his suit pants, but he puts his hand over mine, stilling my movements.

"Cassie, we don't have to do this." His words are quiet, and I lean up, brushing my lips against his before I speak again.

"I want this. I want you."

"But I'm your stepbrother…"

"No, you aren't. We don't know each other like that. You said it already. You don't know me like a stepsister…"

I break off as a thought crashes into my mind. What if he doesn't want me? What if he's scared that I'll tell someone?

"I won't tell." My voice is low, unsure, and I know I've said the wrong thing.

The buzz of my orgasm is fading, and I think he definitely doesn't want me anymore.

"You think that's it?" His face darkens and he sits back, moving away from me. "I don't give a shit who knows about this. We aren't fucking related, but I'm worried what it would do to you if it got out that I'd fucked my stepsister. That I'd tasted her sweet pussy and then slid my cock inside her, taking her virginity, even though I'm older than her. It would ruin you."

"I don't care."

I know I'm being stubborn and childish, but I don't. I want him, and I don't fucking care that he's my stepbrother, or that he's Chase Crawford. All I care about is him and me.

"Chase," I beg, but he shakes his head and buries his face in his hands. "Chase, look at me," I try again, but he shakes his head. For a moment, I sit and watch him. Maybe it's time to get him out of his head.

I crawl over to him and he tries half-heartedly to push me away, but I don't let him. I settle myself on his crotch and slip my hands around him, holding him and running my fingers up and down his back. I can feel his resolve waver as his cock pulses between my thighs and when his lips begin to kiss the sensitive skin on my neck.

"Fuck, Cassie. You're gonna be the death of me."

His lips crash down on mine, and his hands move to my breasts, taking my nipples between his fingers and rolling and teasing them as I rub against his crotch.

His dick twitches, and he pulls me down harder, kissing me firmly and pinching my nipples almost to the point of pain, and I come again with more force than the last time. My head spins and my body clenches against him before he places a gentle kiss on my lips.

"Are you sure, Cassie? We don't have to do this."

My body is slack, but I grin at him and mutter in his ear, "Yes, I want you to fuck me. Hard and fast and give me everything you've got."

His eyes glaze over at my words, and he tugs his underwear down, freeing his cock as he rifles with his other hand through his wallet. He rips the condom he finds open with his teeth and gives his cock two quick pumps before he slides the condom down.

My eyes follow his hands, and he smirks at my wide-eyed expression.

How is that fucking mammoth going to fit inside me?

# Chapter 9

# NO ONE BEFORE

## Chase

MY EYES RAKE OVER HER, and I can't believe what I've done and what I'm about to do. My mind is telling me not to, but my dick needs inside of her.

She's so fucking gorgeous, lying there with her cheeks flushed from the orgasms I've given her, and I know I'm going to savor this moment right here for the rest of my fucking life.

I lean down and watch her face as I lick her bare pussy. She groans, and I lick over and over again, until she's pushing up against me. My cock is throbbing with an aching need, and I can't stop myself now.

Even though I know I'm going to regret this and that it shouldn't be happening, it's all I want.

My heart begins to race as I position myself at her entrance, and her eyes widen as I slowly push into her, inch by inch.

Her fingers contract on my arm and I still, waiting for her to open her eyes and look at me before I move. Slowly, her eyes open, and I can see the pain in them, but I lean down and kiss her as I slowly pull out and then go back in.

Her tight little pussy is heaven, and I never want to leave, but my body has me moving slowly at first and then I begin to pick up the pace, growling in her ear as I slide into her.

"Fuck me, Cass. You're so fucking tight."

She moans my name, and I stare into her eyes as I begin to move faster. My pubic bone is rubbing against her clit, and I push myself against her furiously as my own passion takes over.

Her body starts to shake, and I know she's on the precipice, but I need her to go over with me, so I stop moving again and she whines.

For a moment, we're both still, and then I'm on her lips, like a starving man at a buffet. My cock grinds into her and my tongue devours her when she freezes. She throws her head back and moans softly, but the feel of her coming around my cock throws me over the edge, and I follow her, groaning her name over and over again.

I collapse beside her as my heart races in my chest so fast I think I'm about to have a coronary.

We lie in silence, and I wonder what's going through her head, but before I get a chance to ask, there's a knock at the door and we both spring apart.

The door's locked, but if whoever it is has a key then we're fucked. Cassie plucks up her discarded clothes as I quickly pull up my slacks and search for my shirt. She dives into the bathroom as I do up the buttons of my shirt and snatch her panties from the floor, seconds before Phil opens the door.

He glances at me and comes in with a bottle of my dad's scotch, sitting down at the desk and pouring us both a glass.

I want to get him out of the office, but he raises his glass, tips the contents back, and then stares at me until I do the same. I take the drink, ignoring the burn of the whisky as I watch him, wishing I could think of a reason to get him away, but I have nothing.

We sit and share a few drinks until Calindra comes searching for him and drags him out to their car. As soon as they're gone, I quickly lock the door again and go into the bathroom. Cassie is asleep on the floor.

Her dress is on, but not zipped up, and her hair is fanned out behind her. She is so fucking beautiful, and I almost feel guilty for taking her virginity, but who the fuck could blame me?

She's sweet, kind, caring and doesn't take my shit. In another life, I could really find myself falling for this girl, but as it is, I have to leave her. I know the more I get involved, the harder it's going to be on both of us.

I need to stay away, but I don't know if I have the willpower. Seeing her tonight in that dress blew my fucking mind, and I didn't know what to say in the car. I wanted to tell Stephanie to mind her fucking business, but that would have made it worse.

Saying nothing though was worse, and I saw her cry. It made me feel like shit, and I knew she'd gotten under my skin. My fingers snake under her and I pick her up, stumbling back in my drunkenness, but I manage to stay standing.

I carry her from the study to her bedroom and slip her out of her dress. My mouth waters at the sight of her naked pussy, and I can't resist one more taste. She's fast asleep as I lean down and run my tongue along her seams. I part her folds and kiss her, sucking and licking, and she wakes, shoving on my shoulders and then tugging me closer.

My tongue pushes harder as her hands come down to grip on my hair. Her fingers scratch at my head, and she moans my name, but I don't stop, shoving my tongue in and out of her sweet little cunt until she gushes against my mouth and I lap it up. I milk everything from her, savoring this taste, because I know I have to stop.

"Oh my God, Chase."

Her soft sighs as she falls back against the pillows make me want to sink into her again, so I kick my pants off as she lies wet, wide, and willing on the bed. I move up her body, slipping my tongue into her mouth as my cock glides into her tight pussy.

"Chase, I need…" she moans, and I cut off her words with a slow roll of my hips. My cock pushes against her walls, and she throws her head back with a loud groan, so I put my hand over her lips and whisper *sshh* into her ear before pulling out and slamming back in.

"What do you need, Cass?" My voice is barely a whisper, and her body bucks against mine as I thrust in and out harder and harder.

"You… I… we… more."

Her words are quiet, breathless, and I oblige, moving my hand from her mouth as I pound into her. I stop holding back and fuck her harder and harder until her walls start contracting around me, and my cock pulses inside her.

"Fuck, that was epic."

My fervent kisses and her responsiveness to me burns a bit of her into my soul, and I know I have to leave her. I know that this it because if I don't leave now, I never will. I give her one final kiss, and she turns to stare at me.

"I thought I was dreaming about you, but my dreams are nowhere near as hot as this."

I capture her lips in a soft kiss and pull back, standing up and pulling my boxers on. I turn, watching as she rolls over and falls back to sleep. My eyes stay on her for a while, and I lean over, pressing a soft kiss to the nape of her neck before I shift myself to get up.

She's an addiction I can't have, and one I need to break. I need to leave her alone now or I never will, and as she moans in her sleep, part of me feels like a creep sitting here watching her. I press one last kiss to her neck and sit up, running my hands up her naked body before I slip a shirt over her head and tuck her in, letting my lips linger on her forehead for a moment.

I kiss her once more, gently, and go back to my room where I spend the rest of the night tossing and turning. Eventually, I give up and get up, sitting by the window with my guitar in hand.

I begin to play soft melodies and use my cell to record them after texting my band mates back to reassure them I'm okay.

I see messages from Carla, Holly, and DJ, my regular fuck buddies, but I ignore them. I don't want any of them. Not anymore, and the reason for my change of mood is sleeping a few feet away from me down the hallway.

I miss her already, but I can't do more with her. It'll only hurt her in the long run, so for now, I'm going to stay away from her.

I slip her thong from my pocket and tuck it into the lining of my guitar case, taking it as a memento of us and her first time, but I won't tell her that. She can hate me all she wants, but I'll always have a piece of her with me. No matter where I go or what happens, I'll always be her first.

# Chapter 10

# LIGHTNING STRIKES AGAIN

## Cassie

Five years later

IT'S BEEN four hours since I made the call I swore I'd never make, but I needed someone to be by my side, and he always told me to call if I needed anything.

I never used his cell number, and he updated it frequently, but it's been five years since I last saw Chase.

He's still in Deviant, and they are the biggest selling artists in the world, but other than Happy Birthday, Merry Christmas, and Happy Thanksgiving, I don't hear from him and he doesn't hear from me.

After his dad's funeral, he spent the day shut in his room, and when he left the next day, he hired a car. He left a note propped up in my bed, but all it said was *I'm sorry.*

I finished high school and went to Amherst College but transferred to Stanford. I'd always wanted to go to Stanford, but I wasn't brave enough to leave my mom and go so far away, until things went wrong with Abe, and then I knew I had to do it. I transferred out after my first year, but I only ever went to one other Deviant gig, and he treated me like shit, so I never went back.

My mom moved out to California to be near me, but we still owned the property in New York, or Chase did. I wasn't sure how it worked, but my mom made sure I had enough for school and that I didn't have to work.

She'd gotten a job as a care worker for the elderly and was at her job four days ago when she got ill. She had an aneurysm, and they didn't know if she was going to make it.

I spent four nights sleeping in the hospital room beside her, but this morning, I overheard the doctors talking, and I knew they would be coming in soon to tell me she's dying.

I asked them when they came into the room and they all nodded sadly, so I caved, and I called Chase. My message on his answer-phone was basically me begging him to come to Cedars and help me. I tried Sienna first. She's been my bestie since our first day at Stanford, but she's currently globetrotting, and in the Australian outback. I spoke to her last week and she told me that she was going to be out of cell service, but I had to at least try her first. When I couldn't get her, I called Chase.

I know he's in a relationship, and she seems like a nice girl by all accounts in the press, but I need someone to be by my side, and it has to be him.

My feet pace the room, and I check my cell constantly, but there's nothing. The nurse comes in, and I eye her hopefully, but Chase doesn't appear, and she's busy checking my mom over.

"If there's someone else, you might want to call them. It won't be long now."

I nod at her, but I have no one to call. We have no one. I sit by my mom's bed and cry until I drift into an exhausted sleep.

"Cass," a soft voice says, and I try to open my eyes, but it's when he strokes my face that I manage to get my eyes open. Chase has come.

He dropped everything to come, and the sight of him, older, wiser, and sexier than ever makes my soul sing in a way it hasn't in years.

"Hey, sweetheart," he mutters as he leans forward and presses his lips to my forehead, and time just stops. It's as though no time has passed, yet things are so very different now. For a few moments, my body responds to his touch like it did five years ago, but like five years ago when he left me without a word, reality sets in and someone breaks the moment.

"Oh, Chase. Did you find her okay?" a girl's voice called from the door, and my heart sinks like a stone as I turn to see Belinda Harper at the door. She's like an angel with whisky-colored eyes and honey blonde hair. "Hi, I'm Bel. You must be Chase's stepsister, Cassandra. It's a pleasure to meet you."

Her eyes scan my puffy, make-up free face, ratty t-shirt and loose sweats, and I know she's assessed me as no threat, but I really don't care.

"Hi," I croak in a sleepy whisper, turning back to face my mom to hide the emotion playing on my face. I wanted him to come to help me, but him bringing his girlfriend when my mom is dying doesn't sit right with me. They barely had a relationship, so it's not like he needs the support or anything.

"Bel, can you give us a few minutes, please?"

"What, and wait out there? What if someone recognizes me?"

I clench my hand on my lap, and I know Chase noticed. I can feel his gaze burning into me from where I'm sitting. I don't give a shit if someone recognizes her. I don't even know her, and my mom is going to die, but she doesn't care. My head is about to explode when Chase gets up and speaks tenderly to her.

He speaks to her as though she's someone who needs to be babied. My heart shatters when he leans down and kisses her softly, but I close my eyes and count to ten, then twenty, and then thirty, until I hear the door click closed again.

Chase walks slowly over to sit down beside me, but I can't bear to even look at him, so I sit staring at my mom, watching her slow, steady breaths. A few hours tick by, and Chase sits with me speaking unless someone comes into the room. He's awkward, and it sucks. I asked him to help me, but the memories of his taste and touch are ever present, and the air is thick with unspoken words. When Belinda never reappears, I begin to relax a little.

"So, you're with Belinda?"

He nods, and his eyes scan my face before dropping to his hands.

"How've you been?' I suck at small talk, but the silence is too thick, and I feel like it's suffocating me.

"Good. You?" He doesn't meet my gaze, and I wish he would, but how can I ask him to look at me when I'm afraid of what I'll see in his piercing blue gaze?

"Uh… okay, I guess."

"And school? It was good?"

My mind darts back to school and my relationship with Abe, how it ended, and how I left to come to Stanford after freshman year to escape the memories.

"It was all right. Not much to say."

After that, he goes silent, and I can't think of anything else to say. I turn back to my mom as memories of our last night together wash through me. Rinse, cycle, repeat, like always.

My body thrums because Chase is near me, and I know I've never seriously considered anyone else, even Abe. I knew it wouldn't last with him, so that was why I chose him. He still loved Ella and I never went with anyone else because I realized I like rough sex. I loved him pushing my limits, and although he scared me a little, I really enjoyed our time together.

I shift my gaze back to my mom and guilt washes over me at the fact that I'm sitting beside her, thinking of how much I want Chase. Calling him here was a mistake, and part of me wishes he would leave. He doesn't speak again. He just sits steadily at my side, close enough to feel, but as untouchable as ever.

My eyes don't leave my mom, small as she is in the giant bed and so peaceful looking. Chase wraps his arms around me, holding me as the nurse tells me it won't be too long now. I still don't look at him or say a word though. Not even when I feel his lips brush against my shoulder after the nurse leaves. He moves closer, and I can feel his steady warmth up my back, making my spine tingle, and his lips barely leave my exposed skin. It's wrong. It's so fucked up, but I can't make him move. He's the only thing that's given me any comfort since my mom was brought here.

He breaks the silence in the room first, whispering softly against my neck. It makes me gasp, and he presses small open-mouthed kisses along my skin, licking and sucking on it.

"I missed you, Cass. I know I shouldn't and that it's not the time, but I missed you so fucking much."

My mom opens her eyes when he stops speaking, stares right at Chase and me, smiles, and then drifts back to sleep. I shoot over to her, muttering things and wanting to call the nurse, but then I notice that her body is barely moving.

Her breathing is becoming slower and slower until her breaths stop altogether and I'm all alone. I have no one, and it hits me harder than I ever would have imagined.

My mom is gone. I don't have a dad, and there's no one who cares enough about me to support me through this. Phil moved away after Harvey passed and barely kept in touch until he passed away last year. That was why I called Chase. I needed someone to be there, and although he said he missed me, he still left me. Everyone I love leaves me. Him, Abe, my dad, Harvey, and now my mom. For a while, I just sit and hold my mom's hands as my tears fall. Chase holds me, muttering soft words and apologies into my hair as I sob on his chest and his lips brush against my skin. He doesn't let go of me, but every now and then he'll check his cell like he's got somewhere he needs to be.

When Chase gets up and calls the nurse in, I don't need them to tell me she's gone. I already know. I accept their condolences and sit stroking my mom's hand until it grows colder and stiffer. The nurse comes back in a while later as Chase is typing furiously on his cell. She gives me a kind look and touches my shoulder, giving it a squeeze.

"Cassie, I'm really sorry about your mom. Do you need anything? Is there anyone else I can call or anything I can do for you?"

I shake my head, and she leans down to meet my eyes. Chase is frowning at his cell on the other side of the room, but I barely see him.

"It's almost time to say goodbye. We need to take your mom to the morgue, but take as long as you need, okay?"

I give her a sharp nod and sit staring at her and the tendrils of hair that usually float around her face. She is so at ease, and it makes me feel better knowing she's finally at peace.

"Would you like a coffee and some water?" the nurse asks, and I ignore her, but Chase answers in a soft voice, coming back to sit beside me as she walks towards the door.

"That would be great. Thank you," Chase answers when I don't, and in truth, I could do with a drink. My throat is parched, and I can't remember the last time I ate or drank anything.

The nurses come in and out, and eventually the doctor comes. He's very kind and methodical as he asks us to wait outside. There's no drama or fanfare as he comes out, speaking to me and telling me he needs to leave and that my mom needs to go to the morgue now.

"Go back in and say goodbye," he says softly as his hand grasps mine, "then we need to take her to the mortuary. You need to go home and get some rest. Your friend here can take care of the details from us."

Chase stays outside with the doctor as I go back into the room, laying my head on the bed, ignoring everything else, when Chase speaks again, shattering the silence. His hands haven't stopped touching me since he's come back into the room. His warm hand links with mine and he squeezes it tightly.

"Cass, we should go. I've text Bel to let her know I'm taking you home with me. You shouldn't be alone right now."

He touches my shoulder, and I stare up at him for a second before I shake my head. "No, you can go. It's fine. I'll be fine. Your girlfriend is probably waiting."

His sigh and how he runs his fingers through his hair are familiar to me, and he moves closer to me, so our mouths are almost touching. "I was with Bel at her house when I got your call, and she heard the message. She's kind enough that she wanted to come and help, and I didn't know how to say no to her."

"I'm not complaining. You have your own life. You don't need to be here. I'm fine on my own. Plus, my car's downstairs, so I can go home on my own."

"Please, just let me help, Cassie?"

"Why do you want to help?"

My heart pounds against my ribs as I ask the question, and I don't miss the way he glances away from me before answering, or how he runs his hands over his jeans.

"Because I still care about you. I want to help you and be here for you. Can I just take you home, please? You look exhausted and like you need a break."

I want to say no, but he reaches up, rubbing a tear from my cheek, and I swallow the lust that pools instantly in my stomach at his touch. My heart soars as he leans closer and presses a soft kiss to my forehead and wraps his arms around me, holding me as I break down again at his kindness.

After a few minutes have passed and he's stood up facing me, I shake off the overwhelming grief that hits me again almost as soon as he stands. My mom's dead, and all I can think about is how much I still want him. It's sick and wrong, and I'm disgusted with myself.

"Come on, Cass. Let's go home."

I give my mom one last look before I let him wrap his arm around me and lead me to the door.

As we walk by the nurse who was waiting, she hands me my

mom's purse with all her belongings in it. My throat clogs with tears, and I can't speak as I hold tightly onto her possessions.

My eyes blur as I let Chase take the lead. I'm not even watching where we're going, but when we reach the parking garage, he leads the way to a dark Sedan and opens the back up.

"Cassie, in you get."

His soft hands lift me into the seat and click the belt before he shuts the door and walks around the car to the driver's side.

Belinda's sitting in the front seat of the car, but she's on her cell and doesn't look back as he drives us away from the hospital. I don't look at them as they speak softly in the front, but I hear every word.

"What are you doing? I thought you didn't want to help her. I thought you were going to sit with her for a bit and then we were going to get back to our weekend."

"I'm not talking about this here."

I feel his eyes on me for a moment, but I don't move, react, or flinch. He didn't want to help me. Well, he didn't fucking have to. I was fine on my own. Just fucking fine.

"Chase, I'm sorry, I just got your message. This is my only time off, and now your stepsister is tagging along to my house when I wanted to spend time with you alone."

"I'm taking her to my house, not yours. She needs me."

"I don't care. I thought we were going to fix things and now you're going off with your stepsister. No offence, Catie…" she calls over her shoulder, and I stiffen as Chase automatically corrects her.

"It's Cassie. She's all alone and I won't let her go through this by herself."

"But you said you didn't even want to go to the hospital, that it was a huge imposition and that she should have called someone else."

I gasp as Chase meets my eyes in the mirror. He shakes his head sadly before he turns to her, and the fury in his expression takes my breath away.

"Stop. Stop now."

He turns to face me slowly, and I just stare numbly back at him.

"Cass," he says in a small voice, but I shake my head and lean back against the seat.

"Come on, Chase. We had plans this weekend."

My eyes close, and another tear rolls down my cheek. I try to think of something to say, but I have nothing. I'll get a cab home whenever we get where we're going. I attempt to block her words out, but it's like an earworm, repeating on a loop, and I barely hear Chase as he speaks to her.

"Bel, enough. I'm done talking about this."

His voice is firmer than I've ever heard it, and she sighs loudly, turning the radio up and effectively ending the conversation. My head pounds as I think about how I was so wrong about her. She always seemed so nice in the press and in interviews, when in reality, she's a stuck-up, selfish asshole.

Once we reach the hills, Chase pulls into a drive and idles the car by the curb. He leaves the engine running as he gets out and speaks to her outside the car. I watch her pace around, throw a hissy fit worthy of a toddler, and then storm away into the house as he walks back around the car.

I close my eyes as she walks away and pretend to be asleep because I don't want to face him. As soon as he's in the car, he turns the music off and sits for a moment in silence.

I'm not sure if I've just wrecked his relationship or if they're always like that in private. In public, they're the golden couple.

"Cass, you awake?"

His soft voice makes my skin tingle, but I refuse to answer. I don't even know what to say or how to respond to the fact that his girlfriend is a grade A bitch or that he just stood there and let her speak to him like that.

When I don't answer, he waits a few more seconds before he backs the car out of the drive and begins driving away. My eyes stay closed, and eventually, my exhaustion overwhelms me enough to let me drift off to sleep.

I dream about my mom, and about sitting on the beach in Malibu with her. She's smiling and joking, and it makes my heart happy to see her like that.

I wake as Chase scoops me up from the seat and carries me into a house, placing me in a bedroom by the staircase. My sleepy eyes open when he puts me on the bed and leans over me, brushing his lips against my forehead.

"Go back to sleep, sweetheart. It's okay. You're safe here. You're in my house, and I won't be leaving you again."

Was I safe though, or would he claim another piece of my heart and never give it back? Our eyes hold for a moment, and I can see my desire for him reflected back at me, but he blinks, and it's gone.

"I'll be right outside. I have a few calls to make, but you should rest."

I want to thank him, but the words won't come, so I nod, and he smiles at me in a way that melts my insides and makes my heart stutter.

I know I need to wake up and realize it isn't normal to feel this connected to someone after five years, but I can't help it. *He has a girlfriend, and you just lost your mom.* But it's not lost on me that he looks at me like he did all those years ago. He brushes my hair from my cheek and then steps back before he turns and leaves the room, closing the door.

The room is bright and airy and looks out onto the beach, which, after my dream about my mom, hits me hard in the gut.

My eyes dart to her purse, but I'm not ready to examine the contents, and the pillows on this amazing bed are calling me. I tug up a pale grey comforter and snuggle down, falling asleep almost instantly and waking hours later.

I sit up in the bed with a start, glancing around and taking in the dark grey floors, light grey and white walls, white furniture, and messy bed.

My feet slip on the floor as I stand, and I stare around, hoping to hear some noise, but the house is silent.

I glance down at my clothes and see the four-day-old clothes are dirty and wonder if there's a bathroom I can use to clean up. I'm in desperate need of a shower and to brush my teeth.

My eyes scan the room, and I see a door with a chair in front of it. As I pad across the floor to open it, I hear a noise outside and I see Chase through the window, pacing along the beach.

As I open the door, I see a large, grey-tiled bathroom with a walk-in shower and small bath. My investigation of the room yields shower gel, shampoo, and fluffy towels. My hands shake as my mind goes back to my mom, lying there looking so peaceful she could have been asleep, but I push down the guilt and the pain as I turn the faucet for the shower on.

The water warms quickly, and I step out of my clothes as the first of my tears fall. The water dulls the sounds, and I stand in the shower, sobbing until I'm sitting on the floor.

Eventually, my tears subside, and I stand, washing my hair and my body before getting out and wrapping a fluffy towel around me.

I wrap another towel around my hair and go out into the room, searching for something to wear. I rifle through the drawers, discarding shirts and pants, until I come to one that houses hockey shirts, baseball shirts, and football jerseys.

I grab a Yankees top out and pull it on, letting it fall to cover me as I drop the towel to the floor.

My feet pad across the floor, scooping my purse up, and I sit on a chair by the window, digging out the hair tie from my purse. I also come across a comb and I decide to plait my hair.

It takes time and patience and gives me something to focus on while my heart breaks over and over again.

Each tear that falls drips onto the shirt I'm wearing, but I make no effort to hide them. There isn't any point because they keep coming.

After my hair is almost done, there's a knock at the door, and Chase pops his head in. He gasps when he takes in the bed and steps fully into the room before he spots me sitting on the chair.

"Hey, are you hungry? I was going to get some dinner..."

My eyes drink in the sight of him, tanned, toned, and sexy as hell, but he seems different somehow.

*Am I hungry?*

I can't even remember the last time I properly ate, but my stomach answers for me when it growls loudly, breaking the silence between us.

"Uh, I guess I am. What're you getting?"

His eyes dart to mine and then away as though he's feeling awkward or guilty, and it hurts that he won't even look at me.

"Chinese food okay? Or there's a really good pizza place?"

At the mention of pizza, my mind flips back to sitting with him all those years ago, eating pizza and trying to deny my attraction to him. My face heats as I remember how hard he took my virginity, how much of a force of nature he was then, and how much I wanted him, but he glances down at the floor and all my memories pop at the sight of him staring so hard away from me.

"Uh, whatever. I'll eat anything."

He nods slowly and turns towards the door, stepping outside and closing it with a snap. I guess he doesn't want me to go with him. Maybe he doesn't want me around after all. Maybe I should just go back home and start to organize my mom's funeral.

The thought of doing it alone kills me inside, but it beats the alternative of staying here and having Chase look at me like I'm some stranger.

# Chapter 11

# KISMET OR CLARITY

## Chase

FOR THE PAST FIVE YEARS, I've tried to put her out of my head, to stop myself wanting to go to her and tell her all my secrets. I've had to stop my body reacting to her and force myself to stop looking at her, because it hurts.

It breaks my heart that I don't know the woman she's become. I don't know what her degree is in, or how college was for her. I don't know if she's got a boyfriend or if she's been with anyone else since me.

I spent today speaking to Tony's friend, Kent, who owns a funeral home nearby. I want to take the stress from her and bear the brunt of her pain, but she isn't mine to own or to fix.

I'm with Bel, and I thought I loved her. I really did, until today, and now my head's a mess because Cassie called me when she needed help. She called me, and I know it probably doesn't mean jack shit, but I want it to mean something to her. I want to mean more to her than the guy who took her virginity and then left.

Knowing she's in my bed in my house makes my cock harder

than it's been in years, but I won't cave. I won't let myself trust what I know I'm feeling because, if it's true, then my life these past five years has been a huge fucking lie.

After speaking to Kent and organizing as much as I can without Cassie, I go and sit in my study and nurse a stiff drink, opening the file in my desk that I've had since two years after I left her. The file gives me all the details that I need to know about her life, where she went to school, who she was with, and how she survived without me.

She never knew I had a PI tailing her. She never realized that I had to know if she was okay and that I couldn't let her go. It wasn't like I could ask Janie how Cass was, and when I mentioned her, Janie would end the call or change the subject.

My head swims, and I see my cell light up with message after message from Bel and the guys. I ignore every single one and lean back in my chair, reading the report.

She went to a college for a year, then Stanford and majored in English lit. Al followed her for a few months, and in the report are images of her with her friends, some different guys, and at a few bars. One photo shows them kissing, and my heart explodes with pure fury because the sight of her kissing someone else kills me.

I know she was engaged to a different guy, and the thought of her agreeing to marry someone else makes me murderously angry. I pour myself another drink and try to force myself to calm down. It was years ago that I heard about her engagement, after all, and if they'd still been together, she'd have called him instead of me. Plus, there's no ring on her finger. I checked. I had to.

My eyes close, and I drift off into a drunken doze, waking when I hear the shower going, and I know she's awake.

Knowing she's naked in the next room makes my cock rock solid, I palm my dick through my shorts as I picture her with water running down her tits and between her thighs.

Maybe if I jerk off before I see her, I won't feel this choking tension when I talk to her.

My hand slides into my shorts, and I imagine going into the bathroom and pushing her against the tiles as I slide my cock in and out of her soaking wet pussy. I picture myself fisting her hair and holding her lips to mine while I take what I want, what I need from her, my hips piston up as my balls tingle, and I'm shooting my load over my hands, coming quicker than I have in years. My breathing returns to normal as I sit at the desk, cleaning my hands on a tissue.

I want to talk to her, to find out how her life is, and I want to see how her pussy tastes after all these years, but I can't. I have to stop these thoughts, or I'll never be able to face her. To distract myself, I pick up my cell, which shows a dozen more messages and missed calls from Bel.

I have to call her back. As it rings, I hear the shower shut off, and I swallow the urge to go in there for a taste.

"What?"

Bel's voice snaps me back to the present, and I know she's pissed at me. I totally blew her off today, but if she hadn't been lying beside me when I got the message from Cassie then I never would have told her. "Chase, are you even listening to me?"

"Sorry. I was miles away."

Her sigh sounds down the line, and she speaks in an irritated voice. "We're supposed to be going to the premiere tonight. Are you still coming?"

Fuck. I totally forgot about that. Deviant are on the soundtrack, and I have a cameo in the movie, but I don't want to go anymore. I never really did, but Bel was totally up for going.

"Uh, I…"

"Don't you dare. Don't you dare tell me that you're not coming. I mean it, Chase."

"Bel, come on…"

"No. You come on. We've been planning this for weeks, and now you're blowing me off again because…"

"Because my stepmother died today, and I need to help plan her funeral."

"You didn't even know the woman. Don't even try to act like you're fucking sad about it."

My blood starts to boil, and I know I'm angry at her because she's partly right. I didn't know Janie well, but I cared a lot about her. She always kept in contact with me after my dad died and let me know I could talk to her, as long as I kept my distance from Cassie. I don't really know Cassie anymore, and that kills me.

Her mom finding out we had sex when she was just a teenager ruined any chance I had of getting to know her, and her making me promise to stay away, made my heart break in so many ways over the years.

Why I let her mom push me out of her life, I don't know. Maybe it's because she deserved better. Maybe it's because with her I took what I wanted and didn't care about the consequence, but regardless I can't leave her to do this on her own.

I try playing the guilt card again, but I told Bel about my relationship issues with my dad, and how I barely knew Janie. I never even mentioned Cass to her before today. I couldn't talk about her, not with Bel or the guys. No one knew that I'd screwed my stepsister, that I'd never forgotten the sweet taste of her pussy or how good she felt wrapped around my dick. They never knew that she changed me, and that she saved me that day when she took us away from the funeral. That was the day I think I lost a piece of my soul to her.

Instead of telling anyone about her, I turned to drink, drugs, and fucking, and then I met Belinda. She was like a fucking dream in the bedroom, and she let me do whatever I wanted to her. She rarely said no, but when she did, I didn't push. I'd never been as forceful as I was with Cassie with anyone else, and that worried me. That was part of the reason I didn't push back when Janie told me she knew about Cassie and me.

I hear a thump in the shower, and a mental picture flashes up in my mind of Cassie soapy and wet in the shower. My heart flips over.

*And now my dick's hard again. Way to fucking go, dumbass.*

"Belinda, just stop. I didn't peg you as a selfish brat, but here we are. It's not all about you or about me."

"Are you seriously choosing her over me? Because if you are, you'll be sorry."

"There's no choice to be made. Her mom died this morning, and she needs me."

"Go fuck yourself, Chase."

"Uh huh. Bye then."

I end the call and sit back, running my fingers through my hair. Five minutes Cassie's been back in my life, and I've just dumped my girlfriend of two years, although we've been on the outs for a while.

She cheated on me with Dean Davis six months ago, I caught them in her bed one night. She cried, begged me for another chance, and convinced me it would be a PR nightmare if we split since we were Hollywood's golden couple, but I'd never really forgiven her for it.

After a few minutes, I get up and go to Cassie's room, knocking on the door. She doesn't know it, but she's actually in my bed. This is my room, and I never let anyone, not even Belinda, into my space. I told her the guest room was my bedroom, that I didn't use the backroom, and I locked the door when she was over, but since we spent most of our time at my apartment, it wasn't really an issue.

When I open the door and spot her in one of my shirts, my heart pounds in my chest because she looks damn good in it.

*Get a grip, Chase.*

I try to force myself to concentrate, and to do that, I try not to look at her, but my eyes flicker to her every few seconds. Her understated beauty takes my breath away. She's like the sun; staring at her for too long blinds you, and you have to look away.

When I ask if she's hungry and offer the options, I see the blush on her cheek at the mention of pizza, and I wonder if her mind goes back to when my dad died too.

I can barely look at her, and when I leave to go order the food, I close the door on her. My fingers tap at the app as I lean on the hallway wall outside her room. Just as I'm about to put my cell away, the door opens, and she walks out and into my chest with her arms loaded with laundry that she promptly drops on the floor at our feet.

"Oof, sorry, Chase."

Her legs slip under her and my arm shoots out, steadying her. Our eyes lock as I tug her up to me and I can see she's been crying. Her bloodshot eyes and the swollen lids are a dead giveaway.

"You okay?"

My voice is hoarse, but she stills in my arms and then nods before shaking her head.

"I don't know. I miss her and I just want to call her and have her cook for me as I sit at the table and talk to her. It's just so hard… knowing I'll… never get to see her again and that… she'll never see me get married or have kids…"

Her broken words chill me because she's right.

Our parents should have been there to see us do all those things, and it's so hard that they won't be there to see them.

"It's just so unfair and now… I'm all alone… I have no one left…"

"You have me. You'll always have me, Cass."

I wrap my arms around her and hold her tightly, never wanting to let her go. Her body is stiff at first but relaxes in my embrace, and for the first time in years, I feel like I'm home.

I've been all around the world, slept with my fair share of girls, but never has anyone felt like home, until now.

My lips touch her forehead, and I want to take it further. Fuck, I want to take her into my office and take her six ways from Sunday on my desk, but it's not the time to be doing anything, so I swallow my desire and lead her to my living room, watching her sit down on the sofa.

"You want a drink, Cass?"

She stares at me quizzically for a beat, and I normally wouldn't offer alcohol, but her mom died and she's wound tight as a ball, so I want her to have something that'll help her relax, to open up and to wind down.

She shrugs and I move closer to her.

"What you got?" Her voice is low, playful and teasing, making my cock stir in my pants as my gaze gets lost in her hazel eyes.

"Vodka, gin, wine or scotch."

I want her to drink scotch with me so I can taste it on her lips. I close my eyes for a beat as the vision of her on the bench in the sauna swims before my eyes. Her soft whisper breaks me from my daze.

"Uh, vodka soda, please?"

I give her a brief nod and go out to the hallway, gathering her laundry and dropping it into the machine. My eyes scan the laundry room, and I toss in some fabric softener and soap powder before I go through the door that leads to the kitchen, pouring myself a large scotch and her the drink she asked for. My hands shake as I take it back into her, and just as I put the drink into her hand, my doorbell rings.

I quickly answer it and find Kent and Tony there. I'd forgotten in all the commotion that I'd asked them to come over to make the arrangements.

My heart breaks as I introduce them to Cassie and make sure that she knows that it's covered. I'm paying for everything. It's the least I can do. It takes over an hour, but once it's done and organized, she relaxes against the sofa. Her legs are curled under her and her body is so close to mine that I can't breathe. She turns to face me, and all I can think about is tasting her lips, probing her mouth with my tongue, and running my hands up her thighs until I stroke her naked pussy. Before I can make a move, our food arrives.

We sit in silence and eat, taking sips from our glasses and watching some mind-numbing show on TV.

I'm barely paying attention as I text the boys back and forth about missing tonight. They are a little pissed at me for shirking my responsibilities, but mostly understand. Tony asks if I can just come to the red carpet and then go back home. Show face and all, but I don't want to I'm not going and that's that.

As the show catches my attention, I'm sitting beside Cass on the couch. She's curled on her side, with her head on her arm, and I can see right up the top she has on to the top of her round thighs, with just a hint of her peachy ass on display.

My mind wanders, and I start chatting with Cassie, trying to fill the blanks in for the years that I missed.

"What happened after I left? Why didn't you ever come to see me on tour or come to a show?"

She bites her lip as she surveys me, and my dick hardens. I lean forward to get a drink of soda, and she shifts, giving me a momentary view of her sweet pussy. My hand clenches at my side to stop me reaching out for her when she crosses her legs and sits up.

Her eyes fill with tears, and I want to reach out to her, to comfort her, but what can I say? *I'm sorry I'm a douche? I'm sorry I got scared and ran away from you, from us, because I was worried about what people would think of me banging my stepsister?*

"I did come. Once."

"Wait… what?"

My ears ring, and I turn fully toward her, staring at her in disbelief as her words sound over and over in my ears.

She doesn't answer for a moment, and I watch as a tear rolls down her cheek.

"It was a few months after you'd been home, and I tried to call you. I was having a hard time, and my mom was drinking a lot, but I had a ticket for your show, so I decided to come. I had a backstage pass, but I wasn't sure about it, so I tried to call you and you told me to fuck off and leave you alone."

I remembered. It was when I was drinking a lot and taking so much shit Mason threatened to have me committed to a rehab facility, but the dusty memory rears up and hits me like a punch to the gut. My mouth goes dry and my chest hurts as I watch her take a small sip of her soda before she starts speaking again.

"I came backstage anyway, and I saw…"

I know exactly what she saw. I convinced one of our groupies to give me oral in the green room because of the call, because I felt like shit about leaving her, and about how I'd told her to fuck off.

"Yeah, I know what you saw, and Cassie, I…"

I want to explain to her. I want to tell her I was struggling too. I wanted to come home. I got halfway there earlier that day and forced myself to turn my car around because she deserved better than me. Better than my fucked-up life.

"It's okay. I knew it was a one-time thing with us. You never said otherwise… I just needed…"

She shook off her thoughts and turned the cable box on. I wanted to know what she needed, but her arms folded over her chest and she sat stiffly watching the TV as I stared at her.

During the episode, a character had died, and the cast were singing about the death. Her arms tightened, and I leaned over, tugging her towards me and wrapping my hands around her as her tears fell.

We don't speak, but I rub her shoulders, and she relaxes onto my chest. We sit like that, and I wish I could see into her head and figure out what she's feeling. I'm content and oddly happy because I feel like it's where I'm supposed to be, until my front door barges open and Bel storms in.

She glowers at us as we sit and watch TV, and then starts screaming at Cassie, calling her a slut and a homewrecker.

I feel Cassie tense under me, and I stand up, leading Belinda from my living room. She furiously storms after me and then turns and begins to march back towards Cassie.

"Stop, Bel. What the fuck is wrong with you?"

My voice is cold and commanding, and she stops, spinning towards me with disgust on her face. "Are you fucking her, Chase?"

I wish I was, but I'm not.

"Are you fucking crazy? She's my stepsister, and she's a fucking kid…"

"YOU LOOKED FUCKING COZY TOGETHER, AND SHE'S IN YOUR SHIRT!"

"Because she hasn't been home. I wouldn't touch her. She's almost related to me."

"But she isn't. Do you like her? Do you think she's hot, exotic, tempting because she's almost related to you?"

Her eyes dart back and forth between me and the living room, and I pray Cassie can't hear what I'm about to say because I'll never be able to get her back if she hears me. She'll hate me, and she'll be right to.

"Bel, I wouldn't fuck her if you paid me. She's nothing to me. Nothing at all. She's not my type, and I certainly don't find her attractive. She's too curvy, and her boobs are too big."

I see Bel relax, but when I look up, the first thing I see is Cassie standing by the living room door. Her eyes meet mine, and for a second, I see the pain I've caused her shining in her bright hazel depths, but she shakes her head and closes the door as a tear falls.

# Chapter 12

# HEARTBREAK SOUL SHAKE

## Cassie

HEARING what Chase says to Belinda kills me inside. When he had me wrapped in his arms, I felt safe, whole, and home, but now I feel dirty, cheap, and used. I close the door as his eyes meet mine, and I lean against it for a few moments.

I want to leave, to get as far away from him as I can, but I know if I do, I'll need to deal with everything on my own. My legs shake under me as I ponder my options, but I can't stay here. I can't be here and feel how I feel when I know he doesn't feel the same.

Part of me wonders if he's so disgusted by what we did, and that's why he never reached out or contacted me.

I walk to the sofa and sit down, running my hands over my face and wiping away the tears that have fallen.

*What the fuck am I waiting on?*

I stand up and then sit down.

*Maybe he'll explain. Maybe he'll come in and say he didn't mean it, that he was just saying that to her to protect me.*

*Does it matter?*

My head swims with questions, and I curl my knees up, hugging them to my chest as I sit and stare blankly at the TV.

My ears ring with his words. I know I have to leave, but I'm scared to. I'm scared of being alone, of burying my mom with no one beside me. Maybe I should call Abe, but he's with Ella now, and I don't even know if he'd care.

After a while, I hear the door open behind me, and I don't move. I check the time and see it's a little after six p.m. Chase came back into my life at ten o'clock this morning and already I feel like my life is upside down. I continue to stare blankly at the TV as Chase moves around the room, crossing in front of me in a tux.

He doesn't even look at me as he picks up his cell from the table, and I don't say a word to him as he walks from the room, closing the door with a snap.

I wait a few minutes, swallowing against the pain that lashes at me before I get up and go back into the room I slept in. The closet door is open, and I see his clothes lined up in neat little rows. His shoes are along the floor, and I spin in a circle, searching for something I can borrow.

I open drawers and close them when I find ties, boxers, shirts, and belts, but no joggers or t-shirts. Crossing the room, I frantically search through another dresser, finding a pair of joggers and a loose t-shirt that will do until I can get home.

My hands shake as I tug them on and shrug out of his baseball shirt.

I nab a pair of socks and sit on his bed, pulling them on before shoving my feet into my sneakers and searching around the room for my purse. My eyes find my mom's purse and my heart breaks all over again, but I have to get out.

I can't stand being here. My purse is nowhere to be seen, and I search under the bed, on the dresser, and open and close drawers.

I finally find it in the bottom cupboard in the bathroom and there's a note on top of it.

**Cassie**

**Please stay. I know you're probably desperate to leave, but I swear I'm going to explain everything. Please give me a chance to explain before you leave me.**

**Chase**

---

I ponder what to do, but how can I stay? How can I stay here and let him treat me like this? I'm nothing to him. He said that. He told her I was nothing to him, just another annoyance in his life.

I open my purse and find my cell, powering it on and debating who to call.

Eventually, my fingers hit a number that I know well, but that I haven't called in the longest time. As it rings, I play the conversation out in my mind, but when Ella answers, I almost lose my nerve.

"Hello, Abe's phone. Ella speaking."

My palms sweat and I almost drop my cell, but I suck in a breath as I try to speak around the lump in my throat.

"Uh, Ella, it's um… Cassie. I was wondering… is Abe there?"

Her sharp intake of breath and her cool tone when she answers tells me all I need to know. "No. He's out. Why are you calling him?"

"I just… I needed someone to… you know what, it doesn't matter. It's fine."

There's silence for a beat, and I want to hang up, but something holds me back.

"Cassie, are you okay?"

Ella's voice is softer, quieter, and kinder, and it almost breaks me apart. I really wanted to hate her. I wanted to loathe her for what she did to me, and I hated Abe too for running back to her when we were together, but I know she's better off with him. I never really loved him like I love Chase, and it would never have been fair to him.

"No. I'm uh… my mom died and I'm at my stepbrother's, but he hates me, and I just needed a friend. I'm sorry to have called you."

"Don't be sorry. It's okay. Abe's back now. We can come get you. Are you still in L.A.?"

"Yeah. I transferred to Stanford then moved here when school finished."

"Okay. Where are you?"

"I don't want to put you guys out. It's fine. Honestly."

There's a noise, and then I hear frantic whispering before Abe's voice comes down the line.

"Text me the address, Cassie. I'm coming to get you. I said when we broke up we'd stay friends and I meant it."

His tone tells me there'll be no argument, and my throat clogs with tears as the dial tone sounds in my ears. At least I have a friend I can call. At least he doesn't hate me. He should, but he doesn't and I'm so, so grateful for that. I didn't want to let him go, and I was awful to him when he ended things with me to get back with her.

I find a piece of paper with the address and text it to Abe. He pulls up within thirty minutes, and I leave Chase's house. I don't look back or read the frantic messages on my cell from him, and when he starts calling me an hour later, I silence the call.

Abe and Ella chat with me as they drive me out of Malibu and back across L.A. until they pull up at my mom's house. It's in a quiet little cul-de-sac, and the neighbors' lights are all on.

I thank them both and offer them a cup of coffee, which they turn down, but Abe comes around and gives me a warm hug.

"I'm sorry about your mom, Cassie. Janie was a wonderful woman. Text me the funeral details and I'll make sure we're there."

"Thank you. Thank you for coming to my rescue. You're a good man, Abe. Ella's a lucky girl."

I step back and wave at Ella as she smiles at me from the passenger seat, but Abe looks me square in the face as he answers.

"No. I'm the lucky one. I almost lost her, and she forgave me time and again. I'll never deserve her."

He glances to Ella, and his smile widens so much it hurts to look at.

"You deserve someone like that too. Someone who'd walk through fire for you. Don't let anyone treat you less than you deserve, Cass."

"Do you want us come in?" He nods to Ella and I shake my head. I can cope with some things, but seeing my ex-fiancé with the girl he dumped me for in my mom's house would be too much.

"No. That's okay. Thanks though."

"Hey. It's fine. As long as you're sure."

When I smile at him, he gives my hand a small squeeze and turns back to the car, waiting until I unlock our door and step inside before he drives off.

My eyes water as I glance around the small hallway of our three-bedroom townhouse. It's small, much smaller than Harvey's place, but it's been my home for the past two years, while I've been at school and I love it. I hang my purse by the door and pop my mom's onto the hook, letting my hand linger on it for a moment, but there's a smell of rotting garbage coming from the kitchen.

I go into the kitchen and tidy up, washing my coffee mug and plate, emptying the trash, and cleaning out the fridge.

There's nothing there. No milk or food, and my car is at the hospital. Should I go get it now? Or order a shop online and go get it tomorrow?

I'm not hungry, but I'll need coffee for the morning and some bread, so I decide to take my mom's cell, leaving mine in my purse so I can avoid Chase a little longer, and I order a cab to go get my car.

My Uber arrives within fifteen minutes, and it takes thirty minutes to get back to the hospital. Once I'm in my Prius, I head towards the supermarket and spend time tossing food into the cart.

I tune out the conversation that the cashiers are having and go to my car, loading my groceries into the backseat. My fingers fumble with the dial, and I put on Talk Radio, listening to them talking about the premiere Chase went to.

*"Chase Crawford turned and walked off the red carpet after a disagreement with Belinda Harper. Mason Michaels is apparently furious with him, but is this the end of him and Belinda Harper?"*

*"Well, she certainly didn't look happy, and it was clear that they were arguing all the way up the carpet, but the way he just shook her off and walked away doesn't look good."*

I turn the dial off and begin my drive home. Once I'm home, I pack away all my food and flop onto the sofa, exhausted. It's so hard even doing the simplest of tasks, and my eyes are heavy. Maybe if I close them for a while this will all be a bad dream and I'll wake up to my mom making coffee before her shift.

I let my eyes drift shut and pull the comforter over me as sleep claims me. My sleep is disturbed when there's a loud bang on my door, followed by a yell.

"Cassie, I know you're home. Open the door."

I want to ignore it. I want to go back to sleep, but I can't because the person knocking is now hammering on the wooden door, and I get up, tripping over and hitting my leg on the coffee table as I walk towards it.

I open the lock and peek outside when Chase shoves the door open. He storms inside, slamming it shut behind him. His eyes rake over me as his hands close over my shoulders and hold me tight.

"Why did you leave? Why didn't you wait for me to get back?" I stare sleepily up at him and he gives me a shake. "Cassie, why did you leave me?"

For a moment, I thought it was a dream, but then the events of the past day come back in glorious technicolor and my heart breaks all over again.

I shrug his arms off and step back from him. "Why would I wait? What can you possibly say to me to repair the damage?"

He steps close to me, and I instinctively back up. "Stop. Just listen to me."

His voice cracks and I shake my head. I can't listen. I don't want to. I've been through enough and this is too much to handle.

"Just leave. Please, just leave me alone."

"No. You have to hear me out."

He folds his hands across his chest and stares at me, willing me to relent, but I can't. I won't. After a few minutes of us standing there, he takes a slow step towards me.

"Cassie, I'm so sorry. I didn't mean anything I said to her. You have to believe me."

I want to. I desperately want to believe him, but all the evidence is against him, and I know if I let him back in, I'll get hurt again.

"No. I mean nothing to you. Nothing at all. That's what you said."

"But I only said that to protect you. When you didn't answer me or call me back, I knew I'd fucked up. Please believe me. Please?"

His eyes fill with tears, and it kills me to see him hurting, but as his tears cling to his lashes, I wonder what to say next because I don't believe him. I can't. He reaches out for me before dropping his hands and then running them through his hair as I speak. Every word has an impact on him. Every single one, and I can see the pain I'm feeling reflected back at me.

"I want to. You've no idea how much I want to believe you, but you left me, and you didn't want to see me again, then you said I mean nothing to you."

"Cass," he begins, but I hold up my hand to stop him, and he brushes a tear from my cheek. His touch is warmth, fire, and pain, and I can't take it.

"No. I need you to leave me alone, Chase. I've lost too much already, and I can't deal with this too. Please, just go."

His face falls as he drops his fingers from my skin, and he bites his lip, looking crestfallen as another tear rolls down his cheek.

"I don't want to leave you. Not again. It was hard enough the first time, but there's something you don't know…"

"Does it matter? It doesn't change what you did or how I feel. I need time to grieve and to process what's happened, and I can't do that with you. You consume me, and it hurts. It hurts so fucking bad, Chase."

I have to stop because I'm dangerously close to sobbing. He reaches out and pulls me into his arms, holding me as I break apart. His lips brush against my forehead, my lips, my eyes, and my cheeks, but when my tears subside, he steps back.

"You really want me to leave?"

His voice is a broken whisper, and I don't look at him as I nod, but he leans down, brushing my lips with the gentlest kiss I've ever had before he turns away with his hand on the doorknob. As he twists, he speaks once more before he steps out into the dark summer air.

"Cassie, I'm yours. I have been forever, and when you're ready for me or you need anything from me, I'll be here."

He closes the door behind him, and I drop to my knees, letting the pain overwhelm me. Part of me wants to call him back, but the other, saner part of me lets him go.

# Chapter 13

# PLEASURE & PAIN

## Chase

I CLOSE the door and lean against it as my heart tears in two. She wouldn't listen. I don't blame her, but it still kills me inside.

My eyes are full of tears as I walk slowly to my truck and climb in. I sit for a few minutes and wish I could go back inside.

It's time to tell her everything, but I can't until she's ready. My mind flashes back five years, watching her from afar on the day of the funeral and hiding in my dad's office to escape the insipid people downstairs. They were there to come to the funeral with us and I knew I had to stay away from her, but it wasn't until Janie caught me as the funeral cars arrived that killed any hope I had of having another taste of her.

My cock throbs as the memories of the night of the viewing swim around in my mind because I knew I was supposed to be leaving her alone, but her pussy was too addictive, and maybe, if I got one more taste, I'd be sated. I'd be able to leave her alone.

*I'd just stood up to leave the office when her mom opened the door and walked in.*

"Sit down, Chase."

I automatically sat because she looked as though she was ready to kill me, and her next words shook me to the core.

"I know you and Cassie have had sex and I know you might think you want her now, but you don't stick with any girl."

My heart hammered in my chest as I surveyed her. Her face was tight, and her eyes narrowed at me.

"I... I... she's.... We didn't," I stammered, not even sure what I was going to say, and she laughed humorlessly.

"I know you slept together. I came up to get something last night and heard you. Don't try lying to me."

My palms were slick with sweat, and I rubbed them on my slacks as I tried to answer her, but she frowned at me.

"She's my daughter, my little girl, and she's naive and young, so I'm going to ask you to stay away from her until you leave. She's just lost the only father she's ever known, and you and her together, is sick. What would people think?"

"I don't care..." I began, because I didn't care what people thought about me.

"What about Cassie? Do you care about her? Do you care enough about her to stay away from her, or doesn't her future matter to you?"

I started to shake my head, because I was leaving. I was going away the next day, but a big part of me wanted to sink balls deep into Cassie and stay there. I had to talk to Cassie and explain that I was leaving, not because of her, but because I didn't belong in her world. I didn't get scared of much, but what she was asking hurt and scared me in equal measure. I knew she wanted me to leave without a backward glance, but I couldn't do that to Cassie.

"Please, Chase. I'm begging you. Don't ruin my daughter. Stay away from her and let her forget about you. Don't talk to her, don't look at her, and don't tell her about this. Do the right thing by her."

"No. No. I can't leave her. Not like that. I have to at least explain. She knows I'm going, but I have to tell her that I'm walking away for her."

"Don't you dare. You have to do what's best for her. You have to leave *her alone and let her live her life. You're her stepbrother, and she deserves more than someone who'll ruin her for other guys just because he can."*

*Her eyes held mine and I wanted to protest, but she was right. Cassie was special. A rare gem, and I'd have destroyed her. I always left the girls I liked because I got spooked, so I ran.*

I had to leave, and I had to stay gone, so that was what I did. I didn't speak to her again, and it killed me. I left her a note with a simple *sorry*, because I couldn't lie to her, and I cut all contact. It hurt so fucking much, but I forced myself into work and tried my best not to think of her, but I couldn't not message her on her birthday or at Christmas, so I allowed myself that little contact. I also followed her on Instagram and would snoop on her profile from time to time. I'd stuck to Janie's rules, staying away from Cassie, but I'd fucked up because I loved her.

Something about her called me home, and I hated that I'd let other people's opinions of me form my decisions.

My hands shook, and I opened the door of the truck. I wanted to go back inside but how could I? She asked me to stay away, and I had to respect that.

For ten more minutes I sat outside, ignoring the incessant ringing of my cell, and hoping she'd come out, but she didn't. I eventually answered the call as I started my truck and drove back home.

"Chase, what the fuck?" Tony hissed down the line.

"I couldn't do it. Not anymore. I'm done playing her fucking games."

"Michaels is pissed! I don't know what to tell you."

"I shouldn't have gone. I said I wasn't going, but she forced me into it, and I fucking let her."

"Yeah, you should have just stayed the fuck home."

"Sorry. I know."

"Where are you?"

"I'm driving home from Cassie's."

"Isn't she staying with you?"

His simple words tear the chasm in my chest open, and I struggle to clear my throat so I can answer.

"Not anymore. She went home."

"Is she okay? Poor kid."

*No. She's not okay, but I had to leave her. I had to go home and let her grieve on her own, even though it killed me.*

"She'll be fine. She's strong."

"Yeah, she is. Listen, I'll speak with Michaels. We'll put out a press release saying there was a death in your family and that you just heard. It'll be fine."

"Thanks, man."

He ends the call, and I drive home in silence, wishing I could turn the car around and go back to her. Instead, I have to face the toxic pixie at my house.

When I get there, she's sitting in the limo, but as soon as I pull up, she storms out of the car and comes barreling towards me.

"What the fuck?" she screeches, and I put my hand up to stop her.

"Enough. We're done. In fact, give me my key and get the fuck off my property."

Her eyes glisten, and she comes towards me, but I'm done with her bullshit. I'm done with her lies. I'm just fucking done with her.

"You'll regret it. I mean it."

My shoulders stiffen, and I wonder what I ever saw in her. She's nothing but poison.

"I don't fucking care. Get out of here, right now."

"Chase, you might not care about you, but what about her?"

She holds her cell up, and I see an image of me holding her in the hospital. Her mom is in the background, and my heart thumps as I take in the scene.

"What are you going to do with that? Share it and show everyone the monster you are?"

"No. I'm going to share it and show everyone the sister-fucker you are."

My laugh is loud, and I actually walk towards her, towering over her as I reach her.

"Go right ahead, but one thing you might wanna prepare for is the legal battle I'm gonna bury you with. Defame my character all you want but be prepared to fucking pay."

I want her gone. I don't care anymore about what she says or does and, when she slaps me hard across the face, I just laugh at her.

"Get. The. Fuck. Outta here," I hiss in her face as my cheek stings, and she just laughs as she steps away from me. Her ass swings as she takes exaggerated steps to the limo.

"You'll regret this, Chase."

My eyes stay fixed on hers as she stands by the door and lifts her foot slowly inside, as though she's waiting on me changing my mind.

"I can say with certainty that I fucking won't."

Her gaze darkens, and she climbs in and slams the door. The driver takes off down my street, and I glance back at my house.

I need a scotch and my bed, but I want to see Cassie. I need to see her. Fuck this space between us. I'm over it. I need her and she needs me. My feet carry me back to my truck, and I climb in, blasting the air-con as I make the drive back to her house.

Once I'm there and parked, nerves flutter around my stomach, but I ignore them as I climb out of my truck and march up the steps to her door.

I take a breath and then start banging loudly with my fist in time with my racing pulse. My fingers tap on my thigh as I wait for her to open the door, and when she does, my mouth pops open at her shocked expression.

She opens her mouth to say something, and I step forward, roughly pushing her inside and slanting my mouth over hers, but not quite touching it. I can taste her breath and feel her body quivering against me as I kick the door closed with my foot.

"Tell me to go and I will. Tell me you don't want me like I want you, and I swear, I'll leave and never come back."

Her eyes sparkle and her fingers tense on my arms, digging her nails into me as she holds my hungry gaze.

"I can't," she whispers, and that's all it takes for me to lose control. My tongue presses along the seam of her mouth as I push my way between her thighs, lifting her slightly and holding her up with one hand, while my other is on her neck.

My fingers caress her neck while our lips battle, and she grinds against my hardening cock. My hand moves from her neck, down her shoulder, and over her breast, squeezing her nipple before teasing it between my thumb and forefinger.

"Chase," she moans into my mouth, and I drop her to her feet, pulling down her pants. Her pussy is bare, glistening with moisture, and I stare for a second at it before my lips are on it. I lift her leg over my shoulder and lick and suck her, inserting two fingers inside her and fucking her with them.

Her breathing speeds and I go harder and faster with my fingers and tongue, but it's when I suck her clit into my mouth and then push my tongue roughly against it that she splinters apart, coming so hard her legs shake under her.

Before she's even caught her breath, my pants are down, and I shove her against the wall, driving my cock into her still quivering pussy as I fuck her hard, fast, and furiously. My mouth devours hers, and I know she's what's been missing. Five fucking years I've held back, stopped myself going near her, but there's no stopping me now. As my balls tighten, and my cock pushes into her, pulsing and letting my juices flow, I know that she's it for me. She's my fucking home and I will never let anyone or anything come between us again. It's her and me.

"Fuck, Chase…" she pants against me. I press soft kisses along her neck, her collarbone, and her mouth. I'm afraid to meet her eyes, afraid she'll tell me to go, but more than that, I'm afraid she'll hate me. As my lips meet hers, I want to take her to bed and fuck her slowly.

"Chase, that was… something else…"

Her breathless words give me the confidence to peek up at her, and I see the same feelings reflected back at me.

"Can I stay with you?"

"Do you want to…." she begins as I speak, and we both stop and laugh. She pushes me back with her hands, and I slip out of her, instantly missing the connection, but seeing her walk away in my top is worth it. I step out of my pants, kicking my shoes off, and stand there in my shirt, socks, and nothing else. My dick begins to stir as she slips her fingers into mine and leads me into a room off the hallway.

My eyes scan the room, and I see an unmade bed, clothes littering the floor, and some books stacked upon a table. She leads me to the bed and tugs me onto it with her. I lie facing her and stroke my fingers over her face as she pops my shirt buttons one at a time.

Her hair is tied up in a loose topknot, and her face is free of make-up, but I've never been more turned on. She's fucking beautiful, and she's all mine.

Her hands trace over my chest, and I want to touch her, but when I move, she stops and glowers at me.

"No. Stop, Chase. It's my turn now."

I instantly stop moving and roll onto my back, watching as she climbs onto my crotch and gently touches my abs, my pecs, and down my V. Her body shifts, I can feel her wet heat over my cock. He's straining to get to her, but she slides farther down my legs and wraps her hands around my cock. As she begins to pump, I throw my head back, and a guttural sound makes its way up my throat when she wraps her lips around my cock and sucks gently.

"Cassie, FUCK!"

I moan loudly as she presses her tongue into the underside of my dick, and I hold on to her shoulders as she moves up and down my cock with precision. I lift my hips to meet her and marvel at her gag reflex, or lack of, but I want to come inside her.

"Stop, Cass… FUCK… "

My pulse is sounding loudly in my ears, and I know I'm seconds away from coming, but before I come, she stops and sits up, sliding herself onto me and slowly riding my cock. If her giving me oral was heaven then this is some next level shit because my heart feels like it's about to explode.

"Chase, fuck me," she commands, and I stare in awe at this gorgeous vixen sitting astride my cock and telling me how she wants me.

I growl up at her and flip us, so she's sitting on me as I slip in and out of her. Her moans grow louder, and I twist and squeeze her tits, using my thighs to fuck her harder and faster as our bodies move in sync with each other.

I can feel her orgasm beginning, but before it takes her, I still and hold her against me before I lift her up and stand up.

"On your front, Cass."

My words are met with silence, and I roughly flip her over. Once she's on her front, I tug her thighs, so her ass is in the air, and I spank her gently. Her groan of pleasure tells me she likes it, so I lean down and press a soft kiss to her ass cheek before spanking it again.

"You like that, Cass?" I ask as I stand behind her.

She doesn't answer, so I tap her ass again, harder than before, watching it pink before my eyes.

"Cassie, I'm waiting."

"Yes," she breathes in a low voice, and my palm slaps loudly against her skin as she answers.

"Oh, yes, Chase."

My cock throbs almost painfully, but I'm enjoying seeing what she likes too much to finish yet, so I hit her again and again, until her ass is a bright pink. My hand tingles, and I slide my fingers inside her slick pussy as I lower my tongue to her rim and lick.

Her body convulses on the bed, and I smirk in pleasure.

"Has anyone had this yet?" I ask as I run my finger over the crack of her ass. She shakes her head, and I slip my finger into my mouth, moistening it before sliding it slowly into her ass as I slip two fingers back inside her pussy and press my thumb to her clit. "Good. It's mine. I'll be the first in there too then."

Her loud moan makes the hairs on my neck stand up, and I slowly fuck her ass with one hand, while she rides my fingers.

"God, Cass, the things you make me wanna do to you…"

As her moans become more frequent and louder, I stop and lift her ass up from the bed, slamming my cock inside her and pushing a finger back into her ass. I begin to fuck her slowly, but after a minute, I need to go faster, so I ram into her.

My fingers curl in her hair, and I fuck her harder and harder until she cries out and her pussy clenches around my dick, setting my orgasm off. Her climax goes on and on, and when she collapses onto the bed, I want to lie down with her, but I need to wash up first.

"Where's the bathroom, Cass?"

My voice is low, hoarse, and tired, and she turns to face me. Her eyes are wary, and I can see the fear in the tightness around them and from the frown she has.

"I just need to wash up."

She relaxes against the pillows and mutters in a seductive voice, "Second door on the left. You can't miss it."

I stand, lean up, and kiss her lips firmly before I turn and walk from the room, closing the door gently as I walk to the bathroom on cloud nine. My heartbeat is still pounding furiously as I quickly take a leak and wash my hands and my face. I nab some mouthwash, and I'm mid-gurgle when the bathroom door flies open, making me cough and splutter as I choke at her unexpected arrival in the bathroom.

"What's up, babe?" I ask her breathlessly as I spit the remnants of the mouthwash into the sink, but she surprises me, shoving me hard until I meet her eyes. The sight of her standing there in nothing but my shirt makes me a little hard, but her words and the fierce look on her face knocks my desire away.

"Did you know?"

Her voice is a low hiss, and I stare at her, wondering what the fuck is going on. It's not until she shoves her cell under my face that I register the reason she's so freaking pissed, and after a second, I'm furious too.

"That fucking bitch…" I growl as I stare at the picture of Cassie in my arms. It's clearly from the hospital, and the more I stare at it, the more I can understand why Cassie is furious.

The caption. Oh, the caption…

*Chase Crawford left me tonight. He left me for her. This is nothing. This nonentity… who FYI is his fucking stepsister! He's a sick, twisted sister fucker and I hate him. Anyway, I thought his loyal fans should see the state of Cassie Danson and understand why I'm so fucking done with this complete and utter jackass.*

My blood rushes around my body, and I want to hit something, or someone, but I know it won't help. Cassie snatches her cell back.

"Did you fucking know, Chase?" she snaps, shoving her finger into my chest, and I glance away because I did know. "What the fuck? You knew she was going to do this to me?"

I swallow, about to speak, when her cell starts to ring. It's a blocked number, and I open my mouth to tell her to ignore it, but she puts her hand up and answers.

Her face darkens, and she stares at me in a way that rips my insides to shreds. She doesn't answer, just hangs up and turns to walk away from me.

# Chapter 14

## BETRAYAL BITES

## Cassie

I CAN'T FUCKING BELIEVE this. I can't believe he knew she was going to post something like this on her Instagram about me. Not only has she posted it and tagged him, but somehow, she's tagged me too.

And now my cell is ringing, and reporters are calling me, asking me if I'm really sleeping with my stepbrother and why I'd do that to Belinda.

Chase doesn't speak, and I'm not sure I want to hear his excuse. I just want him gone. If they found my cell, they'll have my address, and if they find him here…

I can't even finish the thought. I want him out. The fact he came here and fucked me, knowing that she was going to do that, infuriates me so much I can't stand to even look at him.

He follows me from the bathroom, and I hear his cell ringing in his pants. As I storm over to pick them up, the ringing stops. My hands shake hard as I shove them into his chest, and he opens his mouth to speak when his cell starts ringing again.

Shaking his head, he rifles through his pockets until he finds his cell, but I can't stand the sight of him anymore. Every time I catch his eyes, a murderous rage takes over my body, and I start shaking in fury.

I have to get away from him, so I go into the living room and plop myself down on the sofa as he follows me, speaking softly into his cell.

I try to tune him out, I really do, but every word is like a loudhailer in my head.

"No, Mason. Of course not." There's a slight pause before he speaks again. "Tony, come on. What the fuck do you take me for? She's a fucking kid and she's my stepsister." He's quiet again, and I watch his distorted reflection in the mirrored cabinet in the corner. "No. I am fucking telling you; I didn't fuck my stepsister. I'm not that fucking desperate or fucked up."

I can hardly bear to see his reflection anymore, and I sit stock still until he ends the call and rushes back into the bedroom. Seconds later, he's out the door, closing it softly behind him. The click makes me jump, and the sound of his truck starting up breaks the sleepy silence like a gunshot as he drives away. He didn't even say goodbye.

My heart breaks all over again, and I tug his top over my head, tossing it to the floor before I drag my tired ass to bed. Thoughts of my mom battle in my head with thoughts of Chase, and I eventually get up and take a sleeping tablet from my mom's cabinet in the bathroom.

Tiredness washes over me, and I sleep longer than I have in months because I have no finals to study for, no job on the horizon, and nothing to get up for.

When I finally wake, I see it's mid-afternoon, and I crawl into the shower, turning the heat up as the water pelts down on me. My skin breaks out in red welts, but I ignore it as I scrub at my skin.

I ignore my cell while I wash my hair and wax, taking my time to make sure I'm all clean and hair free before I get out.

My cell has been ringing incessantly while I've been showering, and I'm almost at breaking point when I glance at it and see that it's Chase. He's also texting me, but his message is so formal that I almost ignore it, until he replies again, saying he needs to talk to me about my mom's funeral.

"Yes!" I answer in my most waspish voice.

"I, uh… I need you to email a list of people who'll attend the funeral."

His tone is so formal, and it hurts to hear him so distant, but before I can say anything, I hear a ruckus outside. My heart stutters, and I miss what he says as I open my living room curtains to see a whole host of people standing outside.

They don't notice me at first, but then the noise level picks up, and I quickly step back, unable to breathe, to think.

"Cassie, are you listening to me?"

I ignore him for a second as I try to regulate my breathing, but then he calls my name again, and this time he sounds angry.

"Cassie!"

"What, Chase? What do you want?" I snap at him as my whole body starts to shake.

"I'll fix this. I'm sorry you got dragged into this, but it's not my fault…"

"Not your fault? Then whose fault is it? I didn't ask for this. I don't want this at my door."

"I know. I'm sorry. I'm so sorry…"

He breaks off and sucks in a breath as my cell beeps in my ear. I glance down at it and see Josiah, my mom's attorney, is calling me.

"Chase, I have to go."

I quickly end the conversation without waiting on him to say anything and answer Josiah's call. It's a brief one to inform me that my mom didn't leave a will, so all her possessions like the house and the cash in her account will come to me, but there's nothing he can do about Harvey's house.

That'll go to Chase. When I ask about my mom's account, he

tells me that there's a little over seventy thousand dollars in total, but the house is paid off. He asks about our past and I tell him about it without going into too much detail.

"She's from Utah originally, but we left when I was two, after my dad bailed, and then she worked as a waitress in a few places before she met Harvey in L.A. when I was eight."

"Okay, that's good. Can you remember anything else?"

I close my eyes and feel like something's clawing at my chest, but I can't figure out what it is, so I ignore it and answer.

"Not really. My earliest memories are of Mom and me in her station wagon, driving, but I don't remember much before the age of five."

"Okay, that's good. Thanks. I'll come out with the paperwork and we can get everything signed, sealed, and off to the courts, okay?"

As he ends the call, I sit back on the sofa and wonder what the feeling was that clawed at my chest. I don't remember what happened when I was small, but every time someone questioned me or my mom, I'd feel nervous, and somehow, afraid.

Trying to distract myself, I get up and focus on cooking some food, but it doesn't work. I want to go for a run, but I can't. When I look outside, there are more trucks and newscasters out there, so I'm stuck inside with painful memories and anxiety clawing at my chest.

As I watch something on TV, I ignore my cell as it rings and beeps and let myself get tuned into the show about vampires. I enjoy the twists and turns of it as the brothers fight for the same girl, but my solitude doesn't last, and eventually, there's a knock at the door that interrupts my ogling the hot vamps.

I don't want to go to the door. In fact, I've almost decided to ignore it when my cell starts to ring. My eyes dart down, and I see Chase is calling me. For a moment, I contemplate not answering, but I know now that I've seen it, I have to know what he wants.

"What is it?" I asked in a voice that crackles with the tiredness

I'm feeling. He sighs before he answers, and my stomach fills with flip flopping butterflies until he speaks again and surprises me.

"Can you let me in?"

I bolt from the sofa to the door and open it to see Chase standing there. Chase looks bored, as I open the door to let him in.

"What are you doing here?" I ask, and he glares at me in a way that makes my insides dance in discomfort.

"Didn't you read my messages?"

His eyes sparkle, and I want to step into him, to have him wrap his arms around my waist and feel his warmth for a moment, but he snarls a curse and shakes his head as I stare at him breaking me from my fantasies.

"What messages?"

"I text you like a dozen messages. I need your mom's outfit for her funeral. Haven't you bothered picking something out for her to wear?"

Tears prickle my eyes at his cruel tone and how blasé he's being.

"No. I ignored my cell."

His eyes blast into mine, and the hatred in the look he's giving me hurts more than I can say.

"Well, that's fucking great. Do you think you can pick something out for her now, or shall we just waste another hour driving to the funeral home and back again?"

My feet are frozen to the ground, and after a second, he growls at me and storms by me, opening my mom's bedroom door.

The smell of her perfume and her bedroom hits me, and I stumble back into the wall as he marches inside, but I can't let him choose her outfit. It's my job as her daughter. No matter how hard it is, I swallow the pain and go into the room.

My tears fall as I take in her perfectly made bed, nightlight still on with her book half-finished on the nightstand beside it.

She'll never finish the book or read the others that are stacked there just waiting to be read, or go to the movies, or the mall, and it's the things she'll miss doing that causes the sob to rise up my chest.

It hurts so much, but I hold it in, picking out a simple black dress with underwear, pantyhose, her favorite shoes, and the jewelry Harvey bought her before he died.

Chase stands by the door looking irritated as I fold and place her clothes into a bag from her favorite store. I also put inside the photo of us from her bedside table, and a coin that she's had for as long as I can remember.

"You nearly done? I have places to be!"

Chase speaks from the door, and I rush over, shoving the bag into his arms as I step outside the bedroom.

Seconds later, the door closes, and he leaves, but he doesn't even glance in my direction. As soon as the door closes, I collapse on the floor, sobbing.

That was by far the hardest thing I've ever done in my life, and I was all alone. Chase might as well not have been there. In fact, his behavior made the whole thing worse, and my sobs wrack my chest, ripping from me in a way that hurts my throat and destroys me completely.

I sob until my eyes are dry, and I go to bed, burrowing under the covers and drifting off to sleep eventually, which is where I spend the whole of the following day.

Chase has organized everything, so all I need to do is show up, but I have two more days. I lie in bed, only getting up to pee or to fill my stomach, but my food supplies are waning, and I need more than Cheetos and candy to eat, but I have no energy left.

My cell sits beside me on my dresser, ignored and forgotten about. I don't look at it. I don't answer when it rings. I ignore the door when it knocks, and I bury myself in my duvet, hoping that it'll all be a bad dream.

Eventually though, I have to use it to order some groceries, but I ignore all my notifications and log in to the grocery store, adding items to my shopping cart.

I'm about to pay when my cell rings, and I accidentally click on answer instead of ignoring it like I meant to.

"Cassie?" Chase asks cautiously, and I swallow the pain again at how he treated me. "I know you probably hate me right now, and to be honest, I hate myself for leaving you like that, for treating you so horribly, but I swear, I was doing it to protect you."

He pauses, but I say nothing. There's nothing to say. There's not a single excuse he could give me that would make up for what he did to me. He hurt me when I needed him most. *Again...*

"I'm so sorry. Tony suspected something, and he was sitting in the car waiting on me. We had a meeting with the label to get to and I was worried about it, so I took it out on you and I'm really, really sorry. Please believe me when I say that hearing you sob when I closed the door broke my heart."

His voice is hoarse, but I can't bring myself to say anything to him.

"Please, talk to me! Please say something."

Another pause, but I can't think what to say.

My mind is empty, broken, desolate, and nothing he says is making me feel any better.

"I really fucking did it this time. Now you hate me. But, Cassie, I'm going to make this up to you. I swear, I'll prove to you how very sorry I am."

I can hear the tears in his voice, and a part of me, a very small part, wants to say something to him to comfort him, but where was my comfort when I needed it? I can't say it. I just can't, and the silence that fills the line is filled with my unsaid words, and the emptiness I'm trying hard to feel. He speaks a few seconds later, begging me to answer him, but I don't. I won't ease his conscience.

"Please let me prove to you how sorry I am. Please let me back in."

No. No way. He can go to hell.

"Goodbye, Chase."

My voice cracks as I speak, and I end the call. I accidentally cancel my grocery order instead of paying for it, and I can't be bothered going back in and adding everything to my cart, so I don't. I shift and lie back on my bed, staring up at the ceiling and until I fall asleep. I wake up a few hours later as my cell beeps again.

My eyes drift to it, and I pick it up, glancing down to see a message from Chase. I rub my tired eyes and try to focus on the words, but I'm too tired, so I get up and go make myself a coffee with the last of my beans.

Didn't I use the last of the coffee? Oh, shit. I think I did. I can't function without it, so I guess I need to go to the store. I get up and sneak out the back door in loose sweats with a cap on and buy a few groceries including my java.

For the next few days I ignore everything and let myself wallow, eating junk food and takeout, but not leaving the house or answering my cell. I text Chase on day one to say I needed some time alone and he's been calling me and then texting after to say he's around if I need him.

I miss him, but I'm trying to shake my addiction to him, so I read the messages, but don't respond to him. I'm almost out of food and cash, but the idea of going to the store and abusing my credit card doesn't appeal to me, so I sit in bed and ignore the grumbling of my stomach for real food. I grab my last bag of Cheetos, hoping they'll tide me over and go back to bed, balancing my newly filled coffee cup on my dresser.

The dresser is overflowing with dishes, and I know my mom would hate the mess, so I quickly tidy away my used crockery before flopping back on my bed and picking up my cell. There are some more messages from Chase, from Abe, and my friends, but I open an email from Chase accidentally and my heart almost drops out of my chest.

---

*Cassie,*

*I know you don't want to speak to me right now, but this guy, Dave Spence, messaged my management team to see if he could track you down. He said you're his daughter Colleen, and that your mom kidnapped you when you were a toddler. He told Tony that he has proof and sent a birth certificate, marriage photos of him and your mom, and his divorce papers. He also apparently had custody of you, your older brother, Grant, who's forty-seven, and your sister, Amira, who's forty-eight.*

*He's given you a contact number to call him on and said he can put you in touch with your grandparents, aunts, and uncles if you like.*

*I've attached the photos and the contact details to the email, but it's entirely up to you what you do with this information.*

*I'm sorry for springing this on you, but I don't know what else to do. I miss you, Cass. I miss you so damn much, it's like someone's ripped my heart from my chest.*

*Can you let me know what you decide to do about Dave? I'll support you no matter what.*

*Chase*

---

I sit in stunned silence for a moment as I process the contents of the email, and when I click on the attachments my low-grade anxiety worsens.

I stare at the man claiming to be my father, and I wonder if he's telling the truth. I don't remember him at all. I don't know why though, but something about him scares me, and I wish I could ask my mom, but I can't.

I scroll through the documents and images and stare at a picture of my mom holding a baby beside two people in their twenties.

The girl is smiling, but the boy looks sullen and forlorn, and my mom's smile is forced. It's nothing like the carefree smile she had my whole life.

I stare for a long time at the picture, but when I scroll down, I see one more image, and I know for a fact that he is telling me the truth because I'm wearing an outfit that I loved in the photo.

My mom is smiling as she runs around the yard, pushing me on my yellow bike.

It's one of my earliest memories, and I remember her laugh and her smile as she played with me. I can't remember anything else, but I remember that day clearly.

I sit and stare at that photo, and I wonder how my mom could leave her other two children behind. How she could lie to me my whole life, and why she didn't tell me, even as an adult, who I was.

My fingers shake as I search Facebook and find my dad online. He's a judge, an engaged member of his local church, and he's posted a picture of me every year on my birthday that people have shared.

I glance at the comments and see people saying my mom was a monster for taking me, that he'll find me someday, and that they can't believe it's been so many years.

Part of me wants to reach out, but something holds me back, and I wish I could talk to someone about all of this.

My finger hovers over Abe's name in my cell phone, but I can't bring myself to call him. He's happy, settled, and moving on with Ella. I can't drag him back into my life when it's so messed up.

Next on my call list is Sienna, but I remember she's still off the grid in Australia. I miss her so much. She's the only person I've ever told about Chase and me, and I wish she was here now.

Lastly, there's Chase. My eyes fill with tears, and I want to call him. He's who I really want to talk to.

I miss him too. I know I shouldn't, but I do, and it sucks.

My finger accidentally presses the call button, and within a moment, the ringing sound fills the room.

"Cass, hey, are you okay? I didn't expect to hear from you!"

His voice is breathless, and I worry I've interrupted something, so I end the call and sit up, scrubbing at my face.

As my hands tug at my hair, my cell rings again, but this time it's a video call, and I take a moment to brush my hair from my face before I answer.

"Hey, sorry. I'm in the gym."

His anxious face fills the screen, and I want to cry. My throat burns, and I can barely get the words out through my tears.

"I… need… someone…"

He stares at me with a sad expression, and I wish he'd say something, but he doesn't for a beat, and then his words rush out.

"I'm in my condo. I'm not at the beach house at the moment, but it's in LA. It's just off Hollywood Boulevard. Why don't I text you the address and you can come over?" I start to shake my head, but he interrupts. "Don't say no, Cass. Please. Just come over. Bring a bag and you can stay for a few days. Or a few weeks. I don't care just come to me, please. I can't come to you because of the fucking vultures outside. They're making it so much worse, and if I come back then they'll spread shit."

"Chase, I don't think it's a good idea. The journalists will see me if I leave."

"I know, babe. I want to come to you, but if I come and stay, or if I come and pick you up, we'll have a tail that won't leave, and I don't want to do that to you. Can you drive? Or do you want to be alone?"

"I want you…"

"Then come here, please. Cass, I want to take care of you."

"Will they not follow me?"

"No. Alone you're not of interest to them. It's me they really want."

"Chase, I don't know."

"Cassie, I don't care about the journalists, I care about you. This is why I stayed away, denied myself what I wanted for so long. I need you too, babe. Come here, please?" He pauses and runs his fingers through his hair before staring at me in a way that unnerves me. His eyes burn into me through the screen, and I want to go to him so badly, but I'm still reticent. "Please. It's safe. I swear. There's underground parking, and the condo is in a different name. You'll be safe here."

I almost say no, and then I think about my anxiety over finding out who my dad is, and how it's all over the internet where I live. People are sharing pictures of my house and my address is everywhere, so I decide to accept.

"Okay. Text me the details. I'll leave soon."

He smiles at me and my heart flutters, but I ignore it as I hang up and begin to pack some things.

My mom's car is in the garage, it's a silver Audi. I can use that and drive out without having anyone try to stop me. My car is still parked out on the drive outside.

I put a few dresses, some jeans, some shirts, underwear, and sweaters into my college rucksack. I also pack my make-up, my hair irons, cell phone charger, and my toiletries, and I throw my MacBook and charger in on a whim.

Next, it's my shoes, I choose my dark healed Jimmy Choo boots that'll go with anything, a pair of Mary Janes, and some sneakers that I toss inside the almost full bag too.

I quickly shower and dress in a pair of jeans and a sweater, shoving my feet into my favorite pair of Nikes as I brush my hair out, wincing at the tugs in it. I French braid it and twist the braid into a knot at my neck before spraying some perfume. Once I'm satisfied that I don't look like something that's been dragged through a hedge backwards, I go into my room and make sure I've got everything I need.

As I'm about to leave, I stop at my mom's bedroom door and walk in. I haven't been in here in days, and I haven't touched anything since Chase came by for her outfit.

I stand and stare around the room and then walk over and sit on her bed. I wish she was here. I wish I could see her, talk to her, hold her one more time.

My eyes dart around the room, and I see her closet is still open from the other day. There's a box on the floor that is half-hidden, but I see it. I must have knocked it over in my haste to get her clothes.

I stand up, leaving my bag on the bed, and walk over to it. The box is old, taped closed, and weighs almost nothing. Part of me wonders what's in it, but another part of me is so angry with my mom that I toss the box across the room where it lands on her bed.

I storm over to it and want to rip it apart when I see my name on it in faded ink. I debate opening it, but if it's about my past, I don't think I want to be alone when I open it. Maybe I should take it to open when Chase is there. Maybe that's a better idea than opening it alone and melting down.

I pick it and my bag up and go out to the garage. My spot is still empty since my car is outside, so I pop the hood of my mom's car and stuff the box and the bag in the trunk.

Lastly, I plug in my cell and put the directions into the sat nav as I back out of the garage. I ignore the few shouts from journalists who are standing around, but I drive away and head towards the interstate.

# Chapter 15

# GUILTY AS SIN

## Chase

I PACE NERVOUSLY UP and down my apartment as I wait on Cassie to arrive. My palms are sweating, and I want nothing more than to down a bottle of scotch before she gets here, but I hold off.

I don't know what I'm in for with her, and after how I treated her, I don't deserve shit from her. I was my usual jackass self, but the look on her face fucking killed me, and as soon as I dropped Tony off with the things, I drove home and tried to call her.

I called over and over again, text her groveling apologies. I even drove over, but the stupid fucking reporters were still outside so I couldn't even go in.

Eventually, I drank myself to oblivion, and the boys came over to kick my ass. I released a press statement the following day, denying the rumors and explaining that she was my stepsister and that she'd just lost her mom.

I even told them that the moment Belinda chose to share was of Cassie's mom dying, but while most backed off, a few didn't care and were still camped out at her house.

The buzzing of my cell interrupts my musings, and I slam into the counter as I rush to grab it.

Cassie's name shows on the screen, and my heart does a somersault in my chest. She's here. She's downstairs. I told her to call me and that I'd go get her from the garage directly. I don't want anything getting out about her being here. I want to protect her and have time to apologize to her, but I'm not sure if she'll want to hear it.

I answer the call quickly and say hello.

"I'm here."

She doesn't say hi or say anything else, but I don't need her to.

"I'll be right down."

My answer is swift, and I use the service elevator in my kitchen to go to the underground garage. I gave her my code and had her park in one of my lots, so she should be fine, but I'm still nervous.

I anxiously bounce on the balls of my feet, much like I do before a show, but for some reason, the anxiety I'm feeling now is so much worse.

As the door opens, I see her standing across the lot. My breath catches as I take her in, and I wish I could go back to when I left. I should have stayed. I should never have left her after I fucked her, but my stupid pride and my ego wouldn't let me.

She glances up at my stare and wraps her arms across her chest, biting her lip as she waits on me to reach her. My heart rate spikes, and I want to pull her into my arms, hold her and never fucking let her go again, but her eyes narrow on me and I know I have a way to go to make things right between us.

"You got anything I can take?"

My voice is low and wobbles at the tension between us, but she nods to the trunk. Her eyes track my movements as I go to the trunk and take out her rucksack.

There's also a box in there, but she snatches it up before I can reach for it. There's an awkward pause as I glance at her, but she turns away from me, holding onto the box for dear life.

Our footsteps echo as I lead her across the lot and into the elevator, pressing my card against the reader to get to my floor.

The ride up is quiet with unsaid words between us, but I don't want to be the one to break it. What the fuck can I say to her?

I'm sorry I was a dick. *Lame.*

I'm sorry I hurt you. *Sucky.*

I'm sorry for leaving. *Which time?*

We step out when we reach my floor and I lead her to my bedroom. I know I'm an asshole, but I hope that her being here means she'll somehow forgive me. She doesn't say a word and walks inside, taking note of my few personal possessions that are dotted about, but I don't have much here. My house in Malibu has most of my belongings.

I clear my throat, and she turns to look at me. For the first time ever, I see fear in her expression. It's a kick in the gut, and I know I deserve it, but it burns right through me.

"I, uh… the bathroom's in there," I say, pointing to a door to my right and then speak again, popping the back onto the small seat by the window.

"I'll be sleeping down the hall. You can order food if you like. My iPad is there with the code on a slip of paper beside it, and my cards are registered."

I flounder because she doesn't give me the slightest indication that she's even listening to me. Her eyes are on the old cardboard box in her arms, and I walk over to her, touching her shoulder gently. I don't expect her reaction. She squeaks and moves away from me.

I knew I'd hurt her but seeing her visibly flinch, rips into me.

I hold my hands up and step away from her, sputtering out an apology as I leave her alone. The next few hours pass with me in my office, answering emails and messages, chatting with the band, and organizing our next studio sessions with Michaels.

I barely leave my office, and I drink a few sodas to stop myself reaching for the scotch. Eventually, my stomach growls, and I go in search of Cassie to see if she wants food.

I find her curled up on my bed, fast asleep with the box still unopened beside her. She hasn't eaten by the looks of things either, so I decide to order a pizza and some garlic sticks with soda to see if I can entice her out of my room.

I pick my comforter from the floor and drape it over her, brushing my hand over her soft skin. She mutters something and turns over onto her stomach. My eyes follow her every move, and I want nothing more than to crawl in beside her, but I can't. For one, it'd be super creepy for her to wake up with me in the bed, and two, she'd probably end me if she woke up and I was beside her.

Instead, I stand for a moment longer, watching her sleep, before I scoop up my iPad and key in the code as I walk to the living room.

Flopping down on the sofa, I order our food and put on *Tiger King* on Netflix. It's my current watch, and I can't believe how crazy it is.

I'm four episodes in and so caught up in it that I don't see her come into the room until she sits beside me on the sofa.

For a while, we don't speak, and I stare at the TV numbly, wishing she'd say something to break the silence, but she doesn't.

Eventually, I turn to her and she has her arms wrapped around her chest, holding tightly as tears stream down her face.

"Cass, come here."

I open my arms, then pull her towards me, but she stiffens, and I almost let go. My fingers loosen, and my eyes sting as I watch her trying to hide her pain.

I scoot closer to her and slide my arm around her back, tugging her gently to my chest and pressing my lips to her forehead.

The contact burns, and I kiss her skin over and over as I mutter apologies into her hair. I want to kiss her, to taste her lips and slide her under me again, but she breaks the contact before I can and darts to the other side of the room.

Her watery gaze pins me to the sofa, and she shakes her head at me.

"No, Chase," she cries as I push myself to the edge of the sofa. "Stop, please. I can't think around you. You really hurt me, and when you touch me, I forget all about it and I want more. It's not fair."

My chuckle fills the room, and she stops me with a glare that makes my dick hard.

"It's not funny, Chase. You really fucking messed me up and I don't want you touching me right now."

Her words make my smile slide from my face, and I sit straight. "Cassie, I am so, so sorry. Tony suspected something, and I knew I had to keep you safe. It's all I've ever wanted, and after your mom warning me off…"

"Wait, what?"

Her face drops as she glowers at me, stepping closer.

"Yeah, I was about to confess to you the other night that she wanted me to stay away from you, but then all that shit happened, and I left, again."

"When… when did she say this to you?" Her voice is cold, brittle, and her eyes are narrowed on my face.

"The day after we slept together. She spoke to me just after my dad's funeral. She was right. It shouldn't have happened then. You were too young, too innocent, but I was too selfish to say no. I take what I want and to hell with the consequences."

"So, it wasn't me? It wasn't that I wasn't enough for you? For five years I've wondered why you hid from me, why you didn't want to see me again…"

I hold my hand up and cut her off. "Cassie, I've wanted to see you every single day of the last five years. I became mean and angry, bitter and cruel because all I wanted to do was to come back to see you."

I slowly make my way toward her and she steps back until her back is flush against the wall. I stalk towards her like a lion hunting a gazelle, and when I reach her, my mouth hovers tantalizingly close to hers, but I won't kiss her until she lets me.

"Chase, we can't." Her voice is husky, and I watch as her tongue darts out to lick at her lips. My whole body clenches with desire and my cock is solid in my pants.

"Why not?" I ask, and I step closer until my body is touching hers. Her tits press against my chest, and all I want is to suck her taut little nipples into my mouth until she's moaning my name.

My lips brush against her cheeks, her nose, her chin, and finally, I press whisper soft kisses to her lips.

Her gasp of pleasure shoots to my dick, and just as I'm about to claim my prize, the pinging sound of the elevator echoes down the hall, interrupting our moment. My low groan in my throat as I rest my head against hers makes her frown.

"Cassie, I gotta go take care of this."

"What? Why?"

Her confused voice makes me want to stay right where I am, but I can't. I kiss her gently and hold her tightly against me. "I just need to sort this all out, but I need you to trust me, okay?"

She nods once at me, and I press one last soft kiss to her lips, savoring the taste and feel of her. I hope it's enough to get me through dealing with Belinda and her craziness, but I don't think even Cassie's kisses will help there.

The sound of the elevator doors opening has me stepping back. My lips burn and my cock aches as I try to get him to go back to sleep. He soon drops as I remember who it is and why she's here breaking my all-consuming Cassie fix.

Cassie looks at me in confusion, and for a moment, I want to stay exactly where I am because the sight of her there, chest heaving, flushed skin, and pebbled nipples entices me like nobody else ever has, but I can't. I need to stop her name getting dragged through the mud.

"Chase? Chase, where are you?" Bel calls out in a babyish voice that grates against my nerves. I run my hands through my hair as I turn away from Cassie. I don't miss her sharp intake of breath when she realizes who is here, and I see her stiffen in the mirror as I pass it.

My feet quickly carry me out into the hallway, and I stop Bel as she reaches the guest room and my office.

I've already set everything up. All I need is for her to talk. My fingers hover on the button I need to push, and my eyes narrow at her wide smile and the air of smugness around her.

"I knew you'd give in. I knew you'd come back to me," she says as I open the door and usher her into my office, closing the door behind us with a snap.

Neither of us has said a word for a few minutes, and I stare at her. My finger clicks the button and I wait. I know she'll cave first. She always does. I turn my head away from her and hear a soft sigh as she comes to where I'm standing at my desk.

I'm leaning on it, staring away from her, and trying to keep as much space between us as possible when she drops to her knees on the floor between my legs.

She's taken her coat off, and she's wearing a tight black corset with a g-string and nothing else. She runs her hands up my thighs and moans in pleasure when I grip her hands tightly.

"This… us… it's not fucking happening," I spit out as I push away from her and step around my desk, sitting down.

"Come on, Chase. I'll let you put your cock in my ass. I know how you like that."

I drop her hands in disgust and push them off me when she tries to run them up my legs. "I said no, Belinda."

She fingers her nipples as I stare at her and shake my head. She moves her hands to the waistband of my joggers and begins to untie them, but I catch her hands and push her off me again.

"No. Stop. That's not why I asked you over."

Her eyes glitter, and I wonder if it was foolish of me to think I could trap her into saying anything. I turn and walk around the table, sitting on my desk chair and wishing I hadn't bothered trying to fix this clusterfuck of a mess now. She interrupts my thoughts as she speaks.

"But it's why I came. I miss your cock and you fucking me. You know you like fucking my ass and how good I am at sucking you off. I know I messed up, but it's in the past."

My eyes burn into hers, and she licks her lips, thinking she's won, but I'm just so disgusted by her that I can barely think straight. What did I ever fucking see in this manipulative bitch in front of me?

"Come on. I'll suck your dick and then you can bend me over the table and fuck me any way you want."

"No. Stop, Bel. I'm not doing this with you. We're done. I told you that."

Her eyes darken as I speak, and she pushes up from the floor, coming around towards me. There's no way out. Behind me is a wall and the window, but as she climbs onto my lap, I want to vomit.

Her cloying perfume suffocates me, and I can barely breathe, but she speaks in a low voice, rubbing herself on my cock as she speaks. "Chase, just give in. You know you want me."

"I don't," I protest, and she sits back and stares down at me, looking surprised by my non-reaction.

"Jesus, you're not still mad about that stepsister thing, are you?"

"Of course I am. She just lost her mom and she's all alone, and rather than you shelving your jealousy so I could help her, you decided to attack her for coming into my life. She's just a kid, and you tried to ruin her because you want me all to yourself."

"Can you blame me?"

Her words make the bile rise in my stomach, but I swallow it down, because I'm almost there. I've almost got what I want from her, and as soon as I get it, she's gone. History.

"Why did you lie about me? I didn't dump you for her and you know it."

"Maybe not, but that's not what everyone else thinks! No one is going to want you now that you're a sister-fucker."

My blood boils and my hands clench onto the arms of my chair to stop myself from hitting her.

"So, you tried to ruin her to stop me from… what? Moving on? Finding someone else? Can't you see how fucked up that is?"

My eyes find hers and she sits back, chewing on her lip as she stares at me. "It doesn't matter. She won't want your help now. I'm all you've got."

I stand up abruptly and she drops to the floor, sliding along the tiles as I lean down and look into her eyes. "Get the fuck out. We're done. You and me… we're over, and I never, ever want to see you again."

"You don't mean that. You want me."

"I wouldn't touch you with a fucking ten-foot pole. Now get your ass out of here before I call the cops."

My tone is ice cold, and I know she can tell I'm serious because her face falls for a second. "You really don't want me anymore?"

I know she's fucked up, and part of me knows that it's because of her past, but I'm done making excuses for her. We're over. The minute she threatened Cassie, that was it. Game over.

Her eyes fill with tears, and for a moment, I almost feel sorry for her, but then I remember what she's put Cassie and I through, and my sympathy vanishes.

"Leave your key," I tell her as she dashes over to her coat and picks it up. A tear falls from her eyes as she puts my apartment key on the couch.

"Chase, I'm sorry. I shouldn't have tried to come between you and her. She's your family and I should have respected that, but I guess I'm just a jealous bitch."

I hold her stare for a second, but it's enough to see that she's acting. I know her tells too well to think she's being genuine.

"It's too late to apologize."

She stares at me in silence for a beat, and I speak again, pissed off because the girl I want is down the hall and I can't have her until I deal with the shitstorm of the past week.

"You can leave now?"

My voice is unkind and impatient, and she huffs, storming towards the door and slamming it behind her. I follow her to make sure she leaves and that she doesn't go into my room or the living room. I don't want her anywhere near Cassie ever again.

I see her into the elevator and call down, banning her from my apartment with Fuller, the building manager, and then I go back into my office and stop recording. I play it back on my laptop and then forward it to my publicist, Leigh, hoping she'll know what to do with it.

Once that's done, I go for a quick shower to wash Belinda off me and then go in search of Cassie.

# Chapter 16

# GHOSTS OF THE PAST

## Cassie

I WATCH Chase almost run away from me, and for a moment, I'm devastated, but then my hurt turns to fury.

What the fuck is she doing here? Why did he ask her here if I'm here?

I stand where he left me for a moment and scrub my hands over my face, trying to stop myself from going after him, but it's no use. I have to go that way to get to my room.

His 'trust me,' runs through my head, but how can I trust him? He hasn't given me much in the way of opportunities to trust him, so I carefully make my way towards him. I hear her talking to him, but before I reach them, he shows her into a room and closes the door.

For a few seconds, I stand and listen at the door, then make my way back to my room and lean on the door, eyeing the box on the bed.

I need a distraction, because while I'm away from Chase, I think clearly. I'm strong and capable, but when he touches me, I seem to lose all sense of self. I become putty in his hands, and all the reasons this is a bad idea leave me. All the things that can come between us float back into my head and make me doubt that I'll ever be enough for him.

For a few minutes, these thoughts go round and round in my head, and I want to run away, but instead, I slowly step towards the bed and sit by the unopened box that I hope has all the answers to my past.

I toy with the tape on the box and end up ripping it open. What's inside will hurt less, I hope, than the thought of him being in that office screaming at her.

No matter what's inside, I can cope. At least, that's what I tell myself as I slowly open the lid and peek inside. My hands brush over some folders, and I pick up the top one, flipping it open, and see it's a court transcript.

My eyes scan the document, and I see that my mom has made notes along the bottom of the pages.

*Dave lied to the court. He made out that I was addicted to pain medication, when in fact, his constant abuse was the reason I was self-medicating.*

My heart pounds in my throat as I sit down and read the document. It states that my mom was deemed too unstable to care for me, and that custody was being given to my dad.

Further down, I see that my mom's parents, Harold and Sue Stevens, also gave evidence against my mom, and that her sister said she was unstable.

The judge ruled in my dad's favor, and when I check the date, I see it's from three months before my mom ran away with me.

Next is the divorce papers where my mom cited irreconcilable differences.

Then there's a note from someone named Kelsey to my mom. My stomach flips as I read the letter, and I begin to understand more why my mom ran away.

*The cash is all here, and you and Colleen have fake names and fake identities. The car should last a while and I'm sorry I can't be with you when you go, but I will always be thinking of you both. Love you both, Kelsey.*

That's it for that folder, so I lay it aside and then open the next. Now that I've started this, I'm desperate for more details.

In the next folder, I find a letter from my mom addressed to me, and one to Grant, and one to Amira. I don't open the letter to me yet, and I set Grant and Amira's letters aside to be dealt with later.

Behind the letters are ER reports. There's at least thirty of them. My mom had broken ribs, a fractured leg, a miscarriage, three broken arms, a shoulder dislocation, and multiple trips to the emergency room, starting from three years before I was born, but worsening in the year before and the two years that followed.

There are images of my mom with bruises on her face, neck, torso, and back. There are reports from nurses working in the hospital that my mom was suffering domestic assault, and police reports that neighbors had called to report screams coming from my parents' house.

My stomach rolls, and I swallow against the horror of what my mom lived through. I decide to open her letter and find out what happened to her all those years ago, and why she ran with me.

My fingers shake as I undo the envelope and stare at my baby pictures. My mom looks happy in them, but there's something off about her. Her shoulders are tense, and her eyes aren't full of the life I was used to seeing in them.

My eyes water for a moment, and I sit back and suck in a breath, hoping I'm strong enough to cope with whatever's in the letter.

Once I feel a bit more composed, I swallow the tears and start reading the letter.

*Cassie*

*My beautiful girl. I'm so sorry that I lied to you for all these years. Today is your eighteenth birthday and you're currently out with your friends at a party. Harvey is off on business, and I know it's time I finally tell you the truth about us and your past.*

*My name is really Alice Spence, and I was brought up in Mansfield, Ohio. That's where I met your dad. He was my best friend for most of the years of our marriage, and I loved him very much, but one incident changed him.*

*We had three kids (before you came along), Amira, Grant, and Taylor. Taylor was our baby boy, and we loved our kids so much. However, not long after Taylor turned eighteen, he was out with friends and was killed in a car accident.*

*After the accident, your father changed. He started to drink more, and since both Grant and Amira were off at college, it was just him and me in the house. Eventually though, he began to get violent with me.*

*At first, I brushed it off, but after a while, he'd beat me up and then force himself on me. I didn't know what to do. He was a well-respected judge, and most of the cops were his friends.*

*I was a nurse, and I worked at the local hospital in the ER, but he made me leave when my colleagues began to question my bruises or missed workdays.*

*I had a miscarriage at forty-two, after your father beat me so badly, and then I fell pregnant with you. I told him I would leave and never come back if he hit me again while I was pregnant, and he stopped for a time. The sexual assaults continued, but he didn't hit me much while I was pregnant, and when we had you a part of the man, I'd fallen in love with peeked back through the awful mask he was wearing.*

*It didn't last though. When you were a few months old, the abuse got worse than ever. By the time you were eighteen months old, I'd been to the ER seventeen times.*

*Just before I had found out I was pregnant with you, I came across an old school friend of mine working in the ER.*

*Her name was Kelsey. She saved me. Saved us. She helped me save up, and eventually, I knew I had to leave. The tipping point was your father getting custody of you. He lied to everyone and everyone believed him. He was a judge, and the police, my parents, and siblings were all falling for* his act. No one would help me. My parents were furious with me for divorcing Dave and refused to listen to me, so I had no one to turn to for help.

For three months he only let me see you one day per week, but then he began to let you sleep over at my house.

On the night I decided to leave, he came by and dropped you off and you had a bruise on your back. That was the final straw. I put you to bed and was about to call Kelsey to arrange our leaving when he showed up and barged drunkenly into my house.

The neighbors heard my screams as he beat and raped me, then the police came, and he was taken away.

As soon as the cops left, I called Kelsey, and she came by and picked us up. We went back to your father's house, packed a few things into bags for you, and I took some of my jewelry that was in the dresser and then we left.

Kelsey's cousin worked in an auto shop, and he let us use his bathroom so I could dye my hair and step into a fat suit, Kelsey changed your hair color with a blonde wig.

We spent a few hours in a motel outside of Mansfield, and then I left with you and the money I'd managed to save.

I drove us for thirty-six hours to Portland where Kelsey's friend from Australia, Becca, lived. We stayed with her for six months. The jewelry was sold to a pawn shop in Florida by Kelsey, and she sent the money, via a check, to Becca.

Eventually, I got a job as a waitress under my new name, Janie Danson, and we called you Cassie instead of Colleen, but you were only two so you accepted it and after a while didn't even remember being called Colleen.

We eventually left Becca's house and moved to Los Angeles, and that was where I met Harvey. He moved us to New York a few months later when things got serious between us. Our life at the start was rough, but I wouldn't change our destination.

I do miss Grant and Amira, but they never knew about the abuse. I hid it from them. I know they probably hate me for leaving them. I didn't have *a choice though. Dave would have killed me if I stayed, and he was hurting you, so I ran with you.*

*I hope you understand and that when you find this all out, you can come and talk to me.*

*Love you so much my girl*

*Always*

*Mom.*

My tears fall when I reach the end of the letter, and I sit back on the bed, wondering why my mom felt the need to run. She had all that evidence, but then I remember that he was a judge and that she had no one.

My eyes scan the box, and I see another letter and one last folder, plus one small jewelry box tucked into the corner.

I take out the final folder and find newspaper clippings. My eyes scan them, and I see they are about Taylor's accident. He was killed by a drunk driver.

In the folder are family photos, and I see some of Grant and Amira. They all look happy, and Taylor was so cute, but in the few there are of me, everyone looks strained, forced, and unhappy.

They look a lot like my mom, and I sit staring at them for a few minutes before I pick up the other letter from the box.

My fingers dance along the seal, and I suck in a breath as I open the letter. Inside is two letters. One is from my mom, and the other is blank on the outside.

Opening the one from my mom, I read as she tells me she knows about me and Chase. She tells me she's sorry for hurting me, but it was better that I let Chase go. He's not the one for me, and I'm better than a drunken one-night stand with my step-brother. The last thing she said stands out though, and my eyes burn with tears. *Cassie, I saw the way you looked at him and how he looked at you, and that all-consuming, soul-altering feeling you have can break you.*

*Just look at what happened to me. I felt that for your father, and he completely destroyed me. While I loved Harvey, and I did, I really did. He put me back together and made me feel like me again, but it was only a shadow of who I had been.*

*My life with your dad was perfect and I loved it. I loved my kids and your dad, but my love wasn't enough, and having that and then it turning is the worst possible pain.*

*I know you probably hate me for it, but I can't let you fall for someone who consumes you that much. You can't make the same mistakes as me because having loved that fully and lost it means you can only ever give a part of your heart away because the rest of it doesn't belong to you anymore."*

That's it. That's all she says, and it hurts so much that she was so blinded by her past she ended up hurting me to protect me. I loved my mom, but part of me wishes she hadn't interfered.

The other letter is folded over, and since I need a distraction, I open it and four more letters fall out. The top one is a note from my mom.

*Cassie, I've put this/ these away from you. I'm sorry, but I really am doing what I think is best. Love Mom.*

I unfold the other notes and see that they're all in same untidy scrawl that was on the note on my bed when Chase left. My heart hammers in my chest as I look at the dates on them. The first is dated my birthday in 2017, and then there are two that don't have dates.

*Cassie, I wish I could come and see you on your birthday. I wish I could give you so much more than a stupid fucking text, but I can't. I made a promise to myself to stay away and let you live your life and I'll keep it, no matter how hard it is for me.*

*I miss you so much and I don't know how you managed to get buried so deep under my skin, but I can't get you out.*

*I hope you have the best birthday and are enjoying college.*
*All my love*
*Chase.*

The second one is from right after I went to find him when he was on tour.

*Cassie,*

*I'm so sorry I was such a dick to you. I loved hearing your voice, but I had to keep my distance. You completely overwhelm me, and I promised to let you live without me. Please don't hate me for being an asshole.*

*It killed me to be so fucking cruel, but it was so good to hear from you.*

*Missing you always,*

*Chase.*

And the last one is from a few months ago when I finished college.

*Cass, Today is your last day of college. I wish I could be there to celebrate with you. Have the best day. You deserve it.*

*Love*

*Chase.*

The tears I've been holding back since I opened this box spill over, cascading down my cheeks, and I lie down on the bed, curling up as I sob over the pain my mom went through and the pain she put me through.

I must have fallen asleep, because when I wake, Chase is sitting beside me in pajama pants with no top on, reading a book. My eyes drink in his toned chest, and I can't help the desire that uncurls in my stomach as I watch him for a few seconds. Then the contents of the box comes back to me, so I sit up and scan the room for it. The box is closed and sits on the floor beside me. The sight of it brings all the pain back, and when I turn back to Chase, it's to find him watching me. He takes one look at my face and opens his arms to me.

I hesitate only for a moment and crawl into his lap, seeking comfort, safety, and peace, and that's exactly what I find.

# Chapter 17

# COMFORT & KISSES

## Chase

I FINISH my shower and go in search of Cassie. She's not in the living room, or the den, or the kitchen, or the spare room, which only leaves my room, because I'm just out of my office and she's definitely not there.

I open the door and peek in, finding her curled up on the bed, surrounded by papers. Her face is red, and I can see from the door that she's been crying, but she's settled and sleeping.

Part of me thinks I should leave her to sleep, but another part wants to be there when she wakes.

I decide to wait it out, and I'm glad I do. I clear all the papers off the bed and place them back in the box, but my eyes can't help scanning some of the things I'm tidying away, and I wince as I see Janie with bruises on her face and torso.

My curiosity is piqued, but I won't pry. I just hope Cassie trusts me enough to tell me what this is all about.

I sit on the bed, but boredom strikes, and I pick up the book on my nightstand, slipping my reading glasses up my nose. It's not very rock and roll, but my head hurts if I read and I don't have them on, so I wear them at home. No one else knows about them, but I don't care if Cassie knows.

I flick through the pages of *The Hobbit* and find the part I'm reading. The party has just reached Rivendale and has been speaking to Lord Elrond. I've been reading it on and off recently. I'm just getting into it when I hear a soft noise beside me, and I turn to see Cassie is awake and staring at me.

She suddenly sits up and her eyes scan the room, only relaxing when she sees the box on the floor. Her body shifts and she turns towards me with a haunted look in her eyes. The sight of her looking so close to breaking unnerves me, and I open my arms to her.

As she crawls onto my lap, I wrap my arms around her and hold her tightly as she begins to cry, softly at first, before full, heaving sobs rip from her chest.

I run my hands over her back, stroking softly at the skin and shushing her, pressing my lips onto her forehead as I speak.

"It's okay, Cass. I got you. You're safe here."

My arms tighten around her as she cries, and then she sits back to look at me.

"He beat her," she tells me in a broken whisper. "She kept the scans, X-rays, and pictures… and he… uh… he…"

"Sssshhh, it's okay. You don't have to tell me."

Her eyes find mine and she holds my gaze for a second before the words rip from her chest.

"He raped her. What if I came from that? How do I live with that?"

For a beat, I'm silent as my head digests her words, and then I lean forward, resting my head on hers.

"Cassie, if that's what happened then your mom must have loved you so much. She took you and ran away with you, so she never blamed you." I press a soft kiss to her lips and then pull back to look at her. "You shouldn't blame yourself either. You didn't choose to be born or how you were born, and your mom loved you very much."

Tears roll down her cheeks, and I wipe at them with the pad of my thumb, tucking her back into my chest afterwards.

Her breathing begins to even out, and I lean back on my pillow, relaxing. Being in bed with a girl is new to me. I usually use the guest room for my dates, and even Belinda never got inside my actual bedroom. Cassie, though, doesn't have to even ask.

I begin to drift off when her lips press against my chest, and she turns so she's lying on top of me. She kisses up my chest, up my neck, and her lips push against mine.

"Cassie," I groan as she slots her warm heat over my hardening erection.

"Make me forget. Please, Chase," she begs, and I can't say no. Where Cassie's concerned, I can never say no.

Our lips clash. Hers desperate, seeking something I'm not sure I can give her, and mine giving everything I have inside.

I slowly strip her shirt over her head and unclasp her bra, revealing her tits. My mouth waters as the sight of them, and I quickly take my glasses off before I lean down, sucking gently on one of her nipples while my other hand caresses the other. She lifts her hips, and I push against her as I nip gently on the pearly peak of her nipple.

When she wraps her fingers in my hair and tugs, I move to the opposite breast and then kiss a trail down to her stomach.

"Chase, oh my God, please?"

Her breathless voice makes me harder, and I tug her pants down, making sure I have her panties too. Her pussy glistens as I lower my mouth to it, licking and sucking until she's writhing on the bed.

When I stop, she whines loudly, and I grin up at her before sliding a finger inside her. I push in and up, reveling in the moan I elicit from her.

I add another finger and lower my mouth back to her clit,

pressing down firmly on it with my tongue as my fingers pump her from below.

Her fingers wrap in my hair as she rides my tongue and fingers until she comes, squeezing my head with her legs. Her juices flow and I lap at them, not stopping until I've milked every single bit of her orgasm from her.

She collapses back on the bed, and I slide up towards her, kissing her body as I go. Once I reach her lips, I thrust my tongue into her mouth, swirling it around so she can taste herself on my lips.

"Chase, I need you inside me," Cassie groans as my erection pushes against her swollen lips.

"Good, because I need to get inside you too."

I grab a pillow and push it under her ass, then tug my pajama pants down, showing her my hard-on.

Her deft fingers stroke at my shaft and roam down, but I want inside her, so I take her hands and pin them over her head.

"Later," I growl before slowly pushing my cock into her. The feel of her tight, wet pussy has my dick throbbing, and I pull out before slowly slamming back in.

I continue this for a while until I can see her breathing speeding up, and then I begin to go harder and faster.

My fingers bite into her hips as I thrust, and my mouth sucks on her soft nipples while my pubic bone rubs against her clit. Just as she's about to come, I still, making her moan loudly.

My eyes meet hers, and I see everything in her heated look; there's love, acceptance, and desire. Part of me wants to tell her how fucking much I love her, but I'm scared she won't feel the same, and the fear of rejection has me holding back what I'm feeling.

She lifts her lips to mine and we kiss, but I wait for a few seconds before I start moving again. This time, I drag one of my hands up, pinching her pebbled nipple between my thumb and forefinger.

I lower my mouth and suck the opposite side into my mouth, gently sucking, teasing, and biting, and my finger pinches the other side. She begins to meet me thrust for thrust, and I know she doesn't have long left.

I don't either as her pussy clenches around me, my balls tingle for a moment until I come so hard lights flash before my eyes. I roll us to the side so I'm still inside her and drag the comforter up the bed, covering us as her eyes drift closed again.

My heartbeat starts to slow, and I drop a soft kiss to her forehead before dropping my head to the pillow and letting myself, for the first time ever, fall asleep with my cock still half buried in my girl.

I sleep for a few hours and wake up after having the most amazing dream.

My cock is rock solid as I dream about Cassie sucking hard on my dick. My hips lift in response, and I swear the dream is so realistic that I feel her tight lips pull me inside her mouth.

I thrust up and her hands tighten on the base of my cock as her teeth scratch the head, and the small jolt of pain-filled pleasure tells me it's not a dream.

My hands go to her hair, and I begin to thrust up as her hand twists and tightens around my dick. I groan, throwing my head back onto the bed. She continues to lick, suck, and toy with me until I come, shooting my load down her throat.

"Good morning, Chase," she mutters as she climbs up my body, pressing her naked tits to my chest as she crashes her lips against mine.

My mouth devours hers and I flip us around so she's beneath me as I slide my cock along her wet pussy, and I mutter into her open mouth.

"You can wake me up like that anytime you like, Cassie!"

She growls as she flexes her hips up and her hands scrape down my back until she reaches my ass. With her nails digging in slightly, she pulls me until I'm sheathed inside her.

"Chase."

Her low growl as I still has my heart beating erratically, sounding loud in my ears as I start thrusting in and out, swallowing her loud moans of pleasure.

I begin to push harder into her, seeking her spot as I squeeze her tits, and she becomes even louder, which encourages me to go faster. My eyes scan her face as she tosses her head back. Her hands grip onto the bedding as I slam into her more furiously, and her thrusts up to meet me tell me she's close. It isn't until I slip my hands between us, pressing down firmly on her clit, that her tight little pussy contracts around me, and she convulses on the bed, breathing hard and chanting my name.

"Chase, oh my God."

Our lips meet, but this time the kiss is soft, tender, as she curls against my side, running her fingers over my pecs as my heart rate slows.

Soft lips brush against my neck, and I glance down to find her eyes scanning my face. "Are you okay?"

Her small voice and the tremble of her hand tells me she's as worried about going to her mom's funeral as I am. It isn't about me. Not today, at least.

"Yeah, I'm good, babe. Are you okay?"

She blinks away tears and swallows a few times before she looks away, then nods as she threads her fingers through mine. "I am right now. I don't know about later, but for now, I'm okay."

My hand goes to her chin, and I lift her face so I can press a tender kiss to her lips. Seeing her in pain guts me, and I want to fix it, but I know that this pain is beyond my power to fix. I have to let her ride it out and try to put her back together when it's over, because there is no way I'm letting her go again. She's mine and that's it.

Our slow kisses begin to wake my cock again, and when I press it against her, she laughs at me.

"You are insatiable, Chase Crawford. Totally insatiable."

I smirk down at her and begin to kiss a trail down her body because, while my cock is playing a good game, he isn't quite there yet. When I reach the apex of her thighs and push her legs apart, she squeals and tries to close her legs.

"Cassie, let me taste you…" I growl at her, and she shakes her head.

"Let me go for a shower first."

Her counter comes fast, and I stare up at her before I quickly flip her over and palm her ass cheeks. My hand smacks one cheek and then the other, making her moan loudly.

"Are you sure you don't want to let me taste you now?"

She squirms on the bed as I slide my fingers up and down her soaking folds.

"You're soaked, babe. Are you liking me spanking you again?" I ask as one of my palms connects with her ass, and her juices coat my hand that's still touching her.

She shakes her head, and I spank her again, feeling more moisture between her legs.

"I think you're lying."

My mouth breaks into a grin, and my palm strokes her delicately pinking skin, making my cock harder.

I shift down the bed and lower my mouth, licking a trail from her ass crack right down to her pussy, slipping my tongue inside as she writhes around on the bed. She tries to move, but I pin her down with my arm and press my finger against her puckered hole.

"This will be mine," I tell her, and she freezes as I slip my tongue into her while pushing my finger gently inside. Her drawn out sigh and how she pushes back onto my face tells me she's enjoying this, and I thrust my tongue in and out of her while keeping my finger pulsing gently in her ass.

"Chase," she moans as she moves on the bed, and then her orgasm hits, and her body stiffens as the sounds coming from her get louder and more breathless. Before her body has a chance to come down, I move my body up against hers and push my dick inside her pussy as it still shudders.

For a few thrusts, it's great, but I slip out, so I decide to move position.

I slip my legs under her and pull her up so she's facing away from me with her legs at either side of me. She lowers herself down as my hands snake around her waist and up to her tits.

As we start to move, I twist and pinch her nipples and she throws her head back on my shoulder.

"God, Chase, yes."

I move one hand down and grab hers, pushing it towards her clit and making her press against it.

"Keep your hand there while I fuck you."

My voice is commanding, and she whines a little as my hand comes back up her body, skimming her breast to her neck.

I hold it gently, and she turns her face so our lips meet. My hand squeezes gently and I hold it as I piston into her, harder and more forcefully, until I splinter apart.

I let go and we both collapse onto the bed, totally and utterly spent, but it's when she speaks in a breathless moan that I turn to see my fingers have left marks on her neck.

"I'm going to the bathroom."

I watch her walk to the bathroom on shaky legs, and I lie there, waiting on my heartbeat to return to normal. The things she does to me make me crazy.

She comes out of the bathroom and climbs back into bed beside me, resting her head on my arm. I glance down at her and press a soft kiss to her forehead, wincing as I see the marks marring her perfect skin.

"I marked your skin," I tell her softly, and she sighs.

"Yeah, I know. I saw."

Her voice is tired, but she speaks again before I can say a word.

"I need to go shopping today. I need something different to

wear tonight to the funeral home, or I'll need to explain why I have these marks on me."

Her words make me stiffen. I don't want her to leave me. I don't want to go outside and face the world. Here in our little bubble, we're safe and protected, but out there, people are cruel and jealous and they will try to tear us apart.

"Okay, babe. Can we go later though?"

My voice is sleepy, and my body relaxes as my eyes flutter closed and she leans up, kissing my jaw before snuggling against me.

"Sure. Later."

I fall asleep and wake up a few hours later to an empty bed. I sit up with a start and stare around, but my body relaxes when I hear the shower running.

For a few seconds, I ponder going in, but my cell rings and I get distracted. I get up and walk out to the hall as I speak to Tony and Mason Michaels about the tour we have coming up.

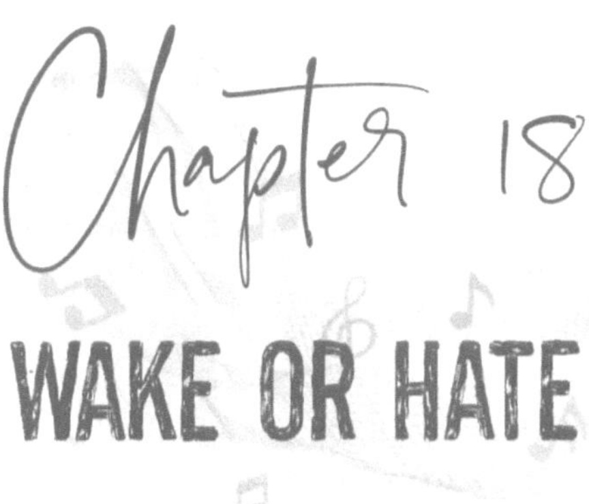

# WAKE OR HATE

## Cassie

I QUICKLY DRY off and pull my clothes on, plaiting my hair before I brush my teeth. I check my neck in the mirror and my body tingles as I remember how rough he was.

My core throbs, and my pussy is achy, but I know I need to go shopping. I can't wear the low-cut dress I brought without people asking why there are fingerprints on my neck.

My thoughts flash back to earlier, and I smile as I touch my lips and stare at my bright eyes with flushed cheeks and swollen lips.

I hear Chase moving about, but he doesn't come into the bathroom, so I finish getting ready and squirt some of my perfume on.

Once I'm dressed, I go in search of Chase, with my stomach growling. That marathon session has made me famished, and it's almost eleven a.m.

On my way to the kitchen, I pass Chase's office and see him sitting by the desk, completely naked, but he doesn't see me. I pause by the door, intending to ask if he wants food, when his voice reaches me.

"Yeah, two weeks on Tuesday. The tour is Asia, Australia, and Europe for four months, and then we're back in the states from January for a break before the next leg kicks off. I know all this."

He's silent for a minute, but I step back away from his office.

I have my Masters starting soon. I can't just take off and go on tour with him, if that's even what he wants. We haven't talked about the future at all. All we've done is have sex, and I'm not sure if he wants a future with me.

He starts speaking again, but I can't listen anymore. My feet carry me numbly back to my room, and I grab my cell and car keys, tucking them into my purse as I go towards the elevator I came up in.

I peek around the door of his office, but he has his back to me, and for a second, I stare at him. The view is breathtaking, and his toned back, perfect ass, and the hint of his cock between his legs sets my core alight, but I have to get out of here.

I need some distance between us because I want to say *screw it*. I want to go with him, and I know I shouldn't. Our relationship is complicated by the fact that I'm his stepsister, and I'm almost ninety-nine percent sure that he won't want me messing up his life or his band.

He runs his fingers through his hair, and his shoulders tense as he speaks again, reiterating that there's nothing between us. I leave him to his call, even though it hurts like hell to be dismissed, and I decide to go to the shops without him.

Of course he doesn't want anything from me. I'm nothing more than a convenient fuck and an annoyance, but the sex is so fucking good.

I drive without thinking, ending up in a mall at the food court. I eat my fill and then go to the shops, taking my time as I pick a cute black dress, blazer, and two scarfs to wear.

I don't check my cell until I'm back in the car, but when I do, I see three missed calls and four missed messages from Chase.

**Hey babe, where'd you go?**

That was from twenty minutes after I left, and then an hour later, he text again.

**Cassie, can you call me please.**

After another half hour, he sent another two messages.

**Hey, are you okay?**

Followed almost immediately by another message.

**I'm getting worried. Can you please answer me?**

Just as I finish reading the messages, my cell starts ringing and I quickly answer it.

"Hey," I begin, but he cuts me off with a growl.

"Where the fuck did you go? Why didn't you wait for me to come with you?"

My insides twist, but I'm not going to let him make me feel bad when he said I don't mean shit to him.

"I went shopping like I told you. You were busy on a call, so I left. I'm on my way back now."

"Yeah, but why didn't you send me a message when you left. I was worried."

My temper flares because he's not my keeper, and I don't need to tell anyone where I'm going.

"You don't need to worry about me. I'm a big girl, and like you said, I mean nothing to you."

I hear his breath catch, and it's a moment before he speaks to me. "Cass, I didn't mean…"

"I got what you meant. Loud and clear. I'm good for a fuck, but nothing else. It's fine."

He's silent for a moment and then he speaks in a low whisper, changing the subject. "How long will you be? I'm going to get some food delivered. Do you want any?"

"No. I'm good. I already ate."

"Okay. Bye then."

The dial tone sounds in my car, and suddenly, my greasy Chinese food threatens to make a reappearance. I swallow and take a few sips out of my water before I make my way to his apartment.

As soon as I go inside, he goes to his office and stays there without speaking to me until it's time for us to go to see my mom's body.

I chose an open casket for tonight, and then the funeral tomorrow, but I'm so nervous, and I feel sick at the thought of standing there alone.

My hand knocks quietly on Chase's office door, and it swings open to show him in his suit and tie.

The sight of him takes my breath away, and I stare at him for a moment until he turns round and meets my heated look with a small smile that melts a little of the ire inside me.

"You ready?"

I can't react because I want to stay in my bubble with him, but I can't. I have to go to view my mom's body, and any problems I have with him will just have to wait.

"Yeah. I think so."

My voice shakes when I speak, but he turns away from me and picks up his cell and wallet, shoving them into his pocket before he turns back to me.

"The cars are here. We need to arrive separately in case there's any press, but I'll be in the car in front, okay? I have a stop to make too at the label and it's better if you're not there because they aren't comfortable with us together."

My head drowns out the rest of this words as the image of doing this all by myself hits me again and again.

He said cars. As in plural. The thought of going there alone sets off my anxiety, and sure enough, when I get downstairs, there are two cars in the garage. One for me and one for him and it hits home that I'll really be alone during this part.

He doesn't notice my panic as he steps into his car and closes the door, but I'm frozen on the sidewalk. I can't do this alone.

For a few seconds, I stand and stare at the car, and the driver who holds the door open looks at me in confusion, but I can't. I just can't.

My feet begin to carry me away, and I've just about reached the elevator when Chase reopens his door.

He takes one look at me breathing hard and climbs from the car.

"What is it?" he asks, and I back away from him as he strides towards me.

"I can't... I can't..."

His hands grip my shoulders. "Cassie, what is it?"

My eyes meet his and I blink back the tears that are threatening, but I can't see him. All I can see is me standing there all alone with no one by my side.

"Please, Cass. Tell me what's wrong?" His voice turns low, pleading with me, and I swallow a deep breath, trying to get control of myself. "It's okay. You're going to be fine."

His hands loosen and he leans down a little, pressing a soft kiss to my forehead, and it's that small moment of compassion that gives me the strength to speak.

"I'm scared, Chase. I can't do this alone."

My honesty makes him freeze, and he wraps his strong hands around my back, holding me tightly to his chest as I begin to calm down.

"You won't be alone, Cassie. I'm right here beside you."

"But you don't want me. I heard you."

His lips brush my ears, and he whispers softly, "I didn't mean what I said to them. I'm scared too. I'm so scared because I fucking love you. I'm so in love with you, Cassie Danson, so I need you to believe me when I tell you that you won't be alone. I'll be right there beside you."

My heart thunders in my ears, and I turn, brushing my lips against his, but he steps back away from me.

"Not here," he mutters in almost a whisper before he turns and leads us to the cars. The drivers are standing looking bored, but he waits until I'm in my car then climbs into his, and we're off.

We reach the funeral home, and I see car after car after car. Some people I know. Some I don't, and I'm stunned when I see how crowded it is. People file in and come to me, gripping my hand and telling me how wonderful my mom was. So many people, but my eyes scan the room and I seek out Chase. His steady gaze gives me strength and I manage to make it through without breaking, but when everyone leaves, I turn to my mom and go over to speak to her.

"Hey, Mom," I mutter. I lean down and brush her hair from her face, smiling at the familiarity of the gesture. "I think I'm in love with Chase. He told me he loves me too, and I know that after Abe, I should be careful, but I think this is it. I think he's really the one for me."

I pause and scan down her outfit, wishing I'd known what she'd like to wear, and I start in surprise when I see a pearl bracelet on her wrist. I didn't give it to Chase, but I'm sure I've seen it before.

Something about it gives me anxiety, and I walk over, slumping down on one of the chairs. I stare at my mom's coffin and wish I could relax, but I can't.

When Chase comes back in a few moments later, I pounce on him and startle him. "Chase, did you give that bracelet for my mom to wear?"

His eyes go to the coffin and he shrugs. "I don't know. I don't think there was a bracelet in the stuff you gave me."

I stand up and begin pacing, ignoring the pains in my feet from my toes being pinched by my shoes.

"Cassie, are you okay?"

I know I'm probably scaring him, but I need to know where that bracelet came from. "No. I need to take that bracelet off her. It's not hers."

My panicked voice and jittery movements make him stop and stare at me. "Come on. Let's go home and get a drink."

Tony comes in with Kent, and they start tidying up the chairs and organizing the rows, but I can't move until I know where that bracelet came from.

I open my mouth to speak, but Chase gives me a sharp look and I close my mouth.

"Come on. I need to get you home."

I don't miss the bite of impatience in his voice, and logically, I know I'm fixated on something totally ridiculous, so I let him lead me out to the cars. He all but throws me into the car and then climbs in after me, but he doesn't speak to me at all on the way back.

We reach the apartment, and he storms into the kitchen, picking up a bottle of scotch and pouring one into a glass. He doesn't offer me one, and I don't ask for one either.

He opens his mouth to speak, stopping when he hears the sound of the elevator, and he glances at me guiltily.

"Cass, can you go in here for a minute?"

He points to the laundry room, and I raise my eyebrow at him, but he grips my arm and pushes me inside, pressing a soft kiss to my forehead as he steps back and closes the door.

I slide down and sit on the floor, kicking my heels off. I take my cell out to text him to find out why I'm hiding in a closet when voices sound in the kitchen.

"So, this is Cassie's dad and siblings," a voice says, and I stiffen as Chase speaks to him.

"Okay, thanks, Tony."

My heartbeat stutters at hearing Chase address Tony. He must have brought them here, thinking I wasn't here, but as my head races with the information, I hear Chase speak and I sit back to listen.

"Hi, I'm her stepbrother, Chase. Nice to meet you all. Can I get you a drink?"

Arsenic? Poison? I think as I hear them discussing options.

My hands ball into fists at my side, and I have to stop myself from going out there as I listen to them make small talk about drinks right outside the door.

There are no footsteps, so I have to assume that they're staying in the kitchen, and part of me wonders if Chase is keeping them there for my benefit. When everyone has their drinks, the conversation turns to me again.

"So, Mr. Crawford, I'm a little concerned. I've come out here to find my daughter, but she's not at home, and I don't know where to look for her."

"So you came to me?" Chase's voice is icy cold, and I wrap my arms around my waist as I listen to them.

"Well, yes. I thought you might know where she is. She belongs with us. We're her family."

I wonder what Chase is thinking as he listens to my 'father', but all I can hear is someone getting annoyed because I'm not where he expected me to be.

"I'm sorry, but I don't know. Cassie and I aren't exactly close. I was there for her when Janie died, but that's it. I don't tend to keep tabs on her. She's her own person."

"She's my daughter and she belongs with us."

I hear a drink being slammed down on the table, and I wonder what's about to happen when a woman's voice breaks the tension.

"Dad, he's right. We don't know her. And we know what lies Mom filled her head with."

My ears start to ring, and I want to go out there and go off on them, but I hold back to hear what they say next.

"We know that Taylor's death broke Mom, and she resented you for what happened, but Chase is right. We don't know her, and she doesn't know us, so going in all guns blazing is just going to push her away."

There is another silence, and then Chase speaks again.

"Look, I'm exhausted, and as you can clearly see, Cassie isn't here." His irritation is clear, and I lean back as someone else speaks.

"Why don't we take this to the living room?" Tony asks, but Chase cuts him off.

"No. Look, I appreciate you coming out here, but do you not think it would be better to let Cassie get in touch with you when she's ready rather than trying to force the issue? How did you get the details anyway because I'm sure it won't have been from Cassie?"

My heart soars at Chase's words, and I know that he's trying to save me from having to meet them.

"I sent them the details because it's still an open legal case. I wasn't sure we had any grounds to keep the information private," Tony intones as another voice speaks.

"We didn't just come out here to see Colleen, but after Tony told us about the details, we had to come. We came for Alice's funeral. She might be a monster, but she was still our mom, and we still loved her."

Grant's voice, I assume, and I run my hands over my face as I realize where the pearl bracelet must have come from. I wish they'd just leave. I don't have it in me to deal with this tonight.

"Look, this is getting us nowhere. Can you call us when you're with her? We're staying at the Marriott a few blocks away."

Amira speaks, and I hear their footsteps as they leave. Chase doesn't open the door, and I'm about to when I hear someone speaking to Chase in a harsh tone.

"I don't know what you think hiding my daughter is going to achieve. I don't like the fact that there are people saying you're with her. It better not be true, or I'll end you…"

His threat is clear, and I wonder what Chase will do. He doesn't seem like the kind of person who'll take a threat lightly. I hear a scuffle and a thump, then Chase speaks in a chilling voice. "You don't get to come into my house and threaten me, and you certainly don't get to comment on my relationships. Cassie and I have nothing to do with you. She's a smart girl who'll make her own decisions, and some guy she probably doesn't even remember isn't going to make decisions for her."

I listen intently as Dave tries to speak again, to reiterate his threat, but Chase cuts him off. "Listen, I didn't get where I am today by letting assholes like you bully, threaten, and intimidate me. Now fuck off. Get out of my house."

There's silence as Dave leaves, and I wish I could go out to see Chase. I want to wrap my arms around him, but I don't move. I have no idea if they've really gone, and until I'm sure, I don't want to risk going out there.

I grab one of the spare duvets down from a shelf to my right and make a nest on the floor, snuggling down and letting my exhaustion carry me off to sleep.

I wake hours later, stiff and sore, and check my purse. My cell is still switched to silent, and I glance down to see that it's a little after four a.m.

Fuck. I need to get up at eight.

Chase didn't come back in to get me, or to wake me, and then I see my message icon blinking.

There are four unread messages. Three from Chase and one from an unknown number. I read the unidentified one first and roll my eyes. I type a response telling him to fuck off, but I delete. That I can deal with later.

**Colleen, this is your father. Get it touch with me soon.**

Next are the three messages from Chase. The first one was a little after nine-thirty, which was when they left, but I read the newest one first.

**I can't do this. It's too much fucking drama. I'm staying at my Malibu house. Stay as long as you like. I won't be there tomorrow. I can't deal with all the shit that comes with you.**

My eyes water and my hand shakes as I scroll to the next message.

**I need air. I won't be long.**

Then the oldest reads:

***Fuck. That was intense. You okay babe?***

I don't respond as I realize that he's just left me. He left me. The pain of facing everything alone washes over me like a tidal wave, and I set an alarm for eight a.m., burrowing down in the blanket and sobbing. I manage to fall back to sleep and wake a few hours later with my alarm sounding.

I quickly get up and roll my neck, but I need to get a shower and dress. I slowly make my way to the bedroom and get my dress, shoes, and blazer for today on his bed.

I'm halfway through my shower when the shower door opens, and warm hands envelop me. I have my eyes closed, so I jump about a mile in the air.

"Ssshhh. It's just me, babe."

His voice is low, and I can taste the whisky on his breath as he tries to kiss me. I shove him away from me.

"Come on, Cass. You know you want me."

He presses against me, and I want to cave, but his words hurt, and I can't do it. I can't let him walk all over me. His lips find my neck, and I almost give in when he licks and kisses a trail up to my earlobe.

"No," I hiss out, pushing him away. I see the confusion and hurt written all over his face, but I can't give in. His forehead crinkles as he watches me from the other side of the shower, but he doesn't make a move towards me.

"What? Why not?"

I ignore him as I rinse my hair off and step out of the shower seconds later, calling over my shoulder, "Maybe check your cell and read your messages to me."

I don't say another word as he stares after me, and I close the door on his startled face, but I don't have time to coddle him. I have to say goodbye to my mom in a few hours and I still need to get dressed.

I quickly dry off, moisturize, and put my underwear on, but just as I'm pulling one of his shirts on to do my make-up, he steps into the room.

My eyes drink in the sight of his body, and I try to ignore the flutters in my stomach when his dark eyes find me staring at him.

"Fuck, Cass. What did I do?"

I shake my head as I watch a droplet of water run down his chest, but when I lift my eyes to his, I want to run away because all I can see in his dark gaze is sex and lust.

"Read your messages to me."

My voice is low and heated, but I won't give in. I fucking won't. I drag my eyes away from him and start blowing out my hair. He stares at me for a minute and then goes back into the bathroom, closing the door with a snap.

I manage to finish drying my hair and have just loosely tied it up in a topknot when he comes back out.

He walks over to me and spins the chair I'm sitting on then drops to his knees between my legs. There's silence as I wait for him to speak, but he doesn't say a word.

He just sits for a moment and then undoes his shirt, leaning forward to press gentle kisses on my waist. With each kiss, he mutters an apology.

"I'm so sorry, babe." Kiss. "Please forgive me. I was just freaked out." Another kiss. "I don't blame you for hating me." More kisses.

My fingers thread into his hair and I feel moisture on my abdomen. He presses one more kiss to my stomach and his voice breaks on his next words.

"I'm a fucking coward and I'm so sorry."

His breathing hitches and his shoulders shake as he sits naked between my legs with his hands wrapped around my waist and his lips on my stomach, but it's when I feel his tears drip onto my legs that I want to cave.

I wrap my hands around his head and lean down to press a soft kiss to his forehead.

"You are not a coward. You got freaked out, but I can't go on like this. You can't keep picking me up and dropping me whenever the mood takes you. I can't do it anymore."

My tears begin to fall, and I know this is it. If he doesn't step up now, then we're done.

"I'm so sorry," he whispers, and his head lifts. Our lips brush gently, and I know that we *are* done. He can't cope with the drama that comes with me, and I can't be his dirty little secret. Not anymore.

"I fucking love you so much, Cassie, but this right here, hurting you and causing you pain kills me and I know it's my fault. That I push and pull at you, but I really do love you. I'm going to stop, I swear. I'm going to be better, to work to deserve you. Just please don't leave me."

He takes another shuddering breath and presses one more soft kiss to my lips.

"I'm not good enough for you, and I'm so sorry that I've led you on, but I won't anymore. I'll keep my distance. When today is over, I'll go back to Malibu, and you can stay here as long as you need."

My heart shatters as he pulls out of my arms and turns away from me. I watch him through tear-filled eyes as he grabs a few things and leaves the room without looking at me. As soon as the door closes, I wrap my arms around my waist and sob. I'm totally alone.

The people who showed up aren't my family, and the only person I want has just walked out on me on the day I need him most. I let myself cry for a few more minutes and then go wash my face. Every step hurts, and I wish I'd never come here because seeing him, loving him, and losing him was hard enough the first time, but this time was so much worse.

# Chapter 19

## CRUSHED DREAMS

## Chase

WALKING out on her when I could see the devastation I'd just caused was the hardest thing I've ever done. It broke my heart, and I stood in my office with my suit and tie, fighting to stop myself from going back in there.

She was right. I couldn't keep taking her on a rollercoaster of emotions. It's the day of her mom's funeral, and she's got this whole new family and she should at least try to get to know them, even if her dad is a giant dick. Her sister seems okay. I don't want to leave her alone to face her father, but I need to work harder to deserve her. I don't want to get in the way of that, but I want her so badly.

I know I'm finally doing what's best for her, but selfishly, I want to keep her for myself. But she'd hate me, and I can't have that. I never again want her to look at me like she did in the shower.

I don't even remember sending that last message telling her I was done and that I wasn't going today, but I will be there for her because I promised. I swore I'd be there for her today and I'm not about to let her go through saying goodbye to her mom alone.

I dress quickly and order some food for us, but I'm too chicken-shit to go into the room. I can't face her tears or the indifference she might show me, so I leave her breakfast at the door and knock, going back to my office and having a croissant and coffee.

Once I'm calmer, I check my cell and re-read my messages from the night before. Another reason I ended things is because I called one of my old flames last night to my house, and I know she's gonna fucking hate me if she finds out. Seeing the messages between us makes me feel sick, and I don't even know what I was thinking.

I remember drinking whisky and hoping she'd call me so I could come home, but when I didn't hear from her, I got drunker and hornier, so in my idiotic drunken wisdom, I called Hannah.

The sex I don't even remember, but I was totally wasted when she arrived, so it could have happened and knowing me it probably did. It wouldn't be the first time I fucked someone when I was too out of my face to even remember it. My only recollection is drunkenly kissing her and then I remember asking her to leave. I was completely tanked, so I went to sleep. I didn't even remember until Cass told me to check my messages, and that was when I saw the messages between Hannah and me.

After I saw them, I read what I said to Cass, and I knew I had to end things. I'd already hurt her enough, but sleeping with Hannah was unforgivable, so I took the coward's way out and finished things.

I waited an hour and knew the cars would be arriving soon, so I went and knocked on my bedroom door.

Cassie opened the door and my heart stopped. She was so fucking beautiful, and I couldn't believe I let her slip through my fingers again.

"Are… uh… are you ready?"

My voice is hoarse as I stammer the words out, and she won't meet my eyes as she nods. Part of me is relieved, but a larger part is gutted.

"Yeah. Let's go."

She steps around me as I stare at her. I trailed after her, wishing I could feel some of the warmth I had yesterday, but knowing I've lost her is eating me alive.

We don't speak in the elevator, or as we reach the cars, but just as she steps inside, I mutter a soft apology again.

Halfway to the funeral home, my cell starts blowing up, and when I see the images of me fucking Hannah, I want to scream.

My cell rings, and I quickly ask Tony to handle it, but then a message pops up from Cass, and I want to run away.

**Is the gossip true?**

That's all she asks, and I slam my hands into my head.

Fuck. Fuck. Fuck.

Another message comes through, and I freeze as I read it.

**I know it is. Now I get why you were full of apologies. You slept with her because my situation freaked you out.**

I never knew how it felt to have loved and lost until that moment, but right then, I knew she'd never want to be near me again.

**Yes, I can't remember it, but I think I did. I am so so sorry. I can explain later.**

My fingers shake as I reply, and she sends one final message back.

**It's fine. I don't need to hear it. You wanted an out and you got one. After today I don't want to see you again.**

I lean my head back on the seat and wish I'd just stayed home with my girl last night. I fucked everything up, just like I always do, but her dad's threat got to me, and when I looked at the door hiding her, I freaked and ran away.

I think I'll regret doing that for the rest of my life. A few tears roll from my eyes, and I quickly wipe at them as we drive up towards the crematorium.

The cars stop, and I get out, but Cassie doesn't look at me. She walks over to a young couple and the guy wraps her in a tender embrace.

My heart pounds as jealousy rips through me, and I clench my hands to stop myself going over there and ripping my girl from his hands.

She walks inside with them and my eyes dart around, spotting her father and siblings standing at the back of the mourners that have gathered.

Tony comes over, and we walk in together, but Cassie is at the front with that guy and his girl beside her, so I slip into a seat at the back. I promised I'd be here for her. No matter how hard this is for her, I'll be here for her.

Everyone files in and the ceremony starts. My eyes don't leave the back of her head as the music starts, and I watch her head bow as the minister talks.

When it comes time for the eulogy, Cassie gets up, and so do I. I slip along the rows until I'm half hidden at the front, but I'm here if she needs me.

Her voice when she speaks is a pained whisper.

"My mom was my hero. She did everything for me. Worked crappy jobs with crappy hours and took us from place to place until we found our home with… with Harvey. He… they…"

It's right then that she sees her father and siblings. She visibly stiffens, losing her place.

She stammers and tries to start again, but her voice cracks, and when she looks at me with pleading eyes, I don't hesitate.

My feet carry me up to the lectern, and I wrap her in a hug as I whisper in her ear. "Do you want me to take over?"

She nods against my chest without looking up. I suck in a breath, give her a tight squeeze, and step up to the microphone.

"Hi everyone. Thanks for coming today to say goodbye to Janie Danson Crawford."

My eyes scan the congregation, and I see a few people I don't know glare towards me as I speak.

I ignore them and think about the girl behind me as I continue.

"When I first met Janie, I was a seventeen-year-old who was adamant I didn't need a stepmom, but my dad didn't care. He was smitten, and when he brought Janie and Cassie into my life, I resented them. I hate to say that I barely let myself get to know them."

Everyone watches me, enraptured, as I speak, and I loosen my clenched hands.

"Years passed, and although Janie contacted me and invited me home, I didn't take her up on it until it was too late to fix things with my dad. She kept trying, and when my dad died, it was Cassie who called me, but Janie was the one who made me feel welcome and told me that my dad was so proud of me…"

I break off as emotion threatens to overwhelm me, but Cassie gently touches my back, and I know I have to do this for her.

"She helped me feel more connected to my dad, and both she and Cassie helped me through it. I will always be so grateful to Janie for how much she was there for me, even after my dad passed. She still checked in with me, and we spoke every year for the last few years, but I wish I'd done more. I wish I'd gotten to know her better and been a better stepson to her, but I won't let her down again. I will be there for Cass. I will make sure that she has someone she can turn to, someone there for her always, and someone who will love her completely."

Everyone is crying, but it's Cassie shaking behind me as I finish that hurts the most. When I turn and wrap my arms around her, the minister rises. Tony approaches and hands me my guitar before he leads Cassie back to her seat as I sing the song I wrote in the weeks after my dad passed. Janie told me it was one of her favorites, but I never told her who it was about.

My fingers strum the chords, and I close my eyes as I begin the song that means so much more now than it did when I wrote it five years ago.

"My heart is beaten, broken on the ground
It's lost without you, and I can't make a sound
I need a moment, a second, a heartbeat
To take you with me and make my life complete
How can I go on, without you by my side?
How can I make it, through this massive loss?
It's killing me slowly, little by little each day
Why won't the loss of you just go away?"

My eyes find hers as she watches me, and I sing it to her. I never told a soul, but I wrote it about leaving her behind.

"I miss our moments, big and small
They say it'll get better.
They say time heals all wounds.
But there's no escape, no reprieve without you.
I want it back.
I want the love, the comfort only you bring
I fight the desire to run…"

I finish the song, and for a second, our gazes hold, but then her eyes turn to the ground and I stand up, glancing around before I step off the podium as *Dancin' in the Sky* starts. I slowly make my way down when Cassie reaches for me and I walk to her. We stand side by side as the curtains close, and she crumples against me. Her tears kill me in a way I've never experienced before, and I wish things were different with us.

I rub her shoulders as she sobs, and I hold her tightly, not wanting to let her go. Kent comes over and directs Cassie and me to the outside, where we stand and thank everyone for coming, but it feels fake, wrong. The line finally starts to slow, and I turn to speak to Cass when I hear footsteps getting closer.

My body stiffens when I see her father coming towards us, and I want to say no. Not now, but he doesn't stop until he's right in front of us.

"Col... uh, Cassie, do you know who I am?"

His voice is sharp, and Cassie's back stiffens as she stares at him. For a moment, she doesn't speak or break her stare with him.

He knows she knows who he is. I can see it in his shoulders and in the way he glowers at us.

"I'm Dave Spence..." he begins, but he's interrupted by the arrival of the rest of the people he came with.

Suddenly, there's a cacophony of noise. Cassie steps closer to me, and I instinctively wrap my arm around her, ignoring the glares from those speaking to her.

My body shifts, and I glance down to see her shaking.

"Are you okay?" I ask in a low whisper, but before she answers, someone rips her away from my hold, and I bristle.

"Let her go!" My voice is a deadly whisper, but it carries as I step between Cassie and her father.

"She's my daughter, and I want to speak to her in private."

"No fucking way."

My curse has an elderly lady gasping, and other people make noises, but there is no way he's going to bully her into talking with him.

Cassie squirms in his grip, making my blood boil. I step closer to him and my eyes narrow even further when he tightens his grip on her.

"I'm warning you. Let her fucking go. Right now."

Someone puts their hand on my arm, but I shake it off. He must see something in my eyes because he drops her arm and steps back from me, but when I turn to Cassie, she's running.

I don't even think for a moment. I just spin around and go after her.

My eyes dart around, and I catch up to her outside as she's having a total meltdown. Her hands are on her knees and her breath is coming in short gasps.

"Cass, are you okay?" My fingers brush her neck, and she flies into my arms. "It's okay. You're safe. I got you."

Holding onto her as I guide us towards the cars, I tell my driver I don't need him, and I usher her into the car. As I close the door, I see her father standing with a murderous expression.

I couldn't care about his hurt feelings. The only priority for me is the girl at my side.

Her breaths are still fast, but she's not as pale, and when I turn to look at her, she meets my gaze with wide, horrified eyes.

Her voice is raspy when she speaks, and I want to go back and rip Dave apart.

"I remembered… I think it was one of my earliest memories."

I can't help reaching out to touch her. My fingers stroke her neck, and I brush my lips across her knuckles.

"He used to beat me. I used to have nightmares about it, and my mom said it was okay. She told me I was safe and that he couldn't hurt me anymore."

Her whole-body shudders as her tears start falling, and I'm totally helpless. I want to fix this for her, make things better, but I don't know how.

"One time was for a broken vase, and another was because I dropped a picture of Taylor. The memories are all coming back."

Her sobs increase, and I just sit with her in my lap as we drive towards her house. We told people to come back there, but I wish we hadn't.

Tony was setting things up for her and for me, but when we get there, neither of us makes any move to get out of the car.

Cass is still in my arms as my lips brush her forehead, but when

I hold my lips there, I feel the shift in the car as she looks up and captures my lips in a kiss that shakes me to my core.

I'm not sure why, but it feels like goodbye, and when she breaks the kiss first to get out, I know I've almost lost her.

# Chapter 20

# BETRAYAL FOR BREAKFAST

## Cassie

SEEING that news on my cell as we drove to my mom's funeral destroyed me. It hurt so badly, and I had to know if it was true. I had to text him, but his reply threw ice cold water over the tiny bit of hope I was holding onto that I was enough for him.

It killed me seeing him, but when he came up to support me, then his song, and then him stepping between me and my father when I froze thawed me a little.

I tried in the car to let it all go but how could I? How could I let the fact he'd left me and went to get laid by someone else?

When I kissed him, I was sure it was for the last time, and I spent the next few hours avoiding his heartbroken looks.

When everyone else is gone and I'm tidying up, he's still here. I leave him in the sitting room to go into the kitchen, dancing to some music on my iPad, when he comes in. I don't see him at first until his hands wrap around me. My heart hammers in my chest as he moves with me, spinning and twirling me around.

After a few songs, he releases me, and we work on washing up together. I don't want to talk, so I sing along with the radio until one of his songs comes on. We both freeze as the song he sang for my mom blasts through the room.

He turns to me, softly singing the words as my body tingles with awareness.

He steps closer, brushing the hair from my eyes as his eyes blaze into mine. His beautiful voice fills the room, and he moves closer, in a way that sets my body alight.

He continues to sing to me in an emotional, raw, unplugged voice. His hands run over my shoulders and his fingers brush along my collarbone.

As he sings the end of the song, he drops to his knees and looks up at me through tear-filled eyes.

"And I'm sorry I left you

I'm sorry I hurt you

I think about it every day

I want to fix what I broke

Take back the words that were spoke

Tear up the note

And learn how to live with you by my side

With you by my side."

My heart stutters at the sight of him on his knees by my feet. I stare down at him with my eyes stinging and the pain of his betrayal in my heart.

I blink, and a tear falls, but I don't bother brushing it away. I just stare at him and wish things could be different.

"I. Am. So. Sorry."

His hands trace patterns on the back of my thighs, and I suck in a breath because I want to crumble. I want to let it go, but I can't.

"I can't. I can't do this. Please, Chase." My voice is low, begging, and his tears fall. It reminds me of the day he saw his dad. How hurt and broken he was.

"I wrote that for you. After I left."

He lifts his eyes to mine, and I slide down to sit beside him. His words knock everything out of me because I hear the words of the song over. The words take on a different meaning, and I turn to face him as he speaks again in a whisper.

"I missed you so much that I could barely function. The guys had to drag me onto the stage and all I wanted was to come back to you."

Tears roll down my cheeks as he sits with me.

"The only thing that helped was writing music and drinking. I had to numb myself so I wouldn't come back and claim you. I did speak to your mom from time to time, and when she told me you were engaged, I swear I thought I was going to break my word and come back for you. I wanted to, so badly, but you moved on and were happy. It was thinking you were happy with someone else that stopped me coming back."

My ears start to ring as I digest his words, but it's when he leans forward and puts his head in his hands for a moment that it hits me how much it hurt him.

"I thought I was happy. I thought he was the one, but I couldn't get you out of my mind, and when he took me to a concert as a surprise and I had to stand there listening to the band singing about how amazing love is, I knew it was time to move on from you. It was killing me inside and I had to try to get over you. I never, ever felt that I was enough to hold on to you, and now I know I'm not."

His hands grip mine firmly and he presses tear filled kisses along my knuckles and then my palm. "You were enough. You are enough. I finally had it all and…" He takes a deep breath as a sob breaks free, and I watch him trying to get control. "And then I finally get you and I fuck it all up. I hurt you again when I swore I wouldn't. I'm no good for you, Cassie. You should want more than me, better than me."

I wish I wanted someone else, someone different, but I don't because I never have.

"I wish I did. It would make this pain, this betrayal, so much easier. I can't be the girl who forgives you for this. I just can't. I love you so much, but knowing you left me last night and then had sex with someone else makes me feel sick."

His breathing hitches, and his eyes crinkle as he fights to hold on to his emotions, but I know he's about to crack because I feel the same.

"I will always regret that. I wish I'd just stayed home with you. I wish I could change it…"

His lips press softly to mine, and I kiss him back because I know that this is the last time I'll ever be his. Our tongues tangle and his fingers wind in my hair as he pulls gently, opening my mouth wider so he can push his tongue deeper inside. His free hand wraps around my waist, and he pulls me around so I'm sitting astride him.

The kiss gets more desperate, and his hand glides up my thigh, stroking my ass through my stockings as he tugs me onto his erection.

"No one else has ever made me feel like you."

His soft words between kisses make me want to forget what's happened, but then the images of them together flash up in my mind's eye and I rear back.

"Stop, Chase. I can't do this."

He freezes, releasing me immediately as I push against his chest and stand up. My chest is heaving because my heart is telling me to let go, to enjoy one last wild ride with Chase, but my head won't shut off. I close my eyes, pressing my fingers to the bridge of my nose and trying to push the headache that's building back down. I hear him stand and feel him staring at me before he speaks in a whisper as the doorbell rings.

"Cass, do you want me to leave?"

I nod, then shake my head, and then nod again.

"I don't… I don't know…"

The doorbell goes again, and this time the person is insistent, pushing hard.

"I'll go, but this, us. We aren't over. We can get through this, but not today."

I swallow the pain again as he stands, brushing my hair from my cheek and pressing his lips to mine before he steps back.

"I'll get it on my way out. Cass, I…" He closes his eyes and swallows hard before he turns and starts to walk away from me without finishing his sentence.

I want to ask him to stay, but I know how unfair that would be of me, so I watch numbly as he backs out of the kitchen. I glance at the mirror above the dining table and see flushed cheeks, bright eyes, and smudged lipstick.

My hands shake as I quickly fix my hair and my face. There are voices in the hallway, and I walk out to ask Chase what's going on when I see my dad and my brother have him pinned to the wall.

"Let him go."

My voice is low, forceful, and furious. Both of them turn to me and shake their heads.

"No. He's done playing with you. He's leaving now."

My dad's voice is deadly serious, but I don't care. This is my home, and I won't let someone I barely even remember dictate who can stay and who can go.

"He's going nowhere, and if you don't let him go this instant, I'll call the cops and have them remove you from the premises."

My dad steps back first, and Chase shoves Grant away from him before he comes back to my side. I know he's not leaving now. I link our fingers and stare at my dad and Grant's livid faces, but I'm not a child, and I won't back down to these ghosts from my past.

"Come in, but don't get comfy. You won't be staying long."

"We need to speak to you, alone," Grant informs me in a heated tone, but Chase bristles by my side until I squeeze his hand, holding him back, and he gives me a gentle squeeze in response.

"No. Chase stays. Anything you have to say to me, you can say to both of us."

My brother rolls his eyes and I see my dad about to say something, so I forestall him.

"I've had a few flashbacks to my early childhood. Some of my earliest memories turned out to be the nightmares I was petrified of when I was growing up."

My father turns his cold stare on me, and I want to shrink back, but with Chase beside me, I'm not scared of him. Not now, not ever.

"Really? What do you remember?" Grant asks, and I meet his gaze steadily as I answer him.

"One of my earliest memories is getting beaten as a baby for knocking over a vase, and another is breaking a picture of Taylor. I took off running into the space in the pantry and he beat me for it when he got me out."

I take a breath as another memory surfaces, and I gasp, taking a step back into Chase's warmth.

"I also remember you raping, Mom. I was supposed to be asleep, and it was just after you took me to her house from your house. We played a little and she was bathing me, but she was crying and telling me how sorry she was. She put me to bed, but I couldn't sleep because I'd left my blankie on the couch. I came out to get it and she was bleeding on the floor with you on top of her. Your face was bleeding, and the coffee table was a mess…"

Another memory hits, and I remember him slamming her head down when she tried to get away.

"You told her you were going to kill her and that you'd get away with it, just like all the other times you had before."

I close my eyes as I try to banish how defeated my mom looked, and when he'd finished, she caught me watching, horrified, by the door. My dad didn't see me, but he staggered up from her, kicked her in the stomach, and then the cops arrived, taking him away.

"That's a nice story your mom filled your head with, but I'm afraid none of it's true."

"Is it not? Then how come you dropped your keys as the cops

took you away. Mom scooped me up and ran as soon as they left. She took my blanket and the few things we had before she went to your house. In the master bedroom there was a safe in the closet, and she took some things from there, packed some clothes and we left."

Once we were at the garage with the woman who could only have been Kelsey, the car was waiting for us. She pulled my short-haired wig on and tucked my hair into a cap as she changed me into boys' clothes. I remember protesting until she handed me a snack, and that's it. I can't remember anything else.

"Is this true?" Grant asks with a horrified glance at my father, but he just shakes his head.

"Of course it's not. It's all your mother's doing. She lied about everything and filled her head with these ridiculous stories."

"But that's true. Your blood was found in her house, along with semen, but they never tested you, did they?"

Grant turns to face his father, and I want them to leave now. I've almost said what I need to say, but it's Grant I address as I speak next.

"Uh, Grant. My mom left a letter for you and one for Amira in her belongings. She also left evidence of her abuse."

My father turns to face me and actually laughs.

"She had no proof then and she has none now. Just where do you get off telling my son lies about me?"

"It's not a lie. And you're the one barging into my life, not the other way around."

"I am your father, and you will speak to me with respect."

My blood boils and I step forward, going toe-to-toe with the man who physically and mentally abused my mom.

"Respect is earned, not commanded."

I don't see the slap coming, but as it connects with my cheek, I'm tossed to the side and Chase punches my father, knocking him back through the open door.

He's furious as he stands over him, holding him by the back of his neck. I'm about to intervene when I see a commotion outside.

The front door is open and those few journalists who waited, get the scoop of a lifetime.

"You ever lay one hand on her again, and I swear it'll be the last thing you ever do."

He drops him to the ground and steps back inside, glaring at Grant.

"Out or in?"

Grant glances longingly at me but steps back, helping his father up from the ground as I lift a hand to my stinging cheek. Chase marches in and slams the door closed before he storms over and examines my cheek.

"Come on. We need to get some ice on that."

His hands are shaking, and I want to say something comforting or tell him how grateful I am, but he won't even look at me as he runs the dishcloth under the faucet. Once it's cold, he comes over and places it gently on my cheek, but his hand shakes even harder.

"I'm sorry. I lost it. They won't want to know you now. It's my fault he found you anyway."

He's silent for a beat, then his eyes meet mine and I want to say something to ease the torment inside them.

His lips shakily press as kiss to my forehead, and he drags my hand up, covering his on my cheek before he steps back. Our eyes stay connected, and I see a single tear fall as he turns to leave.

"Chase," I murmur, and he freezes with his hand on the doorknob.

"Will you stay with me?"

# Chapter 21

# REGRET & REMORSE

## Chase

I PAUSE as I press my lips to her forehead, and my body shudders with the desire and the pain as they battle it out. I hover, wanting to stay, but thinking I should go. Sitting with her on the floor, I thought I had a chance to fix things, but knowing it's not going to happen is tearing me apart.

My fist still aches where I punched her asshole of a father. He doesn't deserve her, and I swear, if he comes after her again, I'll fucking end the douchebag.

As I walk towards the door, I hear her say my name, and I turn back to see her looking at me.

"Will you stay with me?"

Her soft words wipe away my resistance, and it's more than I deserve. I should leave. The sensible thing to do would be to leave, but I've never been sensible where it comes to her.

"Of course, Cassie. I'll always stay with you. No matter what."

I walk back over, sitting in a chair that I move around the dining table so I'm beside her. I slide my arms around her waist, holding her as her dam breaks. Her tears fall onto my shirt, but I don't move. I'm scared she'll take it back. I'm scared she'll let me walk out that door and never let me back in, so I stay, holding her, wanting her, but too scared to have her.

After her tears subside, we just sit, quiet and unmoving. My cell rings over and over. I ignore it, and she does the same.

We move to sit on the sofa and share a bottle of wine as we watch a movie in silence. Neither of us has spoken, but we've been sitting the whole time holding hands.

Her fingers soft, delicate, and warm inside my rough, callused ones make my dick hard and my heart thump loudly.

I've never just sat with a girl and had food with no ulterior motive. Even when I when I was home for my dad's funeral, all I wanted was to forget. Now, I'd do anything to remember every single second I have with her.

Cass comes back in with my cell, tossing it at me, and then goes back into the kitchen to get more wine, I hope. When she doesn't come back in, I glance down at my cell and suppress the growl that builds in my chest.

Message after message lights up the screen from my band mates, from Michaels, and from Tony.

There are calls from Belinda and Hannah. Three from Kami, the label publicist, and Joanna, our A&R person at the label.

Then I see the news items. There are images from the funeral, and the scumbags saying that I was with Hannah yesterday now say I'm with Cassie, and I got violent with her dad when he called me out on it.

Fuck. Fuck. Fuck.

My cell rings again, and I answer with a snap.

"What the fuck is it?"

Michaels, Tony, and Joanna are all on the call, and once they're done reprimanding me, I sit back and just let them talk without interrupting.

There's nothing for me to say. They own my image, and as

much as I want to tell them to fuck off when they suggest I get seen out, I can't because I refuse to throw Cassie to the wolves.

"So, tomorrow, you'll be out on a date with Jamie Stilson. She's America's sweetheart, and it will help your image."

Joanna speaks, having arranged it, and I listen as Tony and Mason agree it's the only way. Joanna and Tony click off, but Michaels is still on the line and I'm waiting on him going off on me when he surprises the shit out of me.

"Chase, I know you have feelings for Cassie. I can see it when you look at her. I don't know what's holding you back from admitting it, but I'm telling you now, don't let the woman you love slip away because of public opinion."

He sucks in a breath and his next words sucker punch me.

"I let my wife get away from me. I didn't fight when I should have, and I missed three months of my son's life. I know shit is more complicated because of who Cassie is, but the gossip will die down with the next news cycle. Nothing, and I do mean nothing, is worth losing the one person who sees you. Trust me, it'll kill you inside, and you'll become bitter and twisted about it."

I open my mouth to speak when Cassie comes back into the room. Her eyes glitter with tears, and I need to find out what's wrong with her.

"Thanks, Mason. I'll keep it in mind."

"Right then. Speak to you later, and make sure you tell her what's going down. Don't let her find out by going online."

He ends the call and Cass sits as far from me as she can get on the sofa.

"Cass," I whisper, but it's too low and she doesn't hear me, so I slide across to her and touch her arm softly. "Cassie, are you okay?"

She nods then shrugs, and then shakes her head as I stare at her, but she won't look at me. I'd love to try and see what's going on in her eyes, but she shifts position.

I try three times and then I move around, flipping my leg over hers and sitting on her lap.

"Chase," she mutters, and her hands push at my chest. I don't budge. I refuse to move until she at least looks at me. I lift her chin so she has no choice but to meet my eye, and she shoves at my chest.

"Move," she hisses, but I just shake my head.

"No. Talk to me. Tell me what's wrong?"

Her gaze darkens and her palm comes up to slap me. The sting of it makes me angry, but I know I deserve this, so I sit tight.

"That all you got, babe?"

I shouldn't goad her, but I know that the quicker she gets her anger out, the quicker we can move past it.

I don't flinch as her hand comes up and smacks my cheek again, nor do I move when she scrapes her nails down my hands, drawing blood.

"Keep going. Let it all out."

Her gaze darkens further, and I let her slap, bite, and scratch me. My hands and wrists are a mess. My lip is bleeding, and her anger is still festering, but I've had enough.

I wrap my hands around her wrists, pinning her beneath me as I sit on her lap. She tries to wriggle, to buck me off and to kick me, but she can't, and then she screams at me.

"I fucking hate you! I loathe you! I wish we'd never met!"

My eyes sting, but I refuse to back down, and I stare down at her as she yells and screams at me in frustration. I let it go on and on until she stills, and tears leak from her eyes. I track them down to her hair, but when I next meet her eyes, she stares at me like she really does hate me. The disgust is evident on her face.

"What is it? Why do you suddenly hate me so much?"

My voice is soft, gentle, and she glowers up at me, unable to move in my hold. She shakes her head and I lean closer so our mouths are a breath apart.

"Tell me, Cassie. Come on. Something's broken you, so tell me what it is!"

Her head bucks forward, and she catches my cheek with her

forehead. It makes my head spin, but I don't let her go. In fact, I hold tighter until she growls at me.

"You made me fall in love with you and then you left me. Then when I need you again, you spring back into my life, in and out like a Jack in the Box. You ran from me to fuck someone else while you're fucking sleeping with me. Now I hear you're going out on a date and I hate it. I hate you for making me feel like this. I hate you so much!"

Her eyes stream with the tears, and I press my lips to hers, ignoring the sting of my lip and my cheeks as I kiss her.

At first, she doesn't respond, and she moves her head, but my arms have her caged in and then she bites down on my lip until I wince in pain. I hiss out a breath as she releases it and sucks it into her mouth.

When she releases it, I slide my tongue into her mouth, taking what I want until she reluctantly gives in. Our tongues battle while I slide my way down her body, gripping her wrists with one hand as I go, keeping our lips firmly attached.

Once my body is wedged between her legs, I slowly push her dress up, pushing my fingers roughly into her panties. My fingers stroke down her folds and she's soaked, panting, and pushing against my head while she tries to shake her head.

"You like this. Admit it. You like that you hate me right now and you want me."

I slip a finger into her pussy as I speak, and she grinds against my hand before she wrenches her lips from mine.

"No. Chase. Stop."

"Are you sure? Your pussy is soaked for me. No one else can have this. This belongs to me." I mutter her against her lips as she moves in time with my thrusts and her mouth opens on a gasp. "Come on. Give up. Tell me how much you want my mouth on your pussy…"

Moisture coats my fingers as I speak, and she shakes her head, moaning softly.

"No. I won't. Stop…"

Her eyes close as I push another finger inside, and she groans, riding my fingers and tugging against my hold on her wrists.

"Chase," she whines, and I push harder, faster and move my thumb so it's on her clit.

"Don't… stop…"

I slam my hand into her over and over, kissing her lips, her cheek, her neck, and then, just as her sweet little pussy begins to tighten, I stop and withdraw my fingers. My hand lifts to my mouth and I suck her juices from my fingers as she watches.

"I want you to come on my tongue before I fuck you over this couch so hard your body will never crave anyone else."

Her dark eyes glisten, and I slip down between her legs, finally letting go of her wrists. She shoves at me, but when my tongue laps at her sweet spot, she stops pushing and winds her fingers into my hair.

"No…. Yes." Her body moves along with my licks. My fingers slide back into her as my tongue licks, sucks, and nibbles on her bud.

Her fingers are tugging on my hair so hard, but I'm so turned on I can't see straight, and my free hand moves across her hips as my fingers move faster. Her body starts to convulse, and I hold myself there, lapping at her like a dying man in the desert who's just found water. She tugs at my hair.

"No," I mutter in a heated whisper as she pleads with me to stop. "I'm not stopping until you scream my name from your fucking lips."

I press my tongue back against her and start licking hard, ignoring her tugs on my hair as three of my fingers push inside her.

My arm holds her down firmly, and her body bucks and writhes on the sofa until she comes again, screaming my name from her lips like a curse.

I stand, unbuttoning my pants and shoving them and my boxers down before I flip her over and slam into her from behind.

She moans loudly as my cock pounds into her and her hands brace against the couch. My palms smack and strike her barely covered ass until it's bright pink and she's moaning my name.

I push into her, gripping her shoulders and pulling her back in to my cock as I give her everything I've got, and before long, I'm spilling my load inside her and she's coming again, moaning loudly. We both collapse on the sofa, her under me and my cock still half inside her.

"Chase, get off me," she commands, and I'm surprised to hear her voice cracking.

"What's wrong, babe?"

My attempt at finding out what's wrong is interrupted by a knock at the door, and I pull out of her, tugging up my pants and boxers as she rights herself and goes to answer the door.

I've just redone my shirt buttons when she comes back into the living room with two cops.

"Chase, these guys are here for you."

Her voice is low, broken, and there's something in her eyes that I can't place, but she watches in silence as they Mirandize and cuff me.

"What did I do?" My voice is brittle, hard because they've just interrupted us.

"You are being arrested for assaulting Dave Spence," one officer tells me as he and his colleague drag me out to the waiting car. My eyes dart back, and I see Cassie standing in the doorway, flushed, and fucking beautiful as she watches them drive me off.

# Chapter 22

## WHAT THE FUCK

### Cassie

MY BODY IS STILL TINGLING after what's just happened, and I'm so confused about whether I wanted that or not. Part of me didn't, but then the sexual part of me is wobbly, turned on, and shaking with how much I enjoyed him dominating me like that.

I go back into the sitting room, but I'm too on edge and I can't settle. Peeking out of the curtains, I see all of the reporters are gone. They obviously can't pass up a chance to see the enigma that is Chase Crawford getting dragged to jail.

Part of me wants to know what it's for, but I know there's nothing I can do but wait. Chase'll tell me soon enough. I decide to shower to pass the time and to distract myself from the pacing I'm doing around my living room. I quickly strip and step into the spray, washing the day from hell from my body. I don't bother washing my hair since I only washed it this morning, but I scrub at my body until I'm red raw and then I stare at myself in the mirror, wondering what the hell is wrong with me.

I spend time at the mirror, moisturizing, preening, and plucking. Then I brush my hair and plait it, before twisting it into a low bun at the base of my neck.

*Why did I let him fuck me when I know he had sex with her last night?*
*Do you know that for sure though?*

This little voice is niggling at me, and I wonder what's going on. I decide to go for a drive and clear my head, so I dress quickly in an old pair of sweats and a loose tee.

My heartbeat thrums as I shove my feet into my sneakers and snatch my purse from the coffee table. Chase's cell is there too, and it's when I see it that I know where to go. I drive to the park my mom and I would frequent and sit for a while, staring out as her death hits me again. As the temperature cools, I decide to take Chase's cell to his apartment. The drive is relatively short, and I park in his vacant spot, not planning on staying long as I let myself in.

My feet carry me through the apartment silently. His office door is closed, and I pause to think about what's happened since I was last here. My body shudders in response to the memory of his rough fingers pushing inside me.

The walk to his room takes courage, and I'm just praying he's not in there, but my relief is tinged with sadness as I gather all my things together.

Our time is over, and while I've no idea what's going on with him or why he's suddenly been arrested, it doesn't matter because we aren't good together. He's my stepbrother, and he has no respect for me saying no. It's not a good combination, and we are highly explosive, so it's best if I just leave him.

He left me alone in his apartment to go and sleep with someone else, which tells me all I need to know about him.

It takes me a while to track all my things down, and I'm just packing my toiletries away when I hear him calling me.

Fuck. I don't want to see him right now. I start shoving everything into my little toiletry bag, but I'm not quick enough, and the door opens wider to reveal a livid Chase standing there.

"Why the fuck are you here and not at home?"

His voice makes my skin break out in gooseflesh, but it's the look in his eyes, wild and furious, that has my insides quivering.

"I'm getting my shit together to leave."

My simple answer causes his back to stiffen, and he brings his fingers up, running them through his hair. "Cassie, don't leave. We can work this out."

His soft words are totally at odds with the look on his face, but my response is involuntary. My spine straightens as he comes into the bathroom towards me.

"Stay with me, please?"

I shake my head as I meet his irritated stare. "No. I can't. I won't."

"Why not? Did I hurt you earlier?"

My eyes scan his face, taking in the scrapes, bruises, and cuts. I did that to him. My heart plummets and I shake my head, firmly staring over his shoulder.

"Look at me, babe."

I want to, but looking at him has me feeling all kinds of guilt over what I did to him, and surprisingly, over what I let him do to me.

His soft fingers brush against my skin, making me sigh, but I push him back. "No. You don't get to touch me again. What happened in my house was a mistake."

My voice is breathless. I can barely hear myself over the roaring of my heartbeat in my ears.

For a moment, there's silence, and then he shoves me back against the counter. His eyes bore into mine in a way that makes my skin tingle and my panties soak. I glare at him, trying to control my reaction to him, but he starts speaking, and I know one thing with startling clarity... our hate fuck from earlier is far from over.

"You love me, you hate me. You want me, you don't. I want you. I fucking love you. How is that not enough for you?"

He grips my arms tightly and crashes his lips down to mine, but

I don't respond. I keep my mouth tightly closed as I shove against his arms.

"Kiss me back."

His forceful words and the way he's holding my shoulders tightly enough to leave a mark make me forget that I should keep my mouth closed.

"No," I say. "I will not."

He kisses me harder, pushing his cock against me. His touch ignites something inside me as I try to simultaneously push him away and pull him closer to me.

"You feel that," he says as he thrusts against me. "This is all for you. Only for you."

I shake my head and he presses soft kisses along my lips, my neck as he grinds against me.

"Chase, I said no."

I try to be firm, but my moan at the end tells him it's not what I really want. His lips attack mine, and his tongue thrusts in as he tugs me against his cock.

"You want me. Just admit it."

I wrench my lips from his, shaking my head.

"I don't. I hate you."

"You hate that you love me."

His lips are back on mine, and he pinches my nipple hard, making me gasp, and he roughly pushes his tongue into my mouth.

For a moment, I lose myself in his kiss, his touch, and I almost forget, but another image of him with her flashes before my eyes and I shove him harder away from me. He relents and steps away from me, but his eyes don't leave mine as I bend over and try to draw air into my lungs.

"What is it? Why don't you want me?"

Part of me wants to lie, to say I never really wanted him, but I can't.

"I can't stop seeing you with her. I can't do this…"

My eyes meet his gaze. He holds my stare, and I see the pain and frustration in his pleading look.

I turn around and run from the bathroom, because I know I'm about to give in to him, to let him walk all over me. I didn't let Abe do it, and I can't let him do it to me anymore. When I say no, I mean it. We're done now. This is over.

I run to the hallway and hear him following me. His warm hands wrap around me and he tugs me to a stop, pushing me hard against the wall. His cock grinds into my ass, and I swallow the sound that threatens.

"Chase, no."

My voice shakes as he tugs down my sweats and panties. His fingers push against me and I feel the moisture he's spreading around.

"Cassie, you want me. Admit it."

I shake my head and writhe against his hold, but he's stronger than me, and when he pushes a finger into me, my resistance folds like a stack of cards. Another finger follows, and he roughly fingers me against the wall with his mouth on my neck, licking, sucking, and biting me.

I still myself against him, refusing to move as his fingers deftly stroke at me, and he growls in my ear. His free hand reaches up, and while his body is still pinning me to the wall, he reaches up my top and squeezes my breast.

"Come on. Just admit you want me."

I shudder and then shake my head, dropping it back onto his shoulder when he pinches my nipple hard again.

He pushes his thumb against my clit as his fingers pump in and out of me, and with the pressure on my nipple, I know I'm close. Just as I'm about to fall over that precipice, he stops, and I whine.

"Chase, please?"

"Please what? Let you come or let you go?"

My frustration at him swells because I don't know. I want to leave, but what he's doing to my body right now feels so good. He's playing me like a well-tuned guitar, and he's strumming me to my climax.

"Well, what do you want? Tell me…"

"I don't…. I don't know…"

At my words, he shoves his fingers roughly inside me and pushes me harder into the wall. "How about now?"

He works my clit with his thumb, slamming his palm against me as his fingers release my nipple, and suddenly, I'm free falling. I come harder than I ever have in my life, and I can barely stand up.

He steps back slightly and then twists me around to capture my lips in a punishing kiss. His rock-solid erection pulses against my stomach, and he breaks the kiss. I startle when he walks further back, but then he scoops me up and throws me over his shoulder, smacking my ass repeatedly as he makes his way into the bedroom. He slips my sweats and panties off, tossing them on the floor as we go.

By the time we reach the bedroom I've never been in before, my ass is stinging and my temper is starting to flare, but it's not until he drops me onto the bed that I really get annoyed.

"Stop, Chase," I tell him, but he doesn't listen. His eyes are wild, hungry, and intense, and he stares at me until I stop talking.

"Turn," he commands in a low whisper, and I shake my head.

"No. Stop."

Again, he ignores me, and his strong hands wrap around my waist, flipping me over until I'm lying on my front, with my bare ass in the air. His palm strikes my ass, and the sting turns me on, making me moan.

"You want me," he informs me as his mouth caresses my neck. "Why won't you admit it?"

I try to shake my head and scoot up the bed when he presses his cock against my ass, eliciting a sound I've never heard before in my life. It's somewhere between a mewl and a moan.

His body weight shifts, and before I can protest, his tongue is licking from my ass crack down and probing me. He sits up for a minute and reaches into the bedside cabinet and pulls some stuff out, but he moves before I can see what it is, and then his mouth is back on me again.

I want to tell him to stop, to run, but he runs his tongue inside me, pushing me higher and higher until I'm about to come and then he pulls out.

"Chase," I whine, and he smacks my ass hard, making me moan in pleasure. He does it again and again until I'm about ready to combust, and then he goes back to my ass and starts to lick.

I've never done anal before. I never wanted to, but having his mouth there turns me on so much that my earlier protests seem feeble and ridiculous.

He pulls back for a second, and I feel something cold and wet against the hole, then something sliding in.

It's small, and it's an unwelcome, yet welcome, intrusion. When he presses a button and it starts to vibrate, I almost convulse off the bed. He pushes it again and it goes faster, leading me higher, and then he stops it again before I come.

"Cassie," he grinds out in a heated voice. "I'm going to fuck you, hard and fast, but I'm not going to let you come until you tell me what you want."

My head spins, and I think I shake my head, but I can't be sure because his cock slams into me, as deep as he can go. With the thing in my ass and his cock inside me, I lose all conscious thought.

"I told you," he mutters as he thrusts in and out, setting the vibrating higher and higher as he punishes me with his cock. "This is mine. You don't get to take it away from me."

His palm strikes my ass, and I swear my clit feels like it's about to combust into flames. He tugs my hair and holds it tightly as his mouth licks and nibbles on my neck.

"Say it," he mutters, pulling on my hair in a way that makes me whimper, but I keep my mouth closed and he thrusts more forcefully into me before he stills.

"Please, please."

He puts the vibrate up a little more and my whole body starts to tense. "Please what? Say it!" He growls into my ear, still not moving as he stops the vibrations and my orgasm recedes.

"You want me to finish you, so fucking tell me."

My head tells me to say nothing, to run far and fast, but then he starts the toy again as he moves his hips in circles.

"Come on, babe. I can feel it building."

He grips me, and somehow moves us so I'm sitting astride him with the toy pushing farther in. He hits the button again and again, and my body responds like he knew it would, but just as I'm about to come again, he stops.

"Say it…"

His fingers pinch my nipple as his other hand wanders down, pushing against my clit, and I lose the little control I had. My voice is a hoarse whisper as I cave into him.

"I want you. I need this. I want you to make me come."

He moves his hand up to grip my neck and turns my face so he can kiss me, plunging his tongue into my mouth before he starts moving again.

He pounds into me harder and faster and turns the toy back on. His finger returns to my clit, and I grip his thighs as he rides me so hard that, this time, when my orgasm comes, I scream his name as wave after wave consumes me, dragging me down, down, down until I collapse against him, but he hasn't come yet.

"Yes, that's it. Come for me, Cassie. Give me all you got," he tells me as continues to impale me on his dick with his fingers, twisting and teasing my nipples until I splinter apart again, screaming his name.

"Fuck," he roars as he comes, and I wince as his fingers grip my nipples so tight that I'm scared they'll come off.

He pushes me down to the bed and pulls the toy out of my ass, tossing it to the floor along with his shirt before he collapses down on the bed beside me.

For a few minutes, we lie silent, and I battle with how much I let him dominate me, and how I let him fuck me against my will.

He doesn't speak, but his eyes track my every movement and I curl up on my side, facing away from him as shame and disgust well up inside me.

After a while longer, his quiet snores fill the room, and I turn to stare at him. I don't know where this domineering, powerful side of him was before, and although I like it, I'm also petrified because he has the power to break me. He has the power to ruin me completely, and I can't give someone that much control over me.

My eyes dart over his toned body, taking in his guitar tattoo and the lyrics that are underneath.

"Come away with me.

Drive into the darkness beside me.

And you'll always be free.

Free to love, free to try, free to be…"

I press a soft kiss to his shoulder, even though I know I shouldn't. Even though I know I should hate him, something about him calls to me, and part of me wonders if it's the fucked-up part of me that saw my mom being raped. He pushed me before, but never this far, and now my heart stutters as my confusion grows.

*Did he rape me?* No. Not really, because I wanted him inside me.

*Did he let me go when I said no?* Also no, but this is what's fucking my head up.

Maybe if I leave, I'll get some space and some clarity, but then again, no one has ever made me come like he just did.

I lean back, thinking about how much of a jumble my head's in. My eyes are stinging with tiredness, but I can't stay here, can I?

I begin to move away from him when he wakes up and takes hold of my hand.

"Stay with me, Cass," his sleepy voice asks, and I start, but his hands drops, and he quickly falls back asleep.

I wait a few more minutes until I'm sure he's asleep, and then I get up and pull on my sweats. I pick up my panties, shoving them into my pocket as I right my bra and walk from the room. My eyes drift back to him, and I wonder if I'm making the right decision, but he consumes me and pushes my boundaries, which is scaring me, so I don't feel like I have a choice.

I go back into the other room, picking up my cell and loading a gossip page to remind myself of why I need to leave.

He's not faithful. Not to anyone, so why would I be any different?

He slept with someone else.

My legs are Jell-O though, and I sit on the edge of the bed as the video from the other night starts to play, and the first thing I notice is that a few of Chase's tattoos are missing.

The one on his arm isn't there, and neither is the one on his back. The video plays over and over, but I sit staring at it, noticing different things that my heartbroken mind couldn't process.

He's slimmer in the video, and his hair isn't as long as it is now, but there's something else. There's something in the bedroom in Malibu that can't possibly still be there because it's on the wall across from me.

My eyes dart to the hung guitar that's signed by so many artists. I go over and stroke the paintwork, wondering if there are two copies of this guitar, but I find that very unlikely, and when I tally up the evidence, I realize two things.

First, Chase didn't cheat on me because we're not together, not really. And second, the girl is lying for whatever reason. Maybe, whoever it is, is using this to detract from the drama I bring to his life.

The knowledge is startling, and part of me wants to go wake him, but part of me still wants to leave.

# Chapter 23

## UNCEREMONIOUS WAKEUP

### Chase

I WAKE up alone in bed with a start. My hand reaches out, seeking her warmth, but she's not there, so I bolt upright.

Fuck, I never should have gone to sleep.

I sit for a moment and wonder if I pushed too hard. I really thought she was enjoying the hate sex, but what if I was wrong? What if she hates me so much she won't even see me now?

"Cassie," I call out in a hoarse whisper, but there's nothing. No sound, no movement, just nothing.

I crawl up from the bed, walking through my apartment with nothing on. My feet hurt as I make my way into my bedroom, and a feeling of complete and utter despair washes over me because it's empty. There are no clothes on the bed, no bags overflowing with her things like there was when I fell asleep, and as I walk farther into the room, the absence of her becomes palpable.

My legs shake beneath me, and I crumple to the floor, thinking I did push too hard. I've always pushed her, ignored her boundaries, but was this one the final straw? Did I fucking lose her again? I was so scared of losing her that I think I lost my mind a little. My eyes sting, and I stand up, walking out of my room and slamming the door. My feet carry me to the living room, and I almost sigh in relief when I see her sitting on the sofa, sipping from a coffee cup as she watches something on TV.

She doesn't look at me as I go and sit in front of her. Her back stiffens as she stares at me, but I'm too afraid to meet her gaze for fear of what I'll see.

"Chase," she begins in a shaky whisper, and I glance up to see tears streaming down her cheeks. I don't think, don't hesitate as I wrap my arms around her, pressing gentle kisses to her forehead.

"What is it, Cass? What can I do?"

My lips brush against hers and she shudders, wrapping her arms around me and holding me tightly as she breaks down sobbing.

"Cassie, talk to me, babe."

My pleading seems to work because, after a few minutes, her sobs lessen. I move onto the couch and lift her to sit on my lap.

I don't care that I'm stark naked and neither does she. Once her breathing is almost back to normal, I lift her chin and press a soft, open-mouthed kiss to her lips.

She doesn't return the kiss, but she doesn't push me away either. I sit in silence, stroking my hands down her hair, her face, and her body, but she doesn't move and then she pushes back from my chest.

Her tearful gaze meets mine, and she takes a deep breath before she finally speaks to me.

"Chase, I think I'm broken."

My confusion must show on my face because she continues speaking.

"I let you do whatever you want to me. I always have, but this is beyond fucked up. I say no to you and you refuse to listen to me. Not only do you not listen to me, but… I like it, and that's so messed up." Her forehead wrinkles as she stares at me in both revulsion and horror. "What if seeing my mom being raped broke me? I mean, how else can you explain me letting you shove me up against a wall and making me come when I tell you no. It's not okay to do that. And for me to enjoy it so much means that something isn't right inside me."

"Cass, I love you, and I'll only push you as far as you're comfortable. I know when we had our first encounters I was a bit pushy, but I knew you wanted me. I didn't know how inexperienced you were at the start, but I loved your taste, your scent and it drove me wild then. If I thought for a minute you were really saying no, even back then, I wouldn't ever have done any of that. At all."

Her eyes meet mine, and I see a small sliver of hope, of love, and it's that tiny sign that keeps me talking to her.

"I knew you wanted me, but you were too fucking stubborn to admit it…"

She sighs, running her fingers through her hair and licking her lips as she watches me stare at her.

"Chase, I hate that I wanted you. It hurts that you'd push me that hard when I was messed up over something that I thought you did."

Her words take a moment to sink in, and I stare at her openmouthed as the meaning of them bounces around in my head.

Something she thought I did… Something she thought I did.

My mouth opens, but no words come out until finally I glance up at her.

"I didn't sleep with Hannah, did I? I mean I remember her coming over, but that's it. I don't remember fucking her."

She shakes her head. "Not this time, but why did you think you did?"

I can't look at her as shame and regret burn through me. I did call Hannah over, but only because I was so freaked out about Cassie.

"Chase?"

Her small voice makes me look at her, and I know if I want us to work then I have to be honest with her. I have to tell her how much it's freaking me out that the public might hate her because she's my stepsister. My hands shake as I ponder what her reaction will be to my confession. It's not that I don't want her, but my life is always under the microscope of the public, and I don't want her getting hurt because of my fans or their opinion of us.

Her soft fingers rub at my arm, and I blink, bringing her back into focus. Her eyes are warm, but there's something in them that scares me because I know she's seconds away from running away from me forever. I swallow a deep breath and lean in, tasting her lips for a second before she pulls back.

"Chase, you need to tell me what's going on or I'm leaving."

Her tone is sharp, and I know she's serious, which breaks my silence.

"I was freaked out, so I called Hannah over. We sat and drank until I can't remember what time, but I was wasted before she even came over. I don't even remember calling her."

Her eyes burrow into mine as she shifts in my lap, and I know this conversation is far from over. I don't say anything as she moves from my lap and stands. For a few minutes, I watch her pacing before she turns to face me. I scan her face, and I see a hardness there that wasn't there before.

"Why did you freak out?"

*No. Ask anything but that.*

She stares at me with her hands folded across her breasts, and my eyes feast on her. Her sexy curves and long brown hair, her beautiful, full and pouty lips, and her gorgeous hazel eyes that I could get lost in.

"Chase, you have ten seconds to answer or I'm leaving. I've already packed my car, and Abe came to get the other car, and he's driving it back to mine."

Abe? Who the fuck…? Then I remember, her ex-fiancé. Her casually mentioning him makes me furious, so I answer her snarkily without meaning to.

"You're my stepsister. In the court of public opinion, what we're doing is fucked up, and my fans might hate it."

She rears back like I slapped her, and I know instantly I made a massive mistake. I didn't explain properly, and she spins away from me and storms away to the elevator, spitting over her shoulder, "Fuck you, Chase. Fuck this, and fuck you."

I sit for a moment, stunned by her outburst before the thought of losing her really hits me. I bolt up from the sofa, running into the kitchen, but the elevator is closing as I beg her to wait.

"Cassie, wait. Please, let me explain."

I get one look at her devastated expression before the door closes on me. I glance down and run to my room, grabbing a pair of sweats and a shirt. I tug them on and run, pressing the elevator by the door.

As I wait for it to come, I shove my feet into my sneakers and grab my cell, wallet, and keys. I bounce on the balls of my feet as I reach the ground floor and then take off running for the stairs, but I'm too late. She's gone before I reach the parking garage.

"Fuck," I hiss as my fist connects with the wall. None of my cars are in the lot, and I stand pondering what to do.

I check my cell and see it's out of battery. Part of me wants to launch it across the room, but my work cell is in my apartment, so I sprint across the parking lot, jabbing my finger at the elevator button impatiently.

I pace in front of it, muttering hello to my neighbors as they step out. My hand throbs as I jab my finger into the console and key in the code for my floor.

I bolt into my apartment, heading straight to my office. My eyes catch sight of me in the mirror, and all I can see is a stupid fucking moron who let the best thing that's ever happened to him leave because he was too proud to explain himself properly.

My cell powers up, and I quickly call Tony, telling him I need a car sent now. He must hear the panic that's threatening to overwhelm me because he tries to talk to me, but I just tell him to hurry the fuck up as my anger overwhelms me.

If she leaves, if she goes somewhere… I try to stop my thoughts, but what if I never see her again? What if she hates me so much that she never wants to even hear me out? I'll never forgive myself for being such a fucking tool to her.

I pace around my apartment until I get a message from Tony that my car is downstairs. I shove my work cell into my pocket and rush from the apartment, heading to Cassie's.

The car makes it in good time, but when I get there, I'm petrified to get out. She might not want to see me.

The car has a charger, and I've already text her to say I'm sorry, but as we sit outside, I quickly send her another message.

**Listen babe, I'm outside. I'm sorry. What I said was true, still is true, but it's only half the story. I'm not scared about opinions of me. I don't give a fuck what they think of me, but the internet is a horrific place and once we're out there, then we become public property. I'm scared for you. They'll tear you apart because they can, and they'll take joy in trying to hurt me through you. I fucking love you too much to let my bullshit fame destroy you and your happiness. Please let me in and let me make it right, because I know one thing for sure now. I've known it since our first time. You are mine and I'm yours.**

I sit in the car, and when she doesn't respond, I move towards the door. Just as my hand closes over the handle, an older woman steps out of her house, and I watch her for a moment as I try to place her.

She's dressed in a fancy designer outfit and carries herself like someone who has money, but it's who follows her that has me propelling myself from the car.

The sight of her father smiling at my girl makes fury burn

through me, and before I can stop myself, I'm at the door, pushing him aside as I step in.

I didn't tell her the whole story yet after getting so caught up in almost losing her. My fists clench as I remember how it was him pressing charges against me and how he had me arrested. I also didn't tell her that he made up some bullshit excuse, saying I punched him for no reason and that he was just trying to see his daughter. My hands clench at my sides in an effort to stop myself from knocking him out because he also claimed that we all knew who they really were and that we aided Janie in hiding.

I couldn't prove we didn't, so I was charged with aiding and abetting a wanted fugitive, with assault and with domestic disturbance. Our lawyer was there within the hour, but it took another three hours of questioning before they finally granted bail.

Cass doesn't try to stop me, but then I see why.

Her brother is there, and so are numerous other people dotted around. Her father tries to step back in, but I step in front of Cassie, pushing her behind me.

"Get the fuck out." My voice is low as fury burns a fire through me.

"No. She's my..."

"I said fucking leave."

"I'm going nowhere without my daughter."

"Does she want to go with you? Does she even want to know you after what you did to Janie?"

He steps towards me and shoves me against the door, but I bounce back and hold his stare.

"Don't talk to me about her. Alice tried to ruin my life once. She didn't succeed, and neither will you. I'll ruin you."

"Oh really? And how will you do that?"

"I have my ways. You won't be keeping my daughter from me anymore."

The audacity of him has me laughing. His glacial look and the way he clenches his fist tells me he's about a second from punching me, but I want him to do it. I'd welcome it, but at the last second, the woman who stepped outside comes back and tugs on his arm.

"Dad, stop. If you hit him then you lose."

Her simple words make him stop, and he turns away, storming out of Cassie's house.

The rest of the people are still standing there, but Grant and another woman go after them. I turn and meet the eyes of the few people still present and order them all out. Cass doesn't intervene, but an elderly lady comes over and speaks to Cassie in a way that makes my blood boil.

"You know, dear, it's not polite to just stand there when 'someone' orders your guests to leave."

Cassie's spine stiffens, and I reach over, brushing my hand along the back of her neck.

"It's also not polite to just show up at someone's door without an invitation."

The lady glowers at me and I snap my teeth together as she turns her nose up at Cassie and marches towards the door.

"We're staying at the Marriott on Hollywood Boulevard. Perhaps you should come there and get away from this…" Her hands sweep around, showing her obvious disdain for Cassie's house. "You come from a well-placed family, Colleen. We gave you space to bury your mom, but that space is over and it's time you come home. You belong with us, with your family."

I open my mouth to say something when Cassie steps forward. Her back is straight, her mouth is a thin line, and I know whatever she's going to say next isn't going to go down well with these people.

# Chapter 24

# OUT OF THE CLOSET

## Cassie

LEAVING CHASE HURTS SO MUCH, but hearing him say that he freaked because I'm his stepsister destroyed me.

He knew that when he took my virginity, and he knew it when he came to my side when my mom was sick. It stings having it thrown back in my face.

Am I not good enough for him? Am I too fat? Too curvy? Not pretty enough?

All these thoughts bounce around in my head as I make my way home. The drive is quick because traffic is light, and before I know it, I'm pulling onto my street. Just as I park, I notice a few more cars than usual dotted around, but I ignore them as I walk dejectedly from the car. I'm just turning my key in the lock when the sound of numerous car doors opening reaches my ears, and I turn around to see my father, my brother, and a few other people marching up my street.

I want to run inside and shut the door, but it's pointless because they've already seen me and I don't have the energy to fight, so I stand and wait as all of them stop and stare at me.

"May we come in?" an older lady with greying hair asks from the back of the group, and I step aside to let them in.

The living room is a mess with the empty bottle of wine, glasses, and clothes dotted around, but I make no effort to clean up as they file in.

"It's small," the same lady mutters, and I can hear the distaste in her voice.

"So, Colleen, this is your sister Amira." He points to a girl with blonde hair in a neat twist, with an upturned nose. "This is my mom, Martha, but you won't remember her. She helped with you when I got custody."

He makes his way around and points out the rest of the family.

"Aunt Audrey, Uncle Johan, Grant, Grandpa Davis, and Aunt Gemma, and your stepmom, Ellen. They are all so excited to meet you finally that I couldn't stop them from coming with me."

I see everyone's eyes on me, and I don't care. I want them all gone. I need some time alone right now. How I can ask them to leave without causing more of a scene? I want them gone, but a sick, curious part of me wants to hear what they have to say for themselves.

They all seem overly enthusiastic and fake, but they want to meet me, so I let them stay. I offer chairs but not one of them sits down, and I make coffee so I can get a bit of breathing space from the chatter, but they all decline.

Everyone talks at me, telling me how much they've missed me, how hard they looked, but not one of them asks me a single question about my life. It's not until they start bad-mouthing my mom that I ask them to leave. I've had enough.

"Can you stop?"

My words echo as everyone around me stops talking and looks at me in stares that range from anger, to disappointment, to irritation.

"I need time and space to come to terms with all of this, and speaking about my mom like this isn't helping. She was my mom and she loved me."

My father stands up and is about to speak, when his mom comes over and grips my arm, hissing up at me. "She stole you away from us. She hid you and didn't let you know your family. She wasn't a good person."

I want to shrug her off, but I simply meet her forceful gaze with a glare of my own.

"I am not a possession. I'm a person. And my mom did what she thought was best. She was living with being abused and no one would help her, so she helped herself."

My grandma's palm stings my cheek, and I drag myself away from her.

"That's enough. Grammy, Colleen's had years of my mom telling her about this abuse. She's had years of hearing how we were all monsters who didn't help when she needed it." Amira comes over and stands in front of me. Her eyes drink in my furious expression, my clenched fists, and my stiff shoulders. "I think it's time we leave and let Colleen have her... uh... house back."

My dad steps towards us, but Amira cuts him off.

"Colleen will come to us when she wants the truth about her past. She belongs with us and she'll need us. Who else does she have? Her stepbrother? He's not going to stick around."

My ears ring at her words, and I don't speak as she leaves. I don't belong to or with anyone. I'm my own person. I walk to the door and hold it open numbly as Amira leaves, but before my dad follows, Chase flies in through the door.

I don't listen as they argue as he orders everyone out, but it's when my newfound grandma starts berating me that my numbness cracks.

"I belong with no one! I'm not a possession, and you all acting like I'm this thing that was taken from you is ridiculous. You ignored what was happening to my mom. You all knew. All of you, but none of you believed my mom."

My eyes dart around each of them, and my disgust for all of them is evident in my tone.

"You don't get to come into my life and tell me who I am or where I belong. I decide that, and I decide who I see, where I'll go, so you all can leave. I don't know what you came here expecting to find, but I do know it wasn't me. I remember the abuse. I remember my mom being raped, and I'm sorry that it doesn't fit in with your picture-perfect family, but I won't apologize for my mom saving me. Now get out of my house. Right now."

I turn to Chase and bury my face in his chest as they all walk out. For the moment, I don't care about what he said. I need comfort and he can give that to me. Still, as they leave, though, I can hear snippets of their conversations, saying things like Stockholm Syndrome, and how they need to get me psychological help, but I don't look round until Chase closes the door on them.

His lips brush my forehead and my cheeks, but I don't say a word. He leads me into the living room and sits down, pulling me onto his lap.

"Cassie," he begins softly as his lips brush against my forehead.

I don't want him to speak. I don't want to hear it.

None of it. Not his apologies or excuses for what he said, nor his response to what happened when he got here, so to stop it from happening, I kiss him.

He hesitates for a long moment, and then he's kissing me back.

"Cassie," he asks as he draws in a breath. "Are you sure you want this?"

I don't answer. Instead, I run my hands over his thickening cock and push my tongue into his mouth. My hand twists and squeezes, and he starts to thrust into me.

"Cassie?" His voice is hoarse, and he stills my hand with his as he meets my gaze. "Are you sure about this, babe?"

I shake my head, and then nod, and then shake my head again.

"Cassie, we don't have to… I should…"

I put my fingers to his lips, stopping him, and lean up to kiss his neck. "Take me to bed, Chase. Make me forget about everything except how it feels to be riding your cock. I need it, please?"

My begging works, and he lifts me, carrying me to my bedroom.

As he lays me down, he looks at me and smiles widely then rips my shirt from me, tossing it over my head.

Next my bra is off and then my pants. His growl when he sees I'm not wearing panties sets off the flutters in my stomach, and when his tongue pushes against my clit, I almost scream.

Before I can say a word, he roughly pushes his fingers inside me and goes to work. Just like that, all my pain, frustration, and worries disappear, and when I come, he doesn't hesitate to thrust into me.

His cock pounds into me at a punishing pace, his lips feasting on me, and his hands play me like a violinist does a fiddle. It's okay for now. We can work through everything as long as we're together.

Our bodies move in sync, and as he thrusts inside, he tells me how much he loves me. We both come, and he collapses, panting beside me, but his hands reach out and he lifts my chin so he can see my face.

"Babe, I know I fucked up. I really fucking messed up, but I love you so much it scares the shit out of me, but I'm here. I'm with you. I'll always be yours. Can we try and work things out?"

I pause for a moment, scanning his face as I press soft kisses to his lips. I don't answer for a moment because I'm a little scared to say yes.

I know I love him, and I trust he loves me too, but I also know we have a lot of issues to work through, but we can do it. I'm sure we can. We belong together. He's mine and I'm his, and it doesn't matter what people say or what people think. As long as I've got him, and he's got me, then we'll be fine.

"Please, Cass. Just try with me. I won't let you down again. I swear. Having you leave me isn't something I want to go through ever again." His fingers brush my lips as he watches me think about us and our future. He blinks back tears, but one breaks free as he begs me again. "Please, just say yes. Give me a chance to prove to you that I love you and that we can be great together. Please, babe?"

"Yes. We can try," I whisper before his mouth closes over mine, and I know this is where I'm supposed to be. I'm his and I always have been.

The next few weeks pass, and Chase and I spent most of our time in the bedroom at his beach house. On the evening before I'm due to pick up my mom's ashes, Chase and I sit down for a heart to heart, because while I'm trying to trust him, it's not easy. I keep expecting him to leave me.

He brings me a glass of wine and we sit on the patio, watching the waves roll and eating an excellent steak dinner that he cooked for us. Once I'm pleasantly full and sleepy, he picks me up and carries me inside, placing me gently on the bed with a soft kiss.

I scoot up the bed and he goes to get another beer for himself, and a glass of wine for me.

He comes back in and his dark hair is pushed back from his forehead, while his eyes glitter with love at the sight of me sitting on the bed waiting for him.

"Cass," he mutters as he passes me my glass, pressing a soft kiss to my lips, and for a moment, we get lost in the kiss. As our kiss gets more frantic and he put our drinks on the side table, his cell rings. My whole body flinches as he sits up to answer it.

"Hey. Yeah, I got it. Just put the damn thing out there. I don't care."

His voice cuts into my thoughts, and he turns to face me, shoulders tense with a thin line on his lips.

"Look, I told you all already, I don't care about the court of public opinion. Cassie is mine…" He breaks off, running his fingers through his hair as he stares at me. His eyes darken for a moment before he stands and starts pacing around the bedroom.

"Just deal with it, and if the guys don't like the fact that I'm in love with my stepsister, then that's too damn fucking bad. She's my girl, and one day, she's gonna be my wife."

I hear a loud noise and Chase growls down the line as my ears ring. We've been together five minutes, and we haven't talked about anything that far ahead. He needs to take a breath before I bolt.

His eyes find mine, and he pins me to the bed with the feral look he gives me. His irritation at the call shines through, and he sighs again, sitting down on the bed as something is said that he doesn't like. His face is hidden, but I can tell from the set of his shoulders that whatever is being said is hurting him.

"No. I won't. I'm not giving her up and…" he breathes in and turns to face me with tears in his eyes. He closes them for a minute and then speaks in a broken whisper. "If that's how they feel, then fine, but she means more to me than any award or accolade, and I can't lose her again. If the boys want me out because of this, then I'm out."

I must make a noise because he turns toward me as a tear rolls down his cheek. I crawl over to him, wrapping my hands around his waist and holding him. His body is shaking and his voice cracks when he speaks again.

"Okay, that's it then. I'm not going to fight. Just put the statement out and you can say whatever about me being out of Deviant. My life is with her and I won't let anyone come between us again."

There's silence for a moment before he holds onto me tightly, muttering goodbye and ending the call.

"Chase, what did you just do?" I ask in a soft voice as he buries his face in my neck. He doesn't look at me for a few minutes, but his shoulders shake, and when he looks at me, I can see the devastation all over his face.

"I think I just quit my band…"

He looks desolate, destroyed, and it's all because of me. I smile up at him, as he glances at me with sadness in his eyes. I still struggle with my confidence around him and my fear that he'll leave me again hasn't gone, but I'm slowly learning to accept his love.

He's been there every step of the way with my issues over the past few weeks, and I wish I could own the fact that he's mine.

"Chase, no. Please don't give up what you love for me. I'm not worth that."

His eyes burn into mine, bright with tears and anguish, but he leans forward and captures my lips in a desperate kiss.

"You are worth that and more, babe. I'm sorry. I'm sorry I left you, that I said there was nothing between us, but this fucking hurts. I've been in that band since I was seventeen, and I don't know what I'm going to do now."

"Call them back. Call them back and tell them no. Please, don't give up your passion for me."

He shakes his head and his hands come up, gripping my neck as he plunders my lips with a fervor I've never felt before.

"No. This. Us. This is my life. You are my life and I lost you once, I won't lose you again, not for them. Not for anything. I love you. I love you so damn much, Cassie."

He closes his mouth over mine and shifts so we're on the bed, me under him and him kissing me like a drowning man sucking in tiny amounts of air. One of his hands holds mine over my head and the other rifles inside a drawer.

His lips trace my mouth, my neck, and then something slips onto my finger. For a moment, I freeze, completely and utterly stunned, but then he stares down at me with warmth in his bright blue eyes.

"Cassie, you stole my soul five years ago, and I didn't know I was missing it until you came back into my life. I love you so much. Will you promise me that one day soon you'll be my wife?"

As he speaks, a metal ring slides down my right hand until it reaches the third finger.

"This isn't a proposal yet, but a promise that one will come. I always planned on doing this tonight, but now, more than ever, I need to show you that you're mine, always and forever."

He leans his head on mine as I nod at him. I'm okay with promising to marry him one day, just not today.

"Yes, Chase. I promise that, one day, I'll marry you. You're it for me too."

His lips crash against mine, and for the rest of the night, we tune out the outside world as our bodies move in sync, making love to each other in a much more soft and gentle way.

It's the gentleness that captures my heart now, but his vulnerability and sex appeal captured my heart at eighteen, and he's never given it back. We might be fucked up, but at least I know he loves me, and for now, that's enough.

# Epilogue

## Chase

Three years later

THE WARM SUN beats down on my skin, and my back is slick with sweat as I stand at the bottom of an aisle, waiting on the girl I love, the woman who's fought by my side for the past three years to come down and claim me. My tie is tight, and my slacks feel like they are cutting off my circulation, but I know it's just my nerves. I can play to stadiums full of people, but it's this that has my hands shaking and my heart sounding loud in my ears.

After she lost her mom and we reconnected, things were rough. I left my band and started as a solo artist, but my success as a recording artist would be nothing without her. She's my heart, my soul, and my person.

Soft music starts to play, and I glance down the aisle to see her walking toward me. She's a vision in a flowing white dress with flowers and ribbons adorning her hair. Her make-up is simple, and her dress is tight enough that you can just see the hint of our baby in her tummy.

She's four months along, and it's the icing on the cake for us. We already have a little boy, Trent, who's sitting with Sienna at the side of the aisle. Tony is here, and he's still my friend, although it took a bit of time for me to forgive him after everything that went down with the band.

Next to Tony is Amira and her husband, Graham, and Grant is beside them with Lizzie, his wife, and their daughter Orla.

My heart bursts with pride and love when Cassie reaches me.

"Hi." She grins up at me as she stretches up on her toes to kiss me.

"Hi. You are so beautiful."

Her smile widens, and I love that she still looks a little like the shy girl who asked me to take her virginity.

"Are you ready?" the officiant asks, and we both turn to face her, because we are.

"We are." We both speak in unison, and I reach over, stroking Cassie's cheek. She leans into my touch and I can't wait to get this part over with, to take her and my boy to our new home. She doesn't know anything about it, but I picked it to give us a fresh start.

The years haven't been easy on us. The initial reaction was as bad as expected, and it took forever to die down, plus, with me leaving Deviant, it was one thing after another, but we made it, and now look at us. I'm about to marry my best friend and soulmate.

"Okay, I believe you have your own vows. Chase, if you will."

I clear my throat and stare at Cassie because this is it. This is the moment I've been waiting my whole life for. She is mine, and after today, it'll be official. The oceanic wind blows a gentle breeze around us, and the smell of flowers is in the air, but none of it matters because she's about to become mine forever.

"Cass, at the start, I was scared of how much I wanted you, and then I had a rather unconventional taste of you."

Her eyes glitter, and I know she's remembering the sauna in my dad's house. My heart thumps for a moment as I remember dropping to my knees and not taking no for answer.

"You became an addiction I couldn't shake, and even though we separated for years, I never stopped craving you. I pushed through all my reservations and fears about loving you, and I'm so glad I did because I got you. I got you, and you are everything I never knew I wanted. I loved you so much then, but now I'm completely and utterly crazy in love with you.

"We've had a hard time getting here, and you've had a few curveballs thrown at you over the years, but I know your mom would be so proud of the woman you've become, and the mother you are to our boy, and the mother you will be to our girl. You are everything to me, and today will be the happiest day of my life because I finally get to say you're mine."

I stop, sliding her ring on before I kiss her. I step back and stare into the eyes of the only person I've ever truly loved, bar my son, and I'm so thankful that our lives brought us back together.

"Cassie, are you ready?"

She nods, swallows, and then clears her throat.

"Chase, you burst into my life, breaking through my barriers, pushing me to admit what I wanted, teased me, and making me fall for you over and over again. I never knew what a soulmate was, what it was like to have someone want me so much, until you.

"You changed me irrevocably. You made me grow, helped me to see what I wanted and to go for it, made me a mom, and help me every day to raise our boy. You gave up everything for me, and when I came back into your life, I was a hot mess, but you didn't care because all you saw was me. The girl you loved, craved. When all the mess happened, you were there to pick up the pieces. I love you, Chase. I always have, and I always will."

The officiant goes through the remainder of the ceremony in what feels like the blink of an eye, and then she says the magic words.

"I now pronounce you husband and wife. Chase, you may kiss your bride."

I grab Cassie and pull her into my arms, slamming my lips against hers and not caring that we have an audience because she's finally mine, all mine, forever. I pull back and grin at her, wishing we were back in our suite so I could bury my cock into her sweet center, but as the cheers grow louder, I sigh and step a little farther back from her.

Our eyes stay locked, and her mouth lifts as she smiles at me. I know that I lost my heart that day I went home. I went home to bury my dad and came away with the heart of the love of my life. Losing my stepsister was the worst thing that happened to me, but she's now where she belongs, right by my side, and she's going nowhere without me for the rest of our lives. She is etched on my heart, and I'm scored on hers, now and forevermore.

*The End*

# ALSO BY STACY MCWILLIAMS

**Step Dilemma Series**

Stepbrother

Stepsister

**San Francisco Rock Romance**

Black Mercy

Broken Mercy

**Other Books**

Destroyed by Deception

Sing me Home

Nothing But The Sheets

# ABOUT THE AUTHOR

Welcome to the rollercoaster world of Stacy McWilliams.
Stacy McWilliams is a Scottish Author who loves romance. All of
her books have a romantic element and her books will keep you on
the edge of your seat, make you want to throw your kindle around
and her characters will make you either love them or loathe them.

Reviews
"...on the edge reading..." Destroyed by Deception
"...hold on tight and hang on for the ride." Black Mercy
"...captivated from the start..." Candlelight
"...kept me intrigued..." Luminosity
"brilliant paranormal story that pulls you into her world of demons
and teenage romance." Ignition
"What can I say... I was left wanting more… More Hunter, more
Savannah, just more of everything."-Pride

Contact her on Facebook or Instagram and she will message back.

If she's not writing, looking after her three boys or spending time
with her hubs, she's reading or watching TV shows such as Lucifer,
The 100 and Supernatural.

She's working on new materials and is hoping to release more
books in 2021. Also check out her Facebook page for updates on
any signings she's attending.

www.ingramcontent.com/pod-product-compliance
Lightning Source LLC
Chambersburg PA
CBHW021948120726
47992CB00001B/198